B

C000176751

hidden talen

Bello is a digital-only imprint of Pan Macmillan,
established to breathe new life into previously published,
classic books.

At Bello we believe in the timeless power of the imagination,
of a good story, narrative and entertainment, and we want to
use digital technology to ensure that many more readers
can enjoy these books into the future.

We publish in ebook and print-on-demand formats
to bring these wonderful books to new audiences.

www.panmacmillan.com/imprint-publishers/bello

B E L L

A. A. Milne

A. A. Milne (Alan Alexander) was born in London in 1882 and educated at Westminster School and Trinity College, Cambridge. In 1902 he was Editor of *Granta*, the University magazine, and moved back to London the following year to enter journalism. By 1906 he was Assistant Editor of *Punch*, a post which he held until the beginning of the First World War when he joined the Royal Warwickshire Regiment. While in the army in 1917 he started on a career writing plays of which his best known are *Mr. Pim Passes By*, *The Dover Road* and an adaptation of Kenneth Grahame's *The Wind in the Willows – Toad of Toad Hall*. He married Dorothy de Selincourt in 1913 and in 1920 had a son, Christopher Robin. By 1924 Milne was a highly successful playwright, and published the first of his four books for children, a set of poems called *When We Were Very Young*, which he wrote for his son. This was followed by the storybook *Winnie-the-Pooh* in 1926, more poems in *Now We Are Six* (1927) and further stories in *The House at Pooh Corner* (1928). In addition to his now famous works, Milne wrote many novels, volumes of essays, a well known detective story *The Red House Mystery* and light verse, works which attracted great success at the time. He continued to be a prolific writer until his death in 1956.

A. A. Milne

A TABLE NEAR
THE BAND

BELL

First published in 1950 by Methuen & Co. Ltd

This edition published 2017 by Bello
an imprint of Pan Macmillan
20 New Wharf Road, London N1 9RR
Associated companies throughout the world

www.panmacmillan.com/imprint-publishers/bello

ISBN 978-1-5098-6965-7 EPUB
ISBN 978-1-5098-6964-0 PB

Copyright © The Estate of the Late Lesley Milne Limited, 1950

The right of A.A. Milne to be identified as the
author of this work has been asserted by him in
accordance with the Copyright, Designs and Patents Act 1988.

All rights reserved. No part of this publication may be reproduced,
stored in a retrieval system, or transmitted, in any form, or by any means
(electronic, mechanical, photocopying, recording or otherwise)
without the prior written permission of the publisher.

This book is a work of fiction. Names, characters, places, organizations
and incidents are either products of the author's imagination or used fictitiously.
Any resemblance to actual events, places, organizations or persons,
living or dead, is entirely coincidental.

This book remains true to the original in every way. Some aspects may appear
out-of-date to modern-day readers. Bello makes no apology for this, as to retrospectively
change any content would be anachronistic and undermine the authenticity of the original.

Pan Macmillan does not have any control over, or any responsibility for,
any author or third-party websites referred to in or on this book.

A CIP catalogue record for this book is available from the British Library.

Typeset by Ellipsis, Glasgow

This book is sold subject to the condition that it shall not, by way of
trade or otherwise, be lent, re-sold, hired out, or otherwise circulated without
the publisher's prior consent in any form of binding or cover other than
that in which it is published and without a similar condition including
this condition being imposed on the subsequent purchaser.

Visit **www.panmacmillan.com** to read more about all our books
and to buy them. You will also find features, author interviews and
news of any author events, and you can sign up for e-newsletters
so that you're always first to hear about our new releases.

To

THE READER

Whose weekly parcel from the Library has included this or that book, either because it has been recommended by a friend or because the author's previous work has recommended itself:

Who has flipped through the pages in happy anticipation and found that it is a book of short stories:

Who has said disappointedly "Oh! short stories", and has put it aside and settled down to one of the other books:

I DEDICATE THIS ONE

At the same time pointing out to her that completely revealing titles which are both attractive and as yet unused are hard to come by, and that after all one should expect

A TABLE NEAR THE BAND

to offer a view of other tables, at each one of which some story may well be in the making.

Contents

A Table Near the Band

I was giving Marcia lunch at the Turandot.

She is a delightful girl to give lunch to; very pretty, very decorative; drawing the eyes, admiring or envious, of all the other lunchers, but not (and this, I think, is her most charming characteristic)—not showing any consciousness of it; devoting herself with all her heart (if any), her soul (probably none) and her eyes (forget-me-not blue) to her companion. With it all, she is amusing, in the sense that after a couple of cocktails she makes you feel that either you or she or somebody is being extremely funny, smiles and easy laughter being the pleasant condiments of the meal. In short, a delightful person to take out to lunch.

It is one of the advantages of lunch that it rarely leads to an unpremeditated proposal of marriage. I have a suspicion, which has never been confirmed, that I did propose to Marcia once, after dinner. If so, she must have refused me, because I am still a bachelor. There is no doubt that up to that evening (a year ago now) I had regarded myself as in love with her, and had assumed that, as a consequence, the moment would arrive when I should suddenly hear myself asking her to marry me. I woke up next morning with the conviction that I had so heard myself. I spent the next six hours trying to imagine our married life together, from dawn to dawn and December to December; and I concluded that the immediate and, indeed, obvious pleasures of such contiguity, enjoyable as they could not fail to be, would have much to contend against. A little nervously I rang her up at tea-time. I am not at my best in a telephone conversation with Marcia, because, even more than most men, I detest telephone conversations, and, even more than most women, she revels in them. She is never handicapped, as I am, by the fear, or even the knowledge, that other people are within hearing. On this occasion I was handicapped further by the uncertainty whether or not I was talking to my betrothed. I gathered fairly soon that I was not, and, a little later, that neither was I a rejected suitor. Our table had been near the band, and I suppose she hadn't heard.

Marcia lives in a highly polished flat in Sloane Street. The economics of this flat are something of a mystery; I mean to me, not, of course, to her. Indeed, the economics of Marcia's whole life are a little mysterious. She has, or has had, a father and a mother. Casual references to one or other of them keep me in touch with their continued existence, but I have never seen them, nor do I know where they live. However, I gather that the father is, or was, in some unnamed profession or business, which permits of his making a quarterly allowance to his daughter; while Marcia herself earns part of her living in some confidential relationship to a firm in Richmond. I know this, because on one or two occasions when she has had to cancel a date with me it has been some sudden need of this firm in Richmond which has so untimely compelled her. 'You seem to forget, David darling, that I am a working woman,' she has said reproachfully; and, looking at her, one has, of course, been inclined to forget it. In addition to this, one must remember that the flat is not actually her own, but has merely been lent to her by a friend, referred to sometimes as Elsa and sometimes as Jane. Doubtless this friend has two Christian names, like most of us. Elsa (or Jane) is either on her honeymoon or exhibiting new dress designs in South America; or, possibly, both. I understand that she is likely to be away for some time. One of my delightful discoveries about Marcia is that she has almost as many women friends as men friends; and they are all eager to lend things to her.

It will be seen, then, that with all these resources Marcia is well able to afford the Sloane Street flat. I am not sure now why I suggested that there was anything mysterious about it. For all I know she may be a rich woman in her own right, with money inherited from an ancestral brewery or a doting godfather. She has not mentioned yet that this is so, but it may well be. In any case it is no business of mine. All that matters to me is that she is a delightful person to give lunch to; and that this is what I was doing at the Turandot one day last week.

At the moment we weren't lunching, we were sitting in the lounge drinking cocktails. They were doubles, of course, because in these days one is apt to mislay a single at the bottom of the glass, and one can't afford to do that. We raised our glasses to each other, and murmured compliments. One of the things which I like about Marcia is that she doesn't expect all the compliments for herself. She is the only woman who has told me that I remind her of Robert Montgomery. She will say 'You look divine in that suit, darling, you ought always to wear brown'— or whatever it is. This is a very endearing habit of hers, and one which none of my female relations has fallen into as yet.

She took the mirror out of her bag; I suppose to see if she was looking as lovely as I had just said she did. She has beautiful hands, and, possibly for that reason, made a good deal of play with this bag, so that I felt impelled to say 'Hallo, I haven't seen that before, have I?' This is a fairly safe line to take with anything of Marcia's, and often gets me credit for that habit of 'noticing' which all women expect from their men.

'This?' she said, holding the bag up at me. 'I shouldn't think so.'

Some comment was called for. Unfortunately bags do very little for me. I never know what to say to a new one; just as, I suppose, a woman wouldn't know what to say to a new cricket-bat. Obviously the thing has got to be the right shape and, in the case of a bag, the appropriate colour, but one can't praise a thing for its obvious qualities. 'It's charming' was the best I could do.

'David!' she said reproachfully. 'This old thing? Oh, but I oughtn't to say that. Let's talk of something else. Wait a moment.' She opened the bag again, seemed to be looking for something, and then, realising that she wouldn't find it, snapped the catch and murmured 'Of course! I was forgetting.'

I took the bag off her lap. I considered both sides of it, and put it back. I saw now that it wasn't new.

'Mother lent it to me,' she explained. This, as it were, gave her mother another six months of life. She was last heard of in the spring.

'But why?' I asked. I felt that she was using up her mother unnecessarily. A bag is as essential to a woman as braces to a man; one doesn't have to explain how one comes to be wearing them.

'Just motherly love, darling,' she smiled.

'Yes, but——'

'Oh, David, don't go on about it, or I shall cry. If I've got a handkerchief,' she added, opening the bag again.

'Marcia, what *is* all this?'

She looked at me pathetically, and her eyes glistened as though she were crying already.

'I didn't want to tell you, and spoil our lovely lunch together, but the most tragic thing has happened.' She emptied her glass, as if to give herself courage to look back on it, and said, 'I lost my bag yesterday. With everything in it. Oh, but *everything*!'

'Clothing coupons?' I asked in horror. It was the first thing I thought of.

'Of *course*! The whole ration book. How do you think I live?'

Well, I didn't know. But thinking it over, I did see that she might want a ration book for breakfast.

'Everything,' she went on quietly. 'Identity card, ration book, driving licence, car insurance, money, latchkey, flap-jack, of course, and lip-stick, everything.' And in a whisper she added 'Including my cigarette-case.'

I knew that cigarette-case. It was in gold and platinum with an 'M' in little diamonds. Desmond had given it to her, just before he went out to Burma, where he was killed. She was to have married him as soon as the war was over. He wouldn't marry her before: he said it wouldn't be fair to her if he were missing.

While I was wondering what to say which didn't sound either callous or sentimental—(after all, he died three years ago)—she

4

added in a smiling voice, 'I felt absolutely naked when I discovered what had happened.'

This took us off the emotional plane, and I asked the obvious question, 'When did you discover?'

'Getting out of the taxi last night. I'd been down to Letty's for the week-end. Morrison paid the man and let me in with his pass-key, and I rang up Victoria at once, of course, but it was one of those trains which goes backwards and forwards all day—darling, what a life!—and it was now on its little way to Brighton again. With my lovely bag in it. Of course, somebody has just taken it.'

'No news of it at Brighton?'

'No. I rang up again this morning.'

'But Marcia, darling—wait a moment, we want some more drinks for this.' I caught a waiter's eye and ordered two more doubles. Marcia gave me her loving, grateful smile—'What I was going to say was, However does a woman leave her bag in the train? It's part of her. I should have thought you'd have felt absolutely naked as soon as you got on to the platform.'

'That was the idiotic part. I'd been reading a magazine in the train, and I'd put my bag down, and then I put the magazine under my arm—oh, David, I know I'm a fool, but it's no good saying it.'

'I wasn't going to, darling. I'm terribly sorry, and I wish I could help.'

'I know. You're sweet.'

'How about all the things you've got to renew? Ration book and licences and all that? Can't I help there?'

'It's lovely of you, David, but it's all what they call "in train".' She laughed and added, 'Like the bag, unfortunately. I've been rushing about like a mad thing all morning.'

'Was there much money in it?'

She shrugged and said, 'About ten pounds, and quarter-day a long way off. I shall have to go carefully for a bit. But, of course, that's the least of it. It's—everything else.' I felt uncomfortably that she was thinking of Desmond again. She must have realised this— she is very quick, bless her—because she said at once, 'I mean the bag itself, it's so hateful to think of my lovely, lovely bag being worn by some horrible woman in Brighton, or wherever she is.'

'Do I remember it?'

'Well, darling, you ought to, seeing that it's the only one I've got. Only I haven't got it.'

I always thought that women had lots of bags, but I suppose it's like men with pipes. We have half a dozen, but the others are always the ones we can't smoke at the moment.

'I seem to remember a black one,' I said tentatively.

'Of course, darling. I always wear a black bag—when I have it. But never mind my silly troubles, tell me about yourself. You wrote that you were spending the weekend with your married sister. How was she?'

Marcia has a very sweet way of taking an interest in people she has never met. I told her that Sylvia was well. We then went in to lunch. It was, for these days, a very good lunch, and we chattered and laughed and said no more of the bag.

Marcia didn't want me after lunch. I took her to where her car was parked, and she went off to Richmond or somewhere; on business for the firm, I suppose, as otherwise she wouldn't have had the petrol. I wasn't sorry to be alone, because I had something I wanted to do.

I had thought of it almost at once, and now I thought of it again; and the more I thought of it, the more I felt that it was up to me to replace that bag. No doubt it was the cigarette-case for which Marcia was really grieving, but Desmond had given it to her, and I couldn't do anything about that. Nor could I have afforded to do anything about it: the economics of my life don't include platinum and gold cigarette-cases. But I thought that they did include a bag on an occasion like this for a very attractive and much-to-be-pitied young woman. After a few enquiries I wasn't so sure. However, I was committed to it now, at whatever cost, and in the end I felt fairly satisfied with the result. Bags, as I think I have said, all look much the same to me; but this one was certainly black and certainly expensive, and presumably, therefore, just what

Marcia wanted. The girl in the shop was sure it was. She said Moddom would rave about it.

And, in fact, Moddom did.

I spent the week-end at Waylands. I am 36, and what is called a commercial artist. No doubt you have seen me among the advertisements: represented as often as not by an athletic young man and a superb young woman in very little on the beach. This can call your attention to anything, from your favourite laxative to your favourite cigarette or soft drink; from National Savings (the holiday you can look forward to, if you save now) to pocket cameras (the holiday you can look back upon afterwards). Altogether I don't do too badly; and the only reason why I am mentioning this is because a bachelor of 36, who is understood not to be doing too badly, gets invited to houses a little out of his social and financial class. It was in this way, and again at this week-end, that I met Maddox.

Maddox, I suppose, is about 50, and something pretty big in the City. He has known Marcia longer than I have, and he talks to me about her whenever we happen to meet; as if I were waiting anxiously for him to talk to me, and this was the only subject of conversation which could possibly interest us both; as, indeed, it is. Then, having put me at my ease, he leaves me as soon as possible for somebody richer or more noble. He has this natural flair for putting people at their ease. If he had met Shakespeare in his prime (Shakespeare's prime) he would have asked him if he were doing any writing just now—thus showing that he was in touch with the literary fashion of the moment—and drifted away without waiting for the answer.

He is not in the least jealous of my friendship with Marcia. The fact that I am a bachelor assures him in some way that there can be no rivalry between us. He himself is married; and the only thing which has prevented him from marrying Marcia (so Marcia tells me) is this wife of his. Either she is a Catholic and won't divorce him, or she is in a Home for Incurables and he can't divorce her.

I forget which, but I know that it is all very hard on him—and, of course, on his wife, if she is in a Home for Incurables.

On this occasion we saw more of each other than usual, because we travelled down together. I stepped into his carriage when it was too late to step out again, and he went through the usual drill of seeming surprised to find me in such good company.

'Hallo, young fellow! You?'

I admitted it.

He nodded, as if to confirm my admission, and gave himself a moment in which to place me. Then he asked if I had seen the little girl lately.

'Marcia?' I asked coldly.

'Who else?'

I said that I had seen her fairly lately.

'You didn't hear what the little idiot had done? No, you couldn't have.'

'What's that?'

'Left her bag in the train, with £20 in it.'

'Good lord!'

'*And,* of course, everything else. What's really worrying the poor girl is the cigarette-case.'

'Cigarette-case?'

'A beauty. Platinum and gold. But the tragic thing is that it's the one Hugh gave her.'

I wanted to say 'Who's Hugh?' because I had never heard of him, but it didn't sound right somehow. It was no matter, because he went on: 'The feller she was engaged to. You wouldn't have met him, you've only known her for the last year.'

'Two years,' I corrected.

'Poor kid, it was a tragedy for her. Hugh was in the Air Force, and they were going to get married as soon as he got a ground job. And then, just at the end of his last tour, on his very last operation, he was shot down over the North Sea. That cigarette-case was all she had had of him. He'd meant to make a will, he had quite a bit to leave, but like a damned young fool he put it off. Tough luck on Marcia.'

'Very tough,' I said. 'I know the cigarette-case, of course, but she's never told me about Hugh. I suppose she wouldn't like to talk about him.'

'That's right. Naturally she told *me*, because—well, that's different.'

'Naturally. No hope of getting the bag back?'

'Well, hardly—with all that in it. Of course, one would gladly give her a cigarette-case to take the place of Hugh's, but——' he gave a little shrug of his shoulders—'one can't, can one?'

I saw that he wanted to be admired for the delicacy of his feelings, so I shook my head and said, 'Too expensive nowadays, with the purchase tax.'

He almost decided to leave me then. He said coldly, 'It's hardly a question of money. I shall certainly give her a cigarette-case at Christmas, but that's different.'

'I see what you mean,' I said quickly. 'You're quite right, of course. Absolutely.'

That soothed him, and he felt that he could take me into his confidence again. For a man who admires himself so much he is curiously eager to be admired by others.

'All the same one had to do something at once. I mean, the poor girl was in tears, and I don't wonder. So I've given her a new bag. Apparently she only had the one, poor kid. She'd actually had to borrow one from her mother! And then losing £20 like that, and quarter-day a long way off, I felt it was the least I could do.'

'It was extremely generous of you,' I said warmly. 'And just what she'd want. I suppose you know all about these things. I mean you would know the sort and the colour and all that. I'm afraid I'm no good at bags.'

'That's right. Well, I had to ask about the colour, of course. She'd naturally want it to be the same colour.' He gave a little chuckle of self-appreciation. 'But I did it very tactfully, so that she couldn't guess anything.'

'I am sure she wouldn't guess. It will be a tremendous surprise. What colour was it? I should have said black, but I'm afraid I never notice bags very much.'

He shook his head with a condescending smile.

'No, no, not black. I knew it wasn't black. Green. As soon as she told me, I remembered. She always carries a green bag.'

A day or two later (which is how these things happen) I was sitting in the smoking-room of my club when young Hargreaves came in. With a shy smile and an apology he leant over me to ring the bell.

'I've just rung it,' I said. 'Have one with me instead.'

He said, 'Oh, I say!' and then, 'I say, that's very decent of you, I'll have a sherry, but look here these are mine,' and as the waitress came in, 'What'll you have?'

I waved him down, and said firmly to the girl, 'Two large sherries, and put them on my luncheon bill.' As she went, I said to Hargreaves, 'I spoke first, you can't get away from that.'

'Oh well, thanks a lot.'

Hargreaves is very young; at least he seems so to me. He has only just joined the club, and as I am ten years older and have been a member twelve years longer, I feel a world-weary veteran when I talk to him. Like so many young men these days he passed straight into the Army from school. On demobilisation he went up to Cambridge, cramming what should have been three leisurely years of graduation in life into a hectic twelvemonth struggle for a book-learning degree. Then he was free to earn a living. Luckier than most, he had a family business to go into, with money to come (I get my gossip from the secretary); so we need not feel too sorry for him. But like all these young people he is a curious mixture of experience and innocence. He has seen half the world, met people of all countries in every class of life, had adventures of which, at his age, we knew nothing. Yet in many of his contacts with civilian life he still has the *naïveté* of a schoolboy.

We sipped our sherries and talked about the weather. The conversation came to its natural end. He pulled out his cigarette-case and offered me one. I called his attention to the pipe I was smoking. He said 'Oh, sorry' and lit one for himself. With this to give him confidence, he began:

'I say, I wish you'd tell me something.'

'If I can.'

'I don't know London very well, I mean I don't know the best places to go to, and all that. What would be the best place to get a bag?'

'What sort of bag? Dressing case?'

'No, no, *you* know, the sort women carry about.'

'Oh, that sort? What Americans call a purse.'

'Extraordinary thing to call it,' he said, opening his blue eyes wide. 'Still,' he added generously, 'if they call braces suspenders, I suppose it isn't so extraordinary. Well, anyway, that sort.'

I gave him the name of the shop at which I had got Marcia's bag, and mentioned one or two other possible places.

'That's grand,' he said, and made a note of them. 'Thanks very much.'

'They're expensive, you know, at that sort of shop. I'm assuming that you want a really good one.'

'Oh, I do.' He hesitated and said, 'Er—about how much?'

'Ten to fifteen pounds.'

'Oh!' He was more than surprised, he was taken aback. His round pink face became even pinker.

'Of course,' I said quickly, 'you can get them much cheaper at some of the big places—well, obviously it depends on the bag.'

'No, it must be a good one, but——' He gave an awkward little laugh. 'I mean fifteen pounds is all right by me, but would the girl—I mean, I've only just met her, and it isn't her birthday or anything, so would she feel— I mean it's quite a present, not like flowers or chocolates or taking her out to lunch. What do you think?'

'I should think she would be delighted,' I said with some confidence. 'I shouldn't worry about that.'

'Oh, good. Then that's all right. And anyway it *is* rather special. I mean there's a special reason for it.'

It was clear that he wanted me to ask what it was, so I asked him. Besides, I was getting interested suddenly.

'Well, you see, she left her bag in the train, with everything in it, and there's no news of it, and it's been a frightful shock for her.

Apart from everything else, she'd just cashed a cheque for fifty pounds——'

'I shouldn't do anything about that.' I put in quickly.

'Well, I could hardly offer her money,' he said with a delightful man-of-the-world air. 'Actually there was something even worse—a gold and platinum cigarette-case with her initials in diamonds—God knows what that cost, but of course it's the sentimental value which made it so precious to her.'

'Of course,' I said. I wasn't surprised.

'You see, she was engaged to a man who was killed just after D-day. He was in Commandos, and he was dropped behind the lines with the Maquis, *you* know——'

'I know,' I said. 'So was I.'

'I say, were you really? I was in the Burma show.'

'So I heard. Sooner you than me.'

'Oh, it wasn't so bad. I should say your job was a much stickier one.'

'I'd lived in Paris for a good many years. I talked French. That was all there was to it. What was this man's name? I may have come across him.' But I didn't think it was very likely.

'She just called him John. I didn't like to ask his other name.'

'Quite right,' I said firmly.

'This was his engagement present to her. They were to be married on his first leave, and then—— Pretty bloody.

'And now she has lost all she had left of him.' He was silent for a little, contemplating life, and then threw his cigarette end into the fire, and said, 'Well, of course I couldn't do anything about that, but I thought I could at least replace the bag.'

'A very nice thought, if I may say so; and one which I'm sure she will appreciate. What colour did you think of getting? They'll help you in the shop with all the rest of it, but you must be able to tell them the colour. Most women have their own special colour.' Or, of course, colours.

'I know. So, to be quite safe, I'm getting one exactly like the one she lost. Luckily she happened to describe it, it just came out accidentally, but I was on to it like a shot. I mean in my own mind, of course. It was yellow.'

'And a very pretty colour too,' I said.

This should have been the end of it, for other people dropped in, and the conversation became general. But he came up to me again, hat in hand, as I sat alone in the lounge after lunch drinking my coffee.

'Thanks very much for that address,' he said; and I thought it was nice of him to seek me out as he was leaving the club, to thank me for so little. But apparently he had something else to ask. Very casually, as if he knew the answer and wanted to see if I did, he said:

'I say, I suppose there's nothing much to choose nowadays between the Berkeley and the Ritz? I mean for dinner.'

'Nothing,' I said. 'You'll be perfectly safe at either.'

'That's what I thought.' He turned to go.

And then I wondered, a little anxiously, if he would be perfectly safe. He is a thoroughly nice boy, and he is going to meet a thoroughly nice girl one day.

'Just a word of advice, if I may,' I called after him.

'Of course!' He came back to me eagerly.

'Get a table near the band if you can.'

He looked surprised, as well as he might be.

'Why?' he asked, very naturally.

'It's safer,' I said.

All the same, I still think that she is a delightful girl to take out to lunch.

The Prettiest Girl in the Room

THE door of her bedroom opened a little way, the tap of knuckles on it a polite afterthought rather than a request for admission.

'Nearly ready, old girl?'

'Just on, dear.'

'I'll go and get the car.'

'Right.'

The door closed. She had another five minutes. The walk to the garage, trying the self-starter, feeling in the dark for the starting-handle, getting out of the car, winding, getting back into the car, starting, backing, coming to the house, turning, stalling, starting again, warming up the engine for the hill, and then a loud whistle like a siren; she knew it all. Going up the hill he would say, 'I hope to God the Traills aren't there,' and she would say, 'Oh, they won't seem so bad after you've had a drink or two,' and he would grunt and be silent until they were turning into the Hewitsons' lane, and then he would say, 'Well, we needn't stay long. Three-quarters of an hour should about see it. Leave at seven-fifteen. All right by you, old girl?' And she would say, 'Of course, darling.' And at eight o'clock she would say, 'Charles! You really *must* come away.' All just as usual.

Sometimes she wished that he didn't call her 'old girl'. She tried to remember if he had always called her so, or only since she had become—well, older. After all, a grandmother, but only just a grandmother, couldn't complain. She wasn't complaining. She had nothing to complain about. She had two delightful grown-up sons, both with jobs, and a married daughter with the sweetest baby. And Charles—everybody liked Charles. It was just that the winter seemed so long in the country, and life so short; and now that Charles had retired, they always seemed to be saying and doing the same things together, and had nothing new to tell each other. Inevitable, of course; but every now and then one got the feeling that life oughtn't to be so inevitable. Not even when you were a grandmother.

He whistled; she whistled back on her fingers, as he had taught her more than thirty years ago. The war-cry of the Allisons, he had called it. Well, you couldn't say that a marriage was a failure when two people had gone on whistling to each other in the same way for thirty years. Could you? She took a last look at herself in the glass—oh, well!—and went down.

'I hope to God the Traills aren't coming,' said Charles, as they went up the hill. 'Can't stand 'em.'

'Never mind, darling, perhaps Betty will be there.'

Charles cocked an eye at her, and they both laughed. Betty was Mrs Hewitson, and it was supposed that Charles was in love with her. Well, you couldn't still be having jokes like that with your husband if your marriage was a failure. Could you?

'Mustn't stay too long.'

'No, darling. Seven-fifteen.'

Considering that it wasn't a party, but just a ring-up and a 'Why don't you come in on Sunday and have a drink?' there seemed to be quite a collection of people. Charles kissed Betty, and winked at his wife, and Mary offered her cheek to Tom; and then they walked into the crowd, and said the usual things to the usual faces. Presently Mary found herself on a sofa with a drink in her hand, listening once again to the General. When he told her that he had got a three at the seventh that morning, she said, 'Oh, but that's marvellous! It's hard enough to get a four there'; because with a husband and two growing sons you couldn't help knowing all about the seventh. When he told her about the political Brains Trust which they were holding in the village next week, she said, 'How interesting! Oh, I must certainly come to that'; having promised to do so after Charles' exhaustive account of it the day before. She talked to other people, and other people talked to her, and it was all just as it always was; and now she looked at her watch and it was 7.15 and there was Charles with a full glass in his hand, chattering away to Willy and Wally Clintock, those inseparable brothers who had resisted the designs of all the local match-makers for twenty years or more. Of course he liked going into other people's houses and getting away from her for a little, only he always made such a fuss about starting. She couldn't see Mr Traill, but there was Mrs Traill in the wrong clothes again, looking as lonely as usual. She got up, meaning to go across to her, but was stopped by Betty.

'No, don't get up, dear,' said Betty, taking her hand and inclining her back to the sofa, 'sit down and talk to Sir John Danvers-Smith. I've been telling him all about you, and he says he's sure he has met you before. I'll get you a drink.'

Mary acknowledged Sir John with a smile, wondering where they had met, and they sat down together. He was a tall, heavily-built man with a close-cut, black moustache going grey, and a head of greying hair going bald; and though his complexion spoke of easy living, his features were still good—a little like a Roman emperor side-face, she thought. She had noticed as he came up behind Betty that he walked firmly with a complete assurance of solid worth. She thought that he was probably older than Charles, but then he would always look older, whatever their ages. He had that 'set' look which Charles had never got. It was difficult to imagine him young and carefree, just as it was difficult to imagine Charles old and important.

'You know,' she smiled, 'I'm afraid I don't remember you, and I think I should if we had met before. Was it a long time ago?'

'Thirty-eight years,' he said, evidently priding himself on remembering anyone so long. 'You were just eighteen.'

It flashed through her mind that he oughtn't to have disclosed so exact a knowledge of her age, and another flash revealed him to her as the sort of man who got on without consideration of what was in the minds of other people. Anyhow she had never bothered to conceal her age.

'What a memory you have! For there must be very little of that girl left to remember.'

'True. But just something. Whatever else you are, Mrs Allison, you are not—ordinary.' (Good gracious, she thought, whatever else is he suggesting I might be?) 'At first I wondered if perhaps I had seen your daughter somewhere——'

'That seems very possible. Or even,' she added, wondering how he would take it, 'my granddaughter.'

He went on as if she had not interrupted him: 'And so I asked our hostess if she knew what your maiden name was. It was what I had expected.' He waited for a moment, and then said, almost in reproof, 'I see that you still have no recollection.'

'I think I must be allowed one or two more questions first, Sir John. We have already decided that it was in this century, and fact not fiction, so I shall now ask, England or abroad?' She said it with a smile, but it was wasted on him.

'At the Prince's Gallery in Piccadilly. A subscription dance in aid of the School Mission. Your family had connections with my old school, I gathered. Am I correct?'

She looked at him. Through thirty-eight years of war and peace, happiness and unhappiness, adversity and prosperity, thrusting its way through a hundred more familiar faces, a face struggled into life. Now she remembered it all: a girl, an evening, a young man: and then she was looking at Sir John Danvers-Smith again, and he was saying, 'Our hostess seems to have forgotten that drink she promised. Let me get it for you.' He moved away from her. She was alone . . . on a chair up against the wall in the Prince's Gallery.

It was her second grown-up dance.

The first one had been on her eighteenth birthday in the Lancaster Gate house. Her hair was up for the first time —oh, the excitement of it! She was surrounded by her friends and her mother's friends in her own home. Everybody wanted to dance with her. She was the toast of the evening, the belle of the ball. 'Mary!' All glasses raised at supper, and 'God bless you, darling' from a suddenly emotional mother. Her first real ring from her godmother; an amethyst necklet from her father. All her own favourite waltzes on the printed programme, and the little orchestra playing encores whenever *she* rushed up and asked them. Oh, all such fun! And everybody said that it was an even better party than the one two years before, when Kathleen came out. And Kathleen had been engaged for three months, so perhaps in eighteen months from now . . . what was it like being engaged?

It was six years before she knew.

Derek's old school was giving a dance to raise money for its mission in Bermondsey. Derek wasn't noticeably interested in missions, but it was a dance, and an opportunity to display Kathleen to all the fabulous Cheesers and Bills and Tuppys of whom she had heard so much. Derek's mother got up a party. Wouldn't it be nice, darling, now that Kathleen's sister was out, to ask her too? So Mary, longing for another triumphal dance, her hair up, wearing all her jewellery, and in her pretty, white coming-out dress with the blue sash, squeezed—oh, so excited—into one of those new taxis with Kathleen and Derek (holding hands, of course) and was driven to Prince's. There she was introduced to Derek's mother, who promptly forgot about her; and in a little while she was sitting on one of the chairs which lined the walls of the gallery, waiting for her first partner.

Of course Kathleen and Derek ought to have looked after her—Cheeser would have been delighted to dance with such a pretty girl—but they went straight off into a trance in each other's arms, and nobody else existed for them. So Mary sat there, an empty seat on each side of her, almost the only young girl among the chaperons, waiting to be chosen. . . .

She couldn't believe it at first. Surely somebody did something. People were introduced to you, or young men, even if they didn't know you, asked you if they could have the pleasure of the next dance, and wrote their names in your programme. Surely among all these young men there should have been somebody who wanted her. She had said to Derek in the taxi, 'Are you going to dance with me, Derek?' almost as a joke, almost as if it would be a favour on her part to dance with a sort of relation who was in love with somebody else. And he had said, 'All right, infant, put me down for the third.' And so when the second dance was beginning, and she was still waiting, she wrote down 'Derek' on her programme, the only name there, and thought, 'Well, anyhow, that's something'; and he and Kathleen had disappeared after the second dance, and she hadn't seen them again until the middle of the third dance, and there they were, right across the room, dancing together . . . .

She didn't know which was worse, sitting there alone when everybody else was dancing, or sitting there alone when everybody else was chattering round her. What should she be trying to do, what sort of face be bravely trying to wear? Look as if she were waiting for a partner who had gone to get her an ice; or as if she were not feeling very well, and thought that she would sit out this one quietly by herself; or as if she didn't dance, being unfortunately lame from birth, but loved watching other people dance? How did one look like any of those things? How did one look anything but what she felt, utterly humiliated? And —oh God, help me!—there was the supper dance to come; and she would have to look as if the doctor had said, 'Now mind, no supper, a glass of hot milk when you get home, but no supper.' Oh God, how does one look like that? How can I sit here for an hour, while everybody else is having supper? . . .

She got up and went into the ladies' room; it was something to do. She passed young men in other rooms: some alone, smoking a cigarette, perhaps longing for a partner too, some in groups, talking, she supposed, about the dear old school. She passed happy couples sitting out. She came back; well, that was another five minutes gone, five minutes when nobody felt sorry for her. She sat down again and studied her programme, with Derek's name, and only Derek's name, on it. This was the eighth dance, and the next was her favourite, the one she had made them play so often at her own dance—and she had thought then that she liked dancing! Never, never would she go to a dance again, never again go through this awful humiliation . . .

Suddenly she knew what she would do. She would sit through

the next one, because it was her favourite tune, and perhaps she could go off into a dream while it was being played, and if she didn't get a partner for the one after that, the tenth, then she would find Kathleen and Derek and tell them that she felt terribly ill, and make them take her home—probably they would like being in a taxi together coming back—and then she wouldn't have to face that awful supper dance. And if everybody was in bed, she would find something in the kitchen, and take it up into her bedroom— oh, the utter joy of being alone in your own dear little room with nobody to look at you and pity you. Yes, that's what she would do. Oh, thank God, that's what she would do! Why hadn't she thought of it before?

With this sudden, though so comparative, happiness in front of her, she lost her self-consciousness. She smiled to herself with the confidence of one who was no longer defenceless. She smiled, and then told herself that she mustn't be smiling if she were to counterfeit a splitting headache or appendicitis pains, and smiled again at that. She was ridiculously pretty when she smiled, and an assured young man, standing for a moment in the doorway, told himself that it was absurd that the prettiest girl in the room should be wasting herself on the empty chairs each side of her, and that the whiskey-and-soda could wait. He came up to her, and bowed.

'I wonder if I might have the pleasure of the next dance?'

She heard the words from a long way off, telling herself that that was what they said to you when they thought that you were pretty, and wanted to know you. That was what they said to the lucky ones. Vaguely she looked up and saw a tall young man bending over her.

'Oh! I beg your pardon! Did you—were you——'

'I was venturing to ask you if we could have the next dance together.'

He was saying it to *her*! In a confusion of wonder and happiness and gratitude she stammered, 'Oh yes, thank you —oh, please, yes!' And then some instinct made her say coldly, 'Well, I hadn't been meaning to, because I feel rather tired, but——'

'Of course we could sit it out, if you were tired.'

20

'Oh no, no!' she cried eagerly. 'It's my favourite waltz. I should love to dance it.'

'That's good. Then let's sit the rest of this one out, if you allow it——'

'Oh yes, please let's!'

'And then we can introduce ourselves properly.' He sat down beside her.

She wouldn't let him see her programme with only Derek's name on it. She couldn't. She put it into the hand furthest away from him, and held it underneath her dress. If he asked for it, she could let it fall, and say, 'Oh dear, I seem to have lost it!'

'My name is—oh, but first you must promise not to laugh.'

She looked at him in surprise.

'Why, is it such a funny name?'

'Well, the police always seem to think so. They always laugh when I tell them. On Boat Race night,' he explained, in case she didn't understand.

'Oh, I see.' She smiled at him confidently. 'All right, I promise not to laugh.'

'And you promise to believe me? Some people don't.'

'Yes!' She nodded eagerly.

'Well, my name is John Smith.'

She laughed; a spontaneous, irresistible, increasing gurgle of laughter, showing the prettiest little teeth; and then, with a remorseful 'Oh!' and her fingers over her mouth, she cut it short.

'You promised not to,' he said reproachfully.

'I know, I'm sorry. But it *is* so funny.'

'I told you it was.'

'Because, you see,' she began to laugh again, 'my name is Brown.'

He looked at her with awe.

'Don't say—no, it's too good to be true—*don't* say it's Mary Brown?'

She nodded delightedly.

'Well! To think that we've never met before. All over the world John Smiths are meeting Mary Browns, and somehow we've missed it. You haven't got an "e" at the end of your name, by any chance or mismanagement?'

'Oh, no!'

'That's good. We are the people, we Smiths and Browns. All these toffs round here'—he waved his hand at the pictures on the walls—'they think no end of their pedigrees, but there's a John the smith or a brown Mary somewhere in every one of them. By the way, you don't know any Robinsons, do you?'

'Well one, sort of. But I don't like him very much.'

'Quite right. An inferior brood.'

Mary laughed. She could have laughed at anything he said.

They danced. The band played her favourite waltz, *Caressante*. Her eyes were closed in happiness. He danced beautifully, and, like a good dancer, was silent. Life had never been so wonderful. Perhaps, she thought, it is like this when you're engaged.

When the band stopped, he murmured, as if to himself, 'The prettiest girl in the room, *and* the best dancer,' and then he looked down at the vivid little face and said, 'Thank you, Mary Brown.' And very shyly, and wondering if she ought to, she said, 'Thank you, John Smith.' Then they both laughed.

'What about an ice?' he asked, as he led her off the floor. 'Or shall we wait till supper?'

Had he really said 'we'? Did he mean—but of course he didn't mean 'we' together, but just 'we' wherever each of them happened to be. So perhaps if she didn't have an ice now, she would never get one at all.

'Well, I think perhaps——'

'You *are* giving me the supper dance, aren't you?'

(Oh, it was true, it was true!)

'It's no good saying you are engaged,' he went on, 'because the man you were going to have it with—I meant to have told you this before—was arrested half an hour ago, poor chap, I saw a couple of policemen taking him away, they would have it that he was Soapy Robinson, the safe-cracker. Was he?'

She shook her head, swallowed a little nervously, and said in a stage whisper, 'Jones, the Confidence King,' hoping that it would please him. It did. He smiled at her, rather as her History mistress used to smile at her when she got one right.

'Then that settles it, we have the supper dance.'

The supper dance was number 12. She had two dances to wait, but waiting meant nothing to her now. She went to the ladies' room again, because she simply had to look at herself in the glass to see why he called her the prettiest girl in the room, and then, of course, she had to make herself a little prettier so as to be ready for him when he claimed her again. Then she went back, happy to sit there, and watch the dancers, and dream.

He was dancing with a tall girl in red. Mary hadn't noticed the girl in red before, so perhaps she had only just come. One couldn't not have noticed her if she were here, because she was so—so different. She made Mary, she made all the others, even Kathleen, seem like schoolgirls. She looked so exciting, like one of those beautiful adventuresses one read about. Not *really* wicked, of course, but very, very grown-up, and knowing everything; and they had to steal papers because they were being blackmailed, and their fathers would be exposed if they didn't. She was talking to him all the time, so probably she didn't dance very well.

As soon as the dance was over he left her, and came over to Mary.

'Miss Brown,' he said, 'I make you all my apologies, but I have just had a message sent round from my rooms, and it means that I have to leave. I was leaving after supper anyway, but now it seems that I must go at once. I am so very sorry to be deprived of the pleasure of having supper with you. Please forgive me.'

With a sick feeling inside Mary said, 'It's all right. I quite understand.'

'It isn't all right, at least not for me. I had been looking forward so much—Now, will you do me a favour, just to show that you forgive me? Will you let me find you a partner for supper, to take my place? I am quite sure that I can.'

She wanted to say, 'Well, as a matter of fact it's really very lucky, because I've just remembered'—but she wasn't quite sure what she remembered, and it would be such a relief to be having somebody for supper after all, anybody was better than nobody, and any girl might be left without a partner if her partner was suddenly called away.

'I expect they're all engaged now,' she smiled bravely.

'Well, if you don't mind waiting here just for a few minutes, we'll see.'

He came back with—was it Cheeser or Tuppy? She never got the name, so put him down as Robinson. He was a shortish young man with a round beaming face and spectacles. They were very shy with each other at first, but by the time they were at the supper table he was in what seemed to be his usual cheerful mood. They sat with a gang of other Cheesers and Tuppy and their girls, all equally cheerful, and they laughed a great deal, and Mary was as brilliant as any of them. And all the other Cheesers and Tuppy wanted to dance with her, it was great fun trying to fit them all in. They didn't dance very well, but they were nice.

The girl in red seemed to have gone . . . .

In the cab going home Mary said:

'Derek, was there anybody called Smith at school with you?'

'Lots, baby, I expect. I can remember two anyway. No, three. Not in my house, though. Why?'

'Oh, a man I danced with. John Smith. Tall. I just wondered.'

'There was a J. D. Smith—are you all right, darling?' This was to Kathleen who said, 'A bit squashed. That's better,' as she rearranged herself. 'He was a toff when I was a squeaker, captain of Cory's and in the Fifteen, that sort of bloke. Would that be the man?'

'I expect so,' said Mary.

'Sure you're all right, darling?' asked Derek, and Kathleen assured him that she was.

J. D. Smith. Mary wondered what 'D' stood for.

She wondered about him a good deal in the months which followed. She wondered why he had been called away so suddenly. Sometimes she thought that he was a war-correspondent; they were always being sent off to the ends of the earth at a moment's notice.

Probably he had had his pith helmet and revolver already packed before he came to the dance, and was just waiting for the summons. In that case she wouldn't see him for a long time, but she could look for his name in the paper and cut out what he had written. Of course it might be a paper which they didn't take in. It would be better if he were a King's Messenger, taking one of the Crown Jewels (strapped to his waist) to a Foreign Monarch for a present, because you couldn't send that sort of thing by post. In that case he would be coming back with a priceless snuff-box, because Monarchs always exchanged gifts in order to keep relations friendly. So she would see him again quite soon. Or, of course, the Prime Minister might have wanted to consult him suddenly about something, or offer him a seat in the Cabinet. Pitt was in the Cabinet when he was twenty-two, and Mr Smith was older than that.

When, and how, would they meet again? They would run into each other suddenly at Harrods. Or she would be in the stalls and see him looking down at her from a box, and she would say, 'Look, there's Mr Smith!' to her mother or whoever she was with, and they would go up to his box in the interval, or would that be rather forward? Better wait in the *foyer* as they came out, and let him see her sort of accidentally. Or perhaps it would be nice if they met at Studland Bay in the summer, swimming in the sea perhaps, or wouldn't he recognize her in a bathing cap, and she would bring him back to lunch. But really, of course, it would be nicest of all if her father said to her mother at breakfast one day, 'Oh, by the way, my love, I'm bringing a young fellow back to dinner to-night, a Mr John D. Smith, very clever young fellow, I think of making him a partner.' Wouldn't he be surprised when he saw her? Of course, if he were a partner, they would get married quite soon. And once they were married she would devote her whole life to him. She didn't know *what* she would have done if he hadn't rescued her, she would have died of shame. Never, never would she stop being grateful; never, never would she leave him out of her prayers . . . .

She left him out a year later. Kathleen was married now, and was telling her how she and Derek had gone to a dance the night before, and there wasn't a proper sit-down supper, so they had slipped out and had supper at the Carlton, such fun. Suddenly Mary knew that that was what Mr Smith and the girl in red had done. Suddenly she Saw it All. A wave of old-age and disillusionment swept over her, leaving her with the life-long conviction that all men were beasts, and you couldn't believe anything they said, and she would never fall in love or marry anybody, or at least not for a long time. It was, in fact, not until she was twenty-four that she married Charles, who had been in love with her for many years, and had almost given up hope . . . .

'Mary dear, Sir John wanted me to make his apologies to you. He had to hurry off. I've brought you a drink.'

Betty sat down beside her, and began a long story about the latest treasure from the village who had come to help, but, as it proved, had only helped herself. Mary hardly needed to listen, she had heard it so often.

So once again he had deserted her! What a blessèd, blessèd comfort it was to know that it mattered no longer. How cosy to feel that there was one man who would never desert you; never grow old and insensitive. Though you would never again be the prettiest girl in the room, though your dancing days were over, how restful it was to know that you were truly poised at last, and that all the turbulent uneasiness and pathetic silliness of youth was behind you. There was much to be said for autumn—with an occasional sweet reminder of spring, a sudden memory which brought the scent of its flowers into the present, yet left you undisturbed.

It was 8 o'clock again. 'Charles, dear, we simply must be going.'

The usual goodbyes, the usual trouble to get the car started, the usual, 'Sure I can't help, old man?' from their host at the door, the usual, 'Don't stand out in the cold, *please*' from Mary. Then they were off, hands waving, the lights from the house caught between the trees as the drive swung round. All as usual—but not quite as usual.

As they came into the road, he said:

26

'Well, old girl, you did it again.'

'Did what again?'

'Knocked 'em all. The prettiest girl in the room, *and* the best dressed.'

'Charles! Darling!' She could hardly believe that he was saying it. To *her*!

He dropped his left hand for a moment on to her thigh and squeezed. 'Proud of you.'

'Darling!' In a bewilderment of crazy happiness she put her fingers to her mouth and gave the war-cry of the Allisons.

'Good God, what's that for?' said a startled Charles. 'Still, if you feel that way——' He gave the answering call, louder, more piercing.

'The whole village will hear us,' said Mary, laughing weakly. 'They'll think we're mad.'

Presently she found that she was not laughing, she was crying.

A Man Greatly Beloved

I AM fifteen, and extremely advanced for my years. This is not self-recommendation which, as the youngest of us has been told much too often, is no praise, but a *précis* of last term's report by Julia Prendergast, Headmistress, on Antonia Fell, Modern VIB. I am Antonia Fell, and most people call me Tony. I do not care for either of these names, and would rather have been christened Amaryllis and called Meriel for short, which is what I should have been if immersed when of riper years. In the novel which I am writing the heroine is so named and is the admiration of all. I have a Father and a Mother, as so often happens to young people, and a little brother of 13, which is not so inevitable. He was christened Charles Robert. Father calls him Robert and Mother calls him Paddy and I call him Bill, which is somewhat confusing for elderly visitors who have just dropped in. However, life goes on just as if they weren't confused.

What I am going to tell you about is the Strange Case of John Anderson. This is not the my Jo John whose bonny brow was brent, but the one who came to live at Essington, which is our village.

I am not quite sure whether I ought to describe the village or Father first. This is the sort of thing which the experienced writer knows by instinct, and I don't; being inexperienced. Probably whichever I do I shall feel when I read it through afterwards that it ought to have been the other one. This will be a pity, because it is too late when you only have one small exercise-book, and the big one is being kept for the novel. So I shall take a chance and start with Father.

Father is the Vicar of Essington. Most of his opinions are out of date, as is natural to a Vicar who has to believe what people believed before they knew that the earth was round and had taken millions of years getting that way; and so we don't agree on quite a lot of things. He doesn't know this, because I am careful not to argue with him. There is no object in arguing unless you want to convince the other person that you are right. I argued with Prendy about getting off net-ball now I was in the Sixth, even if VIB. We remained of our own opinions still, but I did try to convince her that she was wrong, although without visible success. But if I convinced Father that he was wrong, then he would have to resign his living and we should starve, which would be lamentable for all. Of course, when my novel is published and makes a lot of money, then it won't matter so much. So I am really waiting for that. Meanwhile I go to Church twice every Sunday, when I would much sooner be writing my novel.

Father looks like an actor; and though it is a sad thing to say of one's father, a very bad actor at that. Perhaps if he were really an actor, I should say that he looked like a Vicar and a very good Vicar. He has a deep voice, and deep soul-compelling eyes; and his thick black hair, just beginning to go grey at the sides, is full of curls which he ought to have given to me, but hasn't, having wasted them on Bill. Altogether he is the sort of father you feel rather proud of and nervous about simultaneously, wondering whether the new visitor can take it. I mean some people say 'What a handsome man for a Vicar, my dear'; and others raise their eyebrows, as if he had gone too far. It depends on what you're used to. He is very eloquent in the pulpit, if you don't think about what he is saying but only how he says it, and in the home he makes everything sound just as religious and deep meaning, even if he is asking Mother where she left the Slug Death.

Mother is lovely in every way, and I am devoted to her. Bill is a nice little boy, but of course only a child. Mother calls him Paddy, because he was the next best thing, Father having ordered another daughter. There used to be a book called 'Paddy-the-next-best-thing', and the reason why Father didn't want him was because he feared that Vicars' sons always went to the bad. Bill hasn't gone to the bad yet, being a bit young for it and getting a prize for Divinity last term. Next term he will be at Harrow, which is where you generally begin going to the bad if you have any leaning that way. We shall have to wait and see.

Essington is a pleasant little, old-world village, but the only building in it of antiquarian interest to the visitor is Ballards, a charming black-and-white cottage dating from the thirteenth century—photograph on p. 81. That comes from *Rural Rambles Round England*, which I got for half a three-legged race at the sports; and my friends at school were greatly surprised when I showed them the photograph and told them that I had often been inside it. It is not often that one goes inside a photograph in a book. Father was more hurt than surprised, because the author said nothing about his church being of antiquarian interest, and it quite spoilt his breakfast. He kept on asking for the book again, in case a bit about it had got into some other chapter by mistake, and muttering to himself when it didn't. I was hoping that he would decide to take me away from school and send me somewhere where they didn't have sports, but his dislike of *Rural Rambles Round England* didn't seem to go as deep as that, and I went back at the end of September as usual. Of course what I am really hoping is that one day, in a later edition, the author will add: 'My literary readers will doubtless wish to make an excursion to the famous Vicarage where Antonia Fell, our great woman novelist, was born.'

But it looks as though I shall have to wait a little for that.

2

It is now time that our great woman novelist introduced you to the hero of her story. But as I wasn't there all the time, being at school, I must explain first how it is that I can tell you about it. Authors don't do this as a rule, being unable. I read a book once about a woman dying alone on a prairie, and it went on for pages describing her last dying thoughts; and I did wonder, being very young at the time, how the author got to know them so well when he wasn't there and couldn't have been told by anybody. Of course I am aware now that this is the Art of the Novelist. But when he is telling you a true story, and is one of the characters in it, then the Art of the Novelist hasn't got so much scope, and he can't describe people's dying thoughts unless he says 'Probably' or 'It may well be'. Of course his Art encourages him to touch up conversations a little, particularly anything which he said himself, and I shall probably do this, but you will have to guess for yourselves what my characters are thinking. Except when I tell you of my own ruminations.

Well, Father is the Vicar, and has to take a spiritual interest in everybody in the village, which is quite different from being nosey, but has the same result. And Father always tells Mother everything, mostly twice. So when Mother goes into the kitchen to see Rose (who is our cook and has been with us since I was born, which shows what a sweet thing Mother is) naturally they talk about everything including what Father said. In the holidays I spend a good deal of time in the kitchen, because I shall be living in a little flat in Chelsea one day doing my own cooking, and Rose and I are very great friends in consequence. So I really know everything, including when Father gives Mother a melodious cough meaning 'Not before the child'.

I was only ten when old Mrs Hetherington died, but of course I remember her well, and I remember my excitement when I heard that Ballards had been sold, and wondering who the new owner would be, and whether he would have any great influence on my young life; because Ballards is the sweetest cottage, and I was always in and out of it when Mrs Hetherington was alive, and she left me a moonstone necklace which I used to wear in bed, because I was too young to wear it in the daytime, and Father wanted to lock it up until I was older, but Mother said, 'Who would look in a child's bedroom for jewels?' and as the answer was Nobody, I was allowed to keep it under my handkerchiefs when I had any, which is why I wore it in bed when nobody but myself could see; but I don't now, that sort of excitement wearing off very quickly.

(I fear that my memories have run away with me, and I shall try to make my sentences shorter in future.)

Ah me!

How young one was!

'A Mr John Anderson,' said Father at breakfast on that well-remembered morning. He made it sound like the Archbishop of Canterbury.

'Coo! I bet he stinks,' said Bill.

Bill had just inherited this unlovely word from one of the choirboys, and couldn't be separated from it. Father told him to leave the room and not come back until he had learnt to talk like a gentleman. He went out, and should be there still, but being in the middle of his porridge, he began to cry, and Mother brought him back. He was only eight. The conversation was then resumed.

'Married?' asked Mother.

'I presume so,' said Father, as if this state were natural. Little did he know that his only daughter would never marry, an author's books being her progeny.

'When do they move in?'

'Any moment, I understand. The house is in perfect condition, of course.'

'Shall I still be allowed to go there, Mummy?' I asked.

'When I have called, darling, and if Mrs Anderson invites you,' said Mother.

'When will that be?' I piped. I am afraid I was very young then, asking all these silly questions, but I want my readers to feel that I am hiding nothing from them.

'Next holidays, perhaps,' said Mother.

That's the worst of school, it interrupts the holidays so remorselessly. I said, 'Oh dear,' and changed the subject, not caring to think of the coming term.

But I couldn't wait all that time. So in the afternoon I got on my bicycle and rode over to Ballards, which is only three minutes away on a bicycle, and there was Mr John Anderson and a large furniture van, and the one was superintending the unloading of the other. There were furniture men too, but they had aprons, so one knew at once which was Mr Anderson. He was the very big, elderly one.

'Good morning,' I said to him.

'Good morning,' he replied.

'Are you Mr John Anderson?' I asked.

'I am,' he said.

'I am Miss Antonia Fell,' I announced.

He gave me a funny little dip of the head, not having a hat on. He had a sad sort of face, not unhappy-sad, but wistful-sad, like a spaniel's when you have to explain that you can't take him for a walk. I think it is possible that Alfred, Lord Tennyson's cocker spaniel wanted to be taken for a walk just when his master was beginning 'Tears, Idle Tears', and it was this which gave it that yearning sadness.

'My father is the Vicar of this parish,' I said rather grandly. People generally say 'Oh' when I impart this information, but there are many ways of saying it. I should describe his as really wondering more if the wardrobe could possibly make its way into the house, and what he would do if it couldn't.

'Are you married?' I asked.

'No.' He was silent for a long time, as if thinking of something else, and then said, 'Are you?'

'No,' I replied. I didn't say that I was bound to celibacy, not having decided on this at that time, but I did explain that I was only ten, and that in England one couldn't be married until one was fourteen, though in hot climates like India it was different. He didn't seem to know this. Of course I see now that he may have been still wondering about his wardrobe.

I stood, leaning over my bicycle and shifting about from one foot to another (I was very young and *gauche* in those days), and whenever he looked in my direction I smiled at him, and then I rang my bell once or twice to see if it was working, and at last he said, 'Well, thank you very much for calling' and went into the house. So I got on to my bicycle and rode home. Do I need to tell my readers that I am bitterly aware of my lack of poise throughout this encounter, and that though it was not until last Easter that Miss Prendergast informed my parents that I was much more poised this term, I had been uncomfortable about it long before that?

But five years ago I was a carefree child, and you can imagine with what pride I told them all about it at tea. But when I told them that he wasn't married, Father said that I was a very rude little girl to have asked such a personal question; a remark which I attributed at the time to jealousy, because Father asks people if they are saved, which is much more personal.

Well, that was how I met Mr John Anderson, and I didn't see him again until the Christmas holidays, as I had to go back to school. Although I was only ten, I was already going to boarding-school, because I am so advanced for my years.

Of course by Christmas Father and Mother had got to know him, and he was what is called *persona grata* in Essington society. So now I will tell you what I knew about him, both from the inhabitants of the Vicarage and my friends in the village.

He was 55, and had retired from business; but as he hadn't told anybody what business he had retired from, it was thought to be something that one wouldn't want to linger on in conversation. Like suspenders. Because when at a dinner-party one of the guests says, 'I remember when I was Governor of the Bermudas,' it is rather a falling-off and embarrassing for all concerned, if you say at the end of his story, 'That reminds me of when I was making suspenders.' Far better to remark, 'Of course in the business world we often get examples of what you were saying. I remember in 1923,' leaving it possible that you were Lord Mayor of London in 1924.

This was the first time he had lived in the country, he had always wanted to, but if you're in business in the City you cannot unless you go up to London every day, which isn't living in the country, and isn't really country if it is as near to London as that. Of course he might have gone to Nottingham and made lace like the Beaver, but somehow we were sure that London had been his commercial home. And he had brought a man and his wife from London to look after him, a Mr and Mrs Watkins. He had only engaged them a few weeks before coming to Essington, so all their confidences revolved round His Lordship. Mr Watkins had been with His Lordship for years and years, and had only left him because he wanted to be with Mrs Watkins; but when you asked him what Lordship, he suddenly remembered that he hadn't polished the silver, and you had to run along.

Well, that was all we had found out by Christmas, and now I suppose I ought to describe his looks, because if you can't get a picture of him in your mind, this story might as well not have been written. It is very difficult to describe looks. The easiest way would be to say that he looked a little like an overgrown, slightly moth-eaten Uncle James, only then I should have to describe my Uncle James, which would be difficult again. Of course if he looked like the King or Mr Churchill, then that would tell you all you want to know, but people are rarely so obliging.

He was big and slow-moving, and he walked with the fingers of his hands open. I don't know if that matters but he did. He had a big, clean-shaven face, rather like what Long John Silver's must have been. His hair was grey and sort of fuzzy-looking, as if it had been singed, and if you rubbed it, it would all rub off. He had those lost-dog eyes I told you about, but only when he wasn't really talking to you. When he was interested in what you were saying, his eyes were quiet and kind, and suddenly he would be quite boyish, and he would laugh very softly to himself, as if he didn't want to wake his memories. I told myself later on, when I understood life better, that he had lost somebody very near and dear, and was always remembering; and sometimes, if you were lucky, you could make him forget. So I never knew whether he was really a little deaf, as they said, or just remembering.

He was the kindest man I ever knew.

But of course I didn't really know him at all in those holidays, so I shall now pass lightly over two years and come to when I was twelve.

3

Father once preached for twenty minutes on the difference between 'requisite' and 'necessary', the chief one, which he didn't think fit to mention, being that they are spelt differently. My own feeling about this sermon was that it was neither. Of course one can't go on about goodness and Moses Sunday after Sunday, but I did think that he was getting a little out of his depth that morning through not knowing anything about the ways of writers. The author of 'Dearly beloved brethren' used both words, either because (*a*) he liked the sound of them together; or (*b*) meant to cross out one of them when he had made up his mind which, but forgot; or (*c*) was afraid he was on the short side anyway, and didn't want to waste anything. In the same way we need not ask ourselves why I have already written fifteen pages in my exercise-book, and am only just beginning. Every real author knows that the first anxiety of literary composition is how one can possibly drag the story out so that it gets up to the sixth page of one's exercise-book, and that the next is what one will do for another exercise-book when the 32 pages are finished. Because one is suddenly filled with the sustaining knowledge that one could go on for ever. So in future I shall try not to be so discursive, but confine myself to a straightforward narration of events. It will be difficult, because I fear that I am of the same school as Mr Henry Fielding and the Rev. Laurence Sterne, who evidently had all the exercise-books they wanted.

We get most of our news of the great world from *The Spectator* and Miss Viney's Fred, Miss Viney's Fred being the more in touch with events of interest. Miss Viney lives at Rosemount, and I always go to see her on the first day of the summer holidays, which is partly politeness and partly raspberries. She is a very nice lame person, and gets along quickly with a stick in a sort of wriggle from side to side, which makes her seem more bustling than she really is. Fred is her nephew. He works in a Bank in London; and owing to being said Good-morning to by all sorts of influential people, gets to know things like how many husbands Myrna Loy has had and if we have a secret naval base in the Black Sea.

So Miss Viney asked if he knew anything about a Mr John Anderson of London who had lately come to live among us, because of course we were all wanting to know if it really *was* suspenders. I suppose she must have described him very carefully, so it was not surprising that once again Miss Viney's Fred came to our help. Miss Viney showed me his letter, I mean the part she was letting me read.

It said:

'There was a Superintendent John Anderson who retired last year, one of the Big Four at Scotland Yard, would that be the man? Don't you remember the Luton case, the one that first put him on the map? And then the Cave Murders and The Girl in the Cistern, in fact most of the really gory ones. He was badly knocked about by a race gang just before he retired, and I should think, if he's your man, and he sounds just like it, that Essington must seem a haven of peace to him after all he's been through.'

So *that* was who he was! Well, of course, as soon as I had settled with the raspberries I went straight back and asked Rose about the Luton case and the Cave Murders and the Girl in the Cistern, because she reads it all in the Sunday papers and says it gets you out of your groove. I thought Luton was a place, I know it used to be when I was in IVa, but it was the man's name, and he strangled his wife and buried her under the floor of the summerhouse, which is a very good place which nobody thinks of, and was pursued to Morocco; and I was too young to hear about the Cave Murders which were just murders in a cave, and Rose says that the girl whose body was found in the cistern wasn't murdered by the man who was hanged, but by somebody else. I suppose this often happens.

Well, you can imagine how interesting this was, and I just couldn't wait to find out if it was really our Mr Anderson. So I got on my bicycle and went to Ballards. Of course I shouldn't have done this at my present age, but I was only a child.

Mr Anderson and I were great friends by this time, and as soon as he saw me he led the way to the sort of little terrace behind Ballards, and Mr Watkins brought out drinks. I had some orange-squash with ice in it, and he had a glass of sherry. He asked me all about the last term, and I told him, because I never mind this in the first week of the holidays, and only stupid people ask you about it in the last week. Mr Anderson never did. And then, heartened by the orange-squash but a little swallowy, I put my question to him. I must remind my readers that this was a long time ago, and I was only twelve.

'Mr Anderson,' I began, and swallowed.

'Yes, dear?'

'Are you the Superintendent Anderson who solved the Luton case?'

I only asked him about this one, because I didn't want him to think that I knew about the one I was too young for, and even in those distant days I could feel how tactless it would be to ask him about the one when he hanged the wrong man.

He was just going to drink, and he stopped and put his glass of sherry very slowly down on the little table in front of us. Then he picked it up and drank it off.

'Who told you that, Tony?' he said in a sort of muffled voice.

'*Are* you?' I asked obstinately and very rudely.

He shrugged his big shoulders, and said, as if it had nothing to do with him, 'I don't think it can ever be claimed that one man solved a case. It wouldn't be fair to all the others who helped.'

'But you can say that but for one man it *wouldn't* have been solved,' I said rather cleverly.

'Well, yes, sometimes perhaps.'

'And were you that man?'

'If you must have an answer—I suppose I was. Perhaps everybody wouldn't think so. There was a Sergeant Blythe who——' He broke off suddenly and said, 'Are you greatly interested in crime?'

'No!' I said indignantly.

'Neither am I.'

'I think it's silly.'

38

'Most of it is,' he agreed. Of course, he wasn't really agreeing with me, because I meant it was silly to read detective stories like Bill, and he meant it was silly to be a criminal.

The silence got rather oppressive after that, so I said meekly, 'I'm sorry I asked you, but I just wanted to know if that was who you were.'

He nodded, and murmured, 'Miss Viney's Fred,' and I blushed, being liable to this in those days.

'I want you to understand,' he said at last. 'Look!' And he pointed.

'You mean Ballards?'

'Yes.'

'It's just too lovely,' I said, 'because it is the loveliest house I have ever seen.'

'Can you understand that there are horrible things in the world which one mustn't talk about in its presence?'

'Yes,' I whispered.

'And then—look!'

He brought his hand round in a sort of semi-circle, and there was the garden a glory of snapdragons and marigolds and mallows and hollyhocks, and beyond it the quiet meadow going down to the stream, with the brown cows gently swishing their tails, and the hum of bees in the peaceful blueness of the morning. I felt rather choky, it was all so beautiful suddenly.

'Do you understand,' he said, 'that, sitting here, one just can't think of men and women, people like ourselves, shut away, seeing nothing but a little patch of sky through a barred window?'

'But if they were wicked,' I said, 'weren't you right to put them there?'

'Who is to say how wicked each one of us is?' he said gently. 'Who knows but God?'

Somehow when he talked about God like that it seemed real to me, as it never does in Father's voice.

'Yes,' I said.

He poured himself a little more sherry, and drank it. Then he wiped his mouth and said:

'So that is why I am just Mr Anderson here.'

'Yes, Mr Anderson,' I said humbly.

'Or, of course, Uncle John to my little Tony, if she likes' he added, looking down at me with his funny smile.

'Oh!' I cried, and put my arms round him, and kissed him. It was the first time I had kissed him. I am not one of those girls who treat kisses lightly.

'Let's go and look at the raspberries,' he said, getting up and blowing his nose.

Full though I was of raspberries, I went.

4

The news that our Mr Anderson had been one of the Big Four soon became what Mademoiselle Stouffet (more widely known as Stuffy) would call *un secret de polichinelle dans le village*. At least, I think she would. For the benefit of those of my readers who never reached Modern VIB I will translate this as meaning that everybody now knew it but nobody talked about it. In case anybody thinks that it was I who betrayed Mr Anderson's secret, I will merely remark that all Essington knows anything which Miss Viney's Fred has told her, and that it was because of me telling everybody that Mr Anderson didn't want to talk about it that nobody did. For we were all too fond of him to disregard his wishes.

Nevertheless it made a difference in our feeling for him. He had always been everybody's friend, but now he had a sort of halo of authority which made us look up to him. He took a great interest in cricket, though too old to play, and was ever ready to umpire in our matches, which is an unrewarding task, leading to acrimony and disillusion. Yet now he had only to lift a finger up, and all argument was stayed. This is unusual in village cricket. If Mr Prossett of The Three Fishermen was having a little trouble round about closing time, which I understand is when you most often have a little trouble, a hasty message down the road to Mr Anderson, and all was harmonious again. When he was unanimously elected People's Churchwarden, it was at the back of everybody's mind that *he* wouldn't help himself from the plate. I don't wish to imply that Churchwardens generally do this, but it is a thing which it is easy to suspect other people of doing when you haven't the chance of doing it yourself. And I blush for my sex (this is not a real blush, of course) to have to admit that it is mostly the women who suspect other women's husbands of behaving in this nefarious manner.

And to give one last example of our hero's position in the village I will add that when one of the inmates escaped from the County Asylum seven miles away, and was understood to be making in our direction, mothers just said calmly, 'I suppose Mr Anderson has been told,' and went on with their washing. How different from the escape six years earlier when even I was not allowed to leave the Vicarage unattended by Father and a sheep-dog.

Of course Uncle John had been elected Vice President of the Cricket Club, the Football Club, the Horticultural Society, the Archaeological Society and the Girl Guides Association as soon as he arrived in the village, but these are honorary posts entitling the holder to subscribe not less than a guinea a year to the funds of the Society. Now he was promoted to President of most of these organisations and Treasurer of all of them. In fact, he became not only the most loved but the most influential person in Essington. Some would add politely 'After the Vicar, of course.' But I think that he had more influence than Father. When Father said anything, people thought, 'Well, of course, he had to say that, because he's a parson.' But when Mr Anderson said it, he was just a man like themselves, and this made it more believable. His goodness was part of himself. To be with him was to feel it.

5

That was a short chapter, because now I have to tell you that he died. He died quite suddenly a few weeks ago of a stroke. I don't know enough to explain what this is, but it is something which comes suddenly to people of a certain age. It happened on the last day of term, and the first news which greeted me when I got home was that my dear Uncle John was dead. I was very unhappy, even though it was the beginning of the holidays.

Father had a telegram from a solicitor in London asking him to make arrangements for the funeral, and saying that he would come down as soon as he could, but it mightn't be for a few days. So we decided to give him a public funeral; by which I mean that we, and by 'we' I mean the village of Essington, were going to pay for it and not take the money back from the solicitor. So one of the first questions to decide was what we were to put on the tombstone.

'I know!' I said suddenly at supper that night.

'What, darling?' asked Mother.

'"He was a good man and did good things",' I said rather proudly.

Father cleared his throat musically and feared that he did not recognize the text. I was not surprised, because his reading has been different from mine, so I explained that it came from 'The Woodlanders' by Thomas Hardy, and was what Marty said of Giles Winterbourne. Father raised his noticeable eyebrows.

'Thomas Hardy?' he said, in the voice of one who had been expecting Isaiah. 'An unsuitable choice for a churchyard, Antonia.' Mother shook her head gently at me, meaning, 'Don't go on now. I'll explain afterwards.' She often does this.

Mother said rather diffidently, 'Couldn't you just put those few words from Daniel, dear? "A man greatly beloved"?'

'Daniel X. II,' said Father at once. 'As it happens, I had already chosen that as my text on Sunday.'

The funeral was on Saturday, and I could see him feeling a little hurt at Mother's suggestion; because it was such a perfect text for a valedictory sermon, and if it were already ordered for the gravestone, everybody would know about it, and its announcement on Sunday would be less dramatic. Father has to think of these things.

Mother, who always knows what Father is thinking, said, 'There's no real hurry, of course, we can't give orders for the stone until we have seen the solicitor.'

'He has given me a free hand, my love, and it is the village's responsibility.'

'But not to choose the date of his birth, dear.'

'True,' said Father, and he gave her a little smile, partly because he loves her (and who could help it?) and partly because he saw that now his sermon wouldn't be spoilt. So that was what we decided.

A funeral is a terrible thing, even if you don't care much about the person. The grave is so deep, and so concluding. He was my first dead friend, and I could not stop my tears. This is not a thing I like doing in public, but the whole village was there, and everybody was crying, so I did not mind. And on Sunday Father's sermon sounded so beautiful that the tears came again; as they are coming now while I write this. But then they would come anyhow, I expect, even if I were writing about an imaginary person who died in my novel.

On Monday the solicitor arrived. He went into Father's study, and was there for a long time. When they came out, Father looked utterly shattered.

I think I shall put some dots here . . . .

Because Mr Anderson's real name was John Luton. And he strangled his wife . . . .

I thought at first that he had told me lies about himself on that morning three years ago, and I couldn't have borne it. But if you read what I have written, you will see that he didn't. He was in prison for fifteen years, and when he came out he changed his name to Anderson, but I don't think he meant it to be the name of the man who had arrested him. Or perhaps he did. I don't know very much about him. Except that, when I knew him, he was a good man and did good things.

It still says on his tombstone 'A man greatly beloved'. But Father added a text from the 31st Psalm; and though I have often differed from Father, I felt that he had chosen the last perfect words for the story of my dear Uncle John.

'*Into thy hands I commend my spirit: for thou hast redeemed me, O Lord, thou God of truth.*'

The Rise and Fall of Mortimer Scrivens

Extract from 'Readers' Queries' in 'The Literary Weekly':

Q. What is it which determines First Edition values? Is it entirely a question of the author's literary reputation?

A. Not entirely, but obviously to a great extent. An additional factor is the original size of the first edition, which generally means that an established author's earliest books are more valuable than his later ones. Some authors, moreover, are more fashionable than others with bibliophiles, for reasons not always easy to detect; nor does there seem to be any explanation why an author, whose reputation as a writer has never varied, should be highly sought after by collectors at one time, and then suddenly become completely out of fashion. So perhaps all that we can say with confidence is that prices of First Editions, like those of everything else, are determined by the Laws of Supply and Demand.

Mr Henry Winters to Mr Brian Haverhill.

Dear Mr Haverhill,

It may be within your memory that on the occasion of an afternoon visit which you and Mrs Haverhill were good enough to pay us two years ago I was privileged to lend her Chapman's well-known manual on the Viola, which, somewhat surprisingly, she had never come across; I say surprisingly, for undoubtedly he is our greatest authority on the subject. If by any chance she has now read it, I should be

45

very much obliged by its return at your convenience. I would not trouble you in this matter but for the fact that the book is temporarily out of print, and I have been unable therefore to purchase another copy for myself.

Miss Winters is away for a few days, or she would join me in sending compliments to you and Mrs Haverhill.

Yours very truly,
HENRY WINTERS.

Mr Brian Haverhill to Mr Henry Winters.
DEAR WINTERS,

I was much distressed to get your letter this morning and to discover that Sally and I had been behaving so badly. It is probably as much my fault as hers, but she is away with her people in Somerset just now, and I think must have taken your book with her; so for the moment I can do nothing about it but apologise humbly for both of us. I have of course written to her, and asked her to send it back to you at once, or, if it is here in the house, to let me know where she has hidden it.

Again all my apologies,
Yours sincerely,
BRIAN HAVERHILL.

Brian Haverhill to Sally Haverhill.
DARLING,

Read the enclosed and tell me how disgraced you feel — and how annoyed you think Winters is. I don't care for that bit about purchasing another copy for himself. He meant it nasty-like, if you ask me. Still, two years is a long time to take over a book, and you ought to have spelt it out to yourself more quickly. I could have helped you with the longer words.

The funny thing is I don't seem to remember anything about this viola book, nor whether it is the sort you play or the sort you grow, but I do seem to remember some other book which he forced on us—essays of some sort, at a guess.

Can you help? Because if there were two, we ought to send both back together. I have staved him off for a bit by saying that you were so devoted to Chapman that you had taken the damned book with you. It doesn't sound likely to me, but it may to him. And why haven't we seen Winters and his saintly sister for two years? Not that I mind—on the contrary—but I just wondered. Are we cutting them or are they cutting us? One would like to know the drill in case of an accidental meeting in the village.

My love to everybody, and lots of a very different sort to your darling self. Bless you.

Your

Brian.

Sally Haverhill to Brian Haverhill.

Darlingest, I did mean to ring you up last night but our line has broken down or the rent hasn't been paid or something, and I couldn't do it in the village, not properly.

How awful about Mr Winters! It was flowers of course, silly, not musical instruments, because I was talking about violas to him when you were talking about the Litany to Honoria, I remember it perfectly, I was wearing my blue and yellow cotton, and one of her stockings was coming down. But you're quite right about the other one, it was called *Country Filth* and very disappointing. It must be somewhere. Do send them both back at once, darling— you'll find Chapman among the garden books—and say how sorry I am. And then I'll write myself. Yes, I think he's really angry, he's not a very nice man.

No, I don't think we've quarrelled. I did ask them both to our cocktail party a few weeks later, but being strict T.T's which I only found out afterwards, Honoria was rather stiff about it. Don't you remember? And then I asked them to tea, and they were away, and then I sort of felt that it was their turn to write. I'll try again if you like when I come

home . . . .

Brian Haverhill to Sally Haverhill.
Darling Sal,

1. Don't try again.
2. I have found Chapman nestling among the detective stories. I deduced that it would be there as soon as you said garden books.
3. Books aren't called *Country Filth*, not in Honoria's house anyway, and if they were, what would you be hoping that they were like? Tell your mother that I'm surprised at you.
4. There are a thousand books in the library, not to mention hundreds all over the place, and I can't possibly look through them all for one whose title, size, colour and contents are completely unknown to me. So pull yourself together, there's a dear, and send me a telegram with all that you remember about it.
5. I adore you.
Brian.

Sally Haverhill to Brian Haverhill.
Something about country by somebody like Morgan or Rivers sort of ordinary size and either biscuit colour or blue all my love Sal.

Country Tilth: The Prose Ramblings of a Rhymester by Mortimer Scrivens (Street & Co.).

Ramble the First: *A World Washed Clean.*
Long ere His Majesty the Sun had risen in His fiery splendour, and while yet the first faint flush of dawn, rosy herald of His coming, still lingered in the east, I was climbing (but how blithely!) the ribbon of road, pale-hued, which spanned the swelling mother-breasts of the downland. At melodic intervals, with a melancholy which little matched my mood, the lone cry of the whimbrel. . . .

Brian Haverhill to Sally Haverhill.

O Lord, Sally, we're sunk! I've found the damned book—
Country Tilth by Mortimer Scrivens. It's ghastly enough
inside, but outside—darling, there's a large beer-ring such as
could never have been there originally, and looking more like
the ring made by a large beer-mug than any beer-ring ever
did. You can almost smell the beer. I swear I didn't do it, I
don't treat books like that, not even ghastly books, it was
probably Bill when he was last here. Whoever it was, we can't
possibly send it back like this.

What shall I do?

1. Send back Chapman and hope that he has forgotten
   about this one; which seems likely as he didn't mention it
   in his letter.
2. Send both back, and hope that he's a secret beer-drinker
   and made the mark himself.
3. Apologise for the mark, and say I think it must be milk.
4. Get another copy and pass it off as the one he lent us. I
   suppose Warbecks would have it.

What do you advise? I must do something about the viola
book soon, I feel. I wish you were here . . . .

Sally Haverhill to Brian Haverhill.
One and Four darling writing Sal.

Mr Brian Haverhill to Messrs Warbecks Ltd.
DEAR SIRS,

I shall be glad if you can find me a first edition of *Country
Tilth* by Mortimer Scrivens. It was published by Street in
1923. If it is a second-hand copy, it is important that it
should be fairly clean, particularly the cover. I should doubt if
it ever went into a second edition.

Yours faithfully,
BRIAN HAVERHILL.

Mr Brian Haverhill to Mr Henry Winters.

DEAR WINTERS,

I now return your book with our most profound apologies for keeping it so long. I can only hope that you were not greatly inconvenienced by its absence. It is, as you say, undoubtedly the most authoritative work on the subject, and our own violas have profited greatly by your kindness in introducing us to it.

Please give my kindest regards to Miss Winters if she is now with you. I hope you are both enjoying this beautiful weather.

Yours sincerely,

BRIAN HAVERHILL.

Mrs Brian Haverhill to Mr Henry Winters.

DEAR MR WINTERS,

Can you ever forgive me for my unpardonable carelessness in keeping that delightful book so long? I need hardly say that I absorbed every word of it, and then put it carefully away, meaning to return it next morning, but somehow it slipped my memory in the way things do—well, it's no good trying to explain, I must just hope that you will forgive me, and when I come home—I am staying with my people for three weeks— perhaps you will let us show you and Miss Winters how well our violas are doing now— thanks entirely to you!

A very nice message to Miss Winters, please, and try to forgive,

Yours most sincerely,

SARAH HAVERHILL.

Sally Haverhill to Brian Haverhill.

DARLING,

I hope you have sent the book back because I simply grovelled to the man yesterday, and I had to say I hoped they'd come and see our violas when I got back, but of course it doesn't mean anything. What I meant by my telegram was send the book back, which I expect you've done, and try and get a copy of the other just in *case* he remembers later on. If it's such a very bad book it can't cost much. Bill here is for a few days and says that he never makes beer-rings on books, and it must be one of *your* family, probably Tom, and Mother says that there is a way of removing beer-rings from books if only she could remember what it was, which looks as though she must have got the experience from my family not yours, but it doesn't help much. Anyhow I'm sure he's forgotten all about the book, and it was clever of you to find it, darling, and I do hope my telegram helped . . . .

Messrs Warbecks Ltd. to Mr Brian Haverhill.
DEAR SIR,
We have received your instructions re *Country Tilth*, and shall do our best to obtain a copy of the first edition for you. If it is not in stock, we propose to advertise for it. We note that it must be a fairly clean copy.

Assuring you of our best attention at all times,
Yours faithfully,
H. & E. Warbecks Ltd.
(p.p. J. W. F.)

Mr Henry Winters to Mr Brian Haverhill.
DEAR MR HAVERHILL,
I am glad to acknowledge receipt of *The Care of the Viola* by Reynolds Chapman which arrived this morning. My impression was that the copy which I had the pleasure of lending Mrs Haverhill two years ago was a somewhat newer and cleaner edition, but doubtless the passage of so long a period of time would account for the difference. I am not surprised to hear from Mrs Haverhill that the book has been of continued value to her. It has been so to me, whenever in my possession, for a good many years.

Yours very truly,
HENRY WINTERS.

Brian Haverhill to Sally Haverhill.

DARLING SALLY,

Just to get your values right before you come back to me: It is the Haverhills who are cutting the Winterses, and make no mistake about it. I enclose his foul letter. From now on no grovelling. Just a delicate raising of the eyebrows when you meet him, expressing surprise that the authorities have done nothing and he is still about.

Warbecks are trying to get another copy of *Country Tilth*, but I doubt if they will, because I can't see anybody keeping such a damn silly book. Well, I don't mind if they don't. Obviously Winters has forgotten all about it, and after his ill-mannered letter I see no reason for reminding him. . . .

Sally Haverhill to Brian Haverhill.

SWEETIE PIE,

What a *brute* the man is, he never even acknowledged my letter, and I *couldn't* have been nicer. I think you should definitely tell Warbecks that you don't want the book now, and if he *does* ask for it ever, you either say that he never lent it to you, or else send back the copy we've got, and say that the beer-mark was always there because you remember wondering at the time, him being *supposed* not to have beer in the house, which was why you hadn't sent it back before, just seeing it from the outside and not thinking it could possibly be *his* copy. Of *course* I shall never speak to him again, horrible man. Mother says there used to be a Dr Winters in Exeter when she was a girl, and he had to leave the country suddenly, but of course it may not be any relation. . . .

Brian Haverhill to Sally Haverhill.

Sally darling, you're ingenious and sweet and I love you dearly, but you must learn to distinguish between the gentlemanly lies you *can* tell and the other sort. Don't ask your mother to explain this to you, ask your father or Bill.

Not that it matters as far as Winters is concerned. We've finished with him, thank God . . . .

Mr Henry Winters to Messrs Warbecks Ltd.

DEAR SIRS,

My attention has been fortuitously called to your advertisement enquiring for a copy of the 1st edition of Mortimer Scrivens' *Country Tilth*. I am the fortunate possessor of a 1st edition of this much sought-after item, which I shall be willing to sell if we can come to a suitable financial arrangement. I need hardly remind you that 1st editions of Mortimer Scrivens are a considerable rarity in the market, and I shall await your offer with some interest.

Yours faithfully,

HENRY WINTERS.

Mr Henry Winters to Miss Honoria Winters.

DEAR HONORIA,

I trust that your health is profiting by what I still consider to be your unnecessary visit to Harrogate. Do you remember a book of essays by Mortimer Scrivens called *Country Tilth*, which used to be, and had been for upwards of twenty-five years, in the middle shelf on the right-hand side of the fireplace? I have looked for it, not only there but in all the other shelves, without result, and I can only conclude that you have taken it up to your bedroom recently and that it has since been put away in some hiding place of your own. It is of the *utmost importance* that I should have this book AT ONCE, and I shall be obliged by your immediate assistance in the matter.

The weather remains fine, but I am gravely inconvenienced by your absence, and shall be relieved by your return.

Your affec. brother,

HENRY WINTERS.

Miss Honoria Winters to Mr Henry Winters.

DEAR HENRY,

Thank you for your letter. I am much enjoying my stay here, and Frances and I have been making a number of pleasant little 'sorties' to places of interest in the neighbourhood, including one or two charming old churches. Our hotel is very quiet, thanks to the fact that it has no licence to provide intoxicating drink, with the result that an extremely nice class of person comes here. Already we are feeling the beneficial effects of the change, and I hope that when I return—on Monday the 24th—I shall be completely restored to health.

Frances sends her kindest remembrances to you, for although you have never met her, she has so often learnt of you in my letters that she feels that she knows you quite well!

Your affectionate sister,

HONORIA.

P.S. Don't forget to tell Mrs Harding in advance if you are not going to London next Thursday, as this was the day when we had arranged for the window-cleaner to come. She can then arrange for any other day suitable to you. You lent that book to the Haverhills when they came to tea about two years ago, together with your Viola book, I remember because you told me to fetch it for you. I haven't seen it since, so perhaps you lent it afterwards to somebody else.

Messrs Warbecks Ltd. to Mr Brian Haverhill.

DEAR SIR,

re *Country Tilth.*

We have received notice of a copy of the 1st edition of this book in private possession, but before entering into negotiations with the owner it would be necessary to have some idea of the outside price which you would be prepared to pay. We may say that we have had no replies from the trade, and if this copy is not secured, it may be difficult to obtain another. First editions of this author are notoriously scarce, and we should like to feel that, if necessary, we could go as high as £5, while endeavouring, of course, to obtain it for less. Trusting to have your instructions in the matter at your early convenience,

Yours faithfully,

H. & E. Warbecks Ltd.

Mr Brian Haverhill to Messrs Warbecks Ltd.
DEAR SIRS,

Country Tilth.

I had assumed when I wrote to you that a first edition of this book, being of no literary value, would not have cost more than a few shillings, and in any case £1 would have been my limit, including your own commission. In the circumstances I will ask you to let the matter drop, and to send me your account for any expense to which I have put you.

Yours faithfully,

BRIAN HAVERHILL.

Mr Henry Winters to Mr Brian Haverhill.
DEAR SIR,

I now find, as must always have been known to yourself, that at the time of my lending Mrs Haverhill *The Care of the Viola* by Reynolds Chapman, I also lent her, or you, a 1st edition of *Country Tilth* by Mortimer Scrivens. In returning the first named book to me two years later, you ignored the fact that you had this extremely rare book in your possession, presumably in the hope that I should not notice its absence from my shelves. I must ask you therefore to return it *immediately*, before I take other steps in the matter.

Yours faithfully,

HENRY WINTERS.

Mr Brian Haverhill to Messrs Warbecks Ltd.

DEAR SIRS,

This is to confirm my telephone message this morning that I am prepared to pay up to £5 for a 1st edition of *Country Tilth*, provided that it is in reasonably good condition. The matter, I must say again, is of the most urgent importance.

Yours faithfully,

BRIAN HAVERHILL.

Brian Haverhill to Sally Haverhill.

O hell, darling, all is discovered. I had a snorter from that devil this morning, demanding the instant return of *Country Tilth*, and this just after I had told Warbecks not to bother any more! They had written to say that they only knew of one copy in existence (I told you nobody would keep the damn thing) and that the man might want for it. So naturally I said '£5 my foot'. I have now rung them up to withdraw my foot, which I had so rashly put in it, and say '£5'. But £5 for a blasted book which nobody wants to read—and just because of a beer-ring which is its only real contact with life—seems a bit hard. Let this be a lesson to all of us never to borrow books, at least never from T.T's. Alternatively, of course, to return them in less than two years—there is that
. . . .

Messrs Warbecks Ltd. to Mr Henry Winters.

DEAR SIR,

Country Tilth.

If you will forward us your copy of the 1st edn. of this book for our inspection, we shall then be in a position to make what we hope you will consider a very satisfactory offer for it in accordance with its condition. Awaiting a reply at your earliest convenience, as the matter is of some urgency,

Yours faithfully,

H. & E. Warbecks Ltd.

Mr Henry Winters to Mr Brian Haverhill.
SIR,

Country Tilth.

Unless I receive my copy of this book within 24 hours I shall be compelled to consult my solicitors.

Yours faithfully,
HENRY WINTERS.

Mr Brian Haverhill to Messrs Warbecks Ltd.
DEAR SIRS,

Country Tilth.

In confirmation of my telephone message this morning I authorise you to make a firm offer of £10 for the 1st edn. of this book for which you are negotiating, provided that it is delivered within the next 24 hours.

Yours faithfully,
BRIAN HAVERHILL.

Messrs Warbecks Ltd. to Mr Henry Winters.
SIR,

Country Tilth.

We are still awaiting a reply to our letter of the 18th asking you to forward your copy of the 1st edn. of this book for our inspection. We are now authorised by our client to say that he is prepared to pay £10 for your copy, provided that its condition is satisfactory to him, and that we receive delivery of it by the 22nd inst. After that date he will not be interested in the matter.

Yours faithfully,
H. & E. Warbecks Ltd.

Mr Henry Winters to Mr Brian Haverhill.
SIR,

The enclosed copy of a letter from Messrs Warbecks speaks for itself. You have the alternative of returning my book *immediately* or sending me your cheque for £10. Otherwise I shall take legal action.

H. WINTERS.

Sally Haverhill to Brian Haverhill.

Darling one, *what* do you think has happened!!! This morning we drove into Taunton just after you rang up, Mother having suddenly remembered it was Jacqueline's birthday to-morrow, and in a little bookshop down by the river I found a copy of *Country Tilth* in the 6d. box! Quite clean too and no name inside it, so I sent it off at once to Mr Winters, with a little letter just saying how sorry I was to have kept it so long, and not telling a single 'other sort' except for being a little sarcastic which I'm sure is quite a gentlemanly thing to be. So, darling, you needn't bother any more, and after I come back on Monday (HOORAY!) we'll go up to London for a night and spend the £10 I've saved you. What fun! Only of course you must ring up Warbecks *at once* . . . .

Mrs Brian Haverhill to Mr Henry Winters.

DEAR MR WINTERS,

I am sending back the other book you so kindly lent me. I am so sorry I kept it so long, but it had *completely* disappeared, and poor Brian has been looking everywhere for it, and worrying *terribly*, thinking you would think I was trying to steal it or something! Wasn't it crazy of him? As if you would!—and as if the book was worth stealing when I saw a copy of it in the 6d. box at Taunton this very morning! I expect you'll be wondering where I found your copy. Well, it was most odd. I happened to be looking in my dressing-case just now, and there is a flap in the lid which I hardly ever use, and I noticed it was rather bulging—and there was the book! I've been trying to remember when I last used this particular dressing-case, because it looks as though I must have taken the book away with me directly after you so kindly lent it to me, and of course I remembered that it *was* just before I came to see my people, which I do every year at this time, that we came to see you!

I must now write and tell Brian the good news, because after turning the house upside down looking for it, he was actually *advertising* for a copy to replace it, and offering £10—ten *pounds*, think of it, when its actual value is sixpence! Wouldn't it have been awful if some horrible mercenary person who happened to have a copy had taken advantage of his ignorance of book prices and swindled him? But, whatever its value, it doesn't make it any the less kind of you to have lent it to me, or careless of me to have forgotten about it so quickly.

Yours most sincerely,
SARAH HAVERHILL.

P.S. Isn't this hot weather delightful? Just perfect for sun-bathing. I can see you and Miss Winters simply *revelling* in it.

Christmas Party

'OH, there's a letter from Ruth, how nice.'

'What does she say?'

'Wait a moment, dear, I must find my glasses.'

'Telling you the train, I expect. Might I have the marmalade? Some day it will be explained to me why it's always on your side of the table when you don't eat it. Jessie must have a reason, but it escapes me. Thank you. You told Ruth that Raymond and Coral were coming by the 4.50?'

'Yes, but I don't know if Stephen can get off so early. They keep him so late sometimes.'

'In a Government office? That will be news to a lot of people.'

'Now then . . . Oh dear, Penelope has a slight cold.'

'Babies always look as though they had slight colds, I don't see how anyone can tell the difference. You don't mean that they're not coming?'

'Oh no, no. By the 4.50, that's a comfort. So now they can all come together.'

'Better tell Hoskings.'

'I told him yesterday that he'd have to meet Raymond— well yes, perhaps I'd better just give him a ring, or he'll be wondering about the others. I'm so glad Mark is coming by train. I don't like him dashing about the country on that motor-bicycle, particularly at night.'

'Mark? You didn't tell me about that. Has he written? When?'

'This morning, dear. It's here. Just a postcard to say "Coming by 4.50".'

'May I look?'

'It was only a postcard, dear. I thought you would have read it.'

'Never saw it. I was wondering why he hadn't written to me. May I—Thank you. "Coming by 4.50. Mark". Good. You'd better tell Hoskings he'll want both cars— or shall I go and meet them for one?'

'Better leave it to Hoskings, dear. You'll be wanting to make the cocktails.'

'That's true . . . And I must make sure the television set is working. I'm glad I got that in time for Christmas. I don't suppose they've any of them seen one. I know Mark hasn't."

'Yes, dear, but don't let us sit in the dark *all* the time.'

'No, no, of course not. But there it is, if they want it.'

'Yes, and that reminds me, the bedside light in Coral's room has gone. Put in a new bulb for me, Gerald, they always look as if they were waiting to explode when I do it.'

'Right . . . I say, Helen, you do think that Coral will like that what do you call the thing?'

'*Boutonnière*. Oh, I'm sure she will, dear. It was very expensive. And Ruth will love the bedroom slippers.'

'She'd better. I'd put her over my knee and give her a damned good spanking with them if she didn't. Can't do that to Coral unfortunately, not being one's own daughter. She's not exactly——'

'What, dear?'

'Easy. Except on the eye, of course.'

'Well, we know who we wanted Ray to marry, but when you look round at all the extraordinary girls he might have married, I don't think that we must complain.'

'There's still Mark, of course. Not that he'll be thinking of it for some time yet. And who said that I was complaining of Coral? It's a pleasure to look at her. All I say is that she's not exactly one of us. So damned aloof. D'you think they're happy? Why haven't they got any children? Been married two years.'

'Gerald dear, are you suggesting that young married people can't live happily together in a small flat unless they have children; or that they can't have children unless they are happy?'

'Leave it, Helen, leave it. And I'll have half a cup, and I mean half. A little more milk this time, you never give me enough milk.'

'All the same, I think I know what you meant. There, is that better? And peel me an apple, will you, darling? Or, better still, share one with me, I don't really want more than half. You mean that husband and wife don't always agree about children, and if they are quarrelling about it, then they aren't happy.'

'Practically what I said, wasn't it? What does Ruth think?'

'If she thinks about it at all, she thinks that now she has given you a grandchild, any other baby in the family would be a—what's the word?'

'Mistake.'

'No, dear. I could have thought of that for myself. Anti-climax, that's it.'

'Ruth seems to forget that her baby is a Rawson, not a Merridew.'

'I don't suppose she forgets, she just doesn't think it matters.'

'One doesn't want the family to die out.'

'Well, dear, it won't be doing it this morning, so we'll just have to wait and see. You reminded Philbeach to bring in some holly?'

'Of course. Not too much of it about this year, I'm afraid.'

'Oh, I expect he'll find some, he always does. I wish I had a few flowers for Coral's room. Such a bad month.'

'Nothing in the greenhouse?'

'Not for picking. Oh well, she'll understand. And there's the new *Vogue,* she'll like that. The girls had better have breakfast in bed, then there won't be so much pressure on the bathrooms.'

'What will Jessie say to that?'

'I daresay I can make it all right with Jessie. Coral's so decorative in bed, that always appeals to them, and of course she'd do anything for Ruth.'

2

'By the way, Coral, did you write and tell Mother the train?'

'Just as you like, darling.'

'What did you think I said?'

'Yes, darling.'

'Coral, I'm asking you. Did you write and tell Mother the train?'

'Did I write and tell Mother the train? Did—I—write— no, it's no good, sweetie, I'm not with you. The author and I are in a little shack in the Adirondacks, and at any moment the postman will knock twice. It's very difficult being suddenly asked about mothers. What were you saying, darling?'

'Oh, never mind. I was just wondering, I didn't notice you were reading. Sorry.'

'What did you wonder, darling?'

'I just asked if you had written to tell Mother about the train.'

'No, precious, I thought *you* were going to.'

'As a matter of fact, I did.'

'You did?'

'Yes.'

'Ray darling, one of us is definitely going downhill. Taking a long distance view of the situation from my little eyrie in the Adirondacks, it seems to me that if a letter has been written to your mother telling her about the train, our united purpose is achieved. She now knows about the train. Obviously there is a flaw somewhere, but for the moment I don't see it.'

'You told me *you* were going to write. It was just by chance that I happened to mention it.'

'You have mentioned it every day for the last week, darling. It couldn't have been a coincidence every time.'

'I mean just by chance I happened to mention it in my letter to Mother.'

'Ah well, it's the same train whether you mentioned it by chance or by grim purpose, so that's all right. What a very, very ugly word "mention" is. Let's not mention it again.'

'It would have been rather more polite, don't you think, if *you* had written to her, and said how much you were looking forward to coming down for Christmas?'

'More polite, perhaps, but not so truthful, darling. And it still

63

wouldn't have told her what train we were coming by. What train are we, by the way? Something tells me I ought to know.'

'Obviously the 4.50. It's the only good one.'

'Would it be obvious to your mother too? Because if so——'

'Oh God, why do we have to madden each other like this? At least, I suppose I madden you, I know you're maddening me.'

'Am I, sweetie? I'm so very sorry. Let me return to my little shack.'

'Coral darling, what *is* the matter? Would you rather we *didn't* go down to Wheatleys for Christmas?'

'Much.'

'Coral!'

'You didn't really want to know, did you, darling? It was just a rhetorical question. I was supposed to say "Don't be so absurd", and you would have said "Well, then?"'

'I had no idea.'

'That shows what a good wife or a good actress or a good something I am.'

'What's the matter with Wheatleys?'

'As an hotel, darling, nothing. Comfortable beds, central beating, log fires, first class cuisine, fully licensed, constant h. and c., the usual offices conveniently placed— which is always, I think, *so* important—willing service and every possible home comfort. Oh, I nearly left it out— delightful rural surroundings.'

'But you just can't stand the family. Is that it?'

'You want me to continue the inventory? Very well, sweetie. If I had met your father out anywhere, we should have got on madly together, and everybody would have said "Who's Coral's new boy-friend?" As the father of a family in the bosom of his family, and being a bit frightened of me anyway, he doesn't seem to sort of co-operate. I forget now whether I did kiss him or didn't kiss him when we first met, but whichever it was, it must have been wrong. Or done in the wrong way. Your mother naturally doesn't like me. She probably had a girl in her mind for you— you must tell me about her one day—and is always comparing me with her, and thinking how much nicer it would have been if only little Margot had been coming down to them for Christmas. Mark is a thoroughly nice person, but I should like him more if he weren't always telling me about the girl he is in love with. This is always slightly annoying for anybody moderately good-looking, but it is more annoying when you have just worked yourself up into taking an interest in Betty and telling yourself that she can't be as frightful as she sounds, and then find that it isn't Betty any longer, it's Sally. All this is rather silly and personal, I know, because Mark is an extremely attractive boy—or would be, if he weren't always moaning for somebody else when I see him. Stephen is all right; naturally I have a strong feeling for him as a fellow-alien. But I've seen so many Stephens with watch-chains and striped trousers and a dispatch-case in the cloaks that I don't really get much of a kick out of them. He explained the Gap to me last time we dined there, and I felt it yawning between us more and more widely as the evening wore on. Still, I think I like him more than any of you do. No man bores me all the time: there's always something. As for Penelope, she's just like any other baby of that age. One says *"Isn't* she sweet?" or "*Hasn't* she grown?" whichever sounds the less unlikely, and looks around for somebody else. Oh, I was forgetting Jessie. Jessie and I get on very well together. I'm taking her down an old dress of mine. She'll look ghastly in it, but she won't know. There!'

'You haven't mentioned Ruth.'

'No, darling, I thought I'd better not.'

'You mean you hate her?'

'No, sweetie, it's just that Ruth and I took one look at each other three years ago, and rushed off to Reno and got a divorce for incompatibility.'

'I always felt that she was rather unenthusiastic about *you*, but I thought you liked *her* well enough.'

'That, darling, is one of the incompatibles. Our idea of good manners.'

'I admit she is a little outspoken——'

'She admits it too in the most charmingly outspoken way. I suppose all those years in the Sergeants' Mess saying "Eyes right"——'

'She was a Section Officer.'

'Was she, darling? Somehow I always see her in the Sergeants' Mess.'

'Well, thank you for being so frank about us all.'

'*Vous l'avez voulu, Georges Dandin.*'

'So now we know where we are.'

'Well, darling, I'm not sure about that, but at least we know where we shall be for Christmas.'

'What I don't know is where you'd *like* to be.'

'The reason why you don't know, sweetie, is that you have never asked me.'

'All right, I'm asking you now—at least, it's too late now, of course, but suppose I'd said a month ago "Darling, where would you like to go for Christmas?" what would you have said?'

'Oh, Raymond, my idiot child, don't you see that if you *had* said that, then it wouldn't have mattered *where* we went? I'd probably have said "Wouldn't you like to go to Wheatleys, darling, because if you'd like it very much——" and perhaps I should have found that you didn't really like it as much as all that, and would rather have been going off alone with me to a little inn in the Cotswolds or an hotel in Paris, or—oh, I don't know, but it would have been fun talking it over. And if I had felt that you couldn't bear Christmas anywhere but at Wheatleys, and were just being sweetly unselfish about it, why of course I would have said "Oh, darling, let's go to Wheatleys." But—oh, well.'

'Yes . . . I see . . . I'm sorry, darling.'

'Sweetie!'

'Next year——'

'Yes, next year. Ray . . . *Darling? This isn't the Adirondacks!* Help, help!'

3

'Stephen!'

'Yes?'

'Come here a moment, old thing.'

'What is it?'

'Steve—*ern*!'

'Damn. Oh, all right . . . What is it?'

'You haven't upset anything?'

'Not that I know of. Did you want me to?'

'Silly old boy, I just wondered what the damn was about. Oh, I don't mind, one gets used to swearing in the Army. Did a bit of it myself if it comes to that. I wondered if you had spilt the ink.'

'I haven't.'

'Well, are you busy at the moment?'

'I am trying, in the face of constant interruption, to finish that report.'

'Oh well, you've missed the post now. Look, old man, the point is, which of your dressing-cases are you taking? Because, if you take the big one, then we can fill up with the presents and one or two things of mine and Baby's. *You* won't want much.'

'No, not much. Only my dressing-case to myself.'

'Play the game, old thing. We're all in this together. Naturally if I had any room left over in mine for anything of yours—all I want to know is which dressing-case you're taking, and then I shall be able to make my own plans. Don't forget that I've got Baby to think of.'

'I wish you would think of her as a unit and not as a species. The name is Penelope.'

'Time enough for that, old man, when she knows we're talking about her.'

'I frequently refer to you as "Ruth" rather than "Woman" when you don't know that I am talking about you. The cases seem to be parallel.'

'Yes, well, I can't discuss parallelograms now, I've got to do the packing. You're taking the big dressing-case, is that all right?'

'No, I'm taking the small one.'

'Aren't you being just a little bit obstructive, old man? Why is it so necessary for you to take the smaller one, when the whole side benefits if you take the larger one?'

'I might say, my dear Ruth, that the smaller one was your wedding-present to me, and that I cannot bear to spend a single night away from it. What I do say is that the other one isn't really a dressing-case at all. It has none of those invaluable partitions for brushes, combs, nail-scissors, tweezers and the now unfashionable razor-strop. Only when fortified by the companionship of your dressing-case do I feel sufficiently sure of myself to face a week-end at Wheatleys.'

'It's a damned good one, though I say it myself. It put me back eighty-five guineas.'

'Indeed? Not a sum to be lightly left behind in the box-room. I shall take it with me.'

'Oh well, if you're going to play for yourself and not for the side——What did you mean by "facing" a week-end at Wheatleys? It sounds as if you didn't *like* going there.'

'I hope so. I couldn't dislike it more.'

'My dear old thing, what *do* you mean?'

'When, as a very young member, I was first privileged to enter the Athenaeum, I felt like a new boy at school. Nobody talked to me. Everybody seemed to know everybody except myself. The only place where I didn't feel an outcast was in the lavatory. By repairing thither every few minutes and washing my hands vigorously and in obvious haste, I managed to give myself, and I hope others, a continuous impression that I was on my way to be the life and soul of the party in some more social corner of the club. Making the necessary allowances for the difference in the intellectual atmosphere and the size of the lavatory, I have felt much the same at Wheatleys.'

'Oh, nonsense, Stephen. You get on well enough with Coral, anyhow. Don't think I haven't noticed it.'

'Coral and I are as friendly as any two castaways would be who accidentally found themselves in the same caravan in an Esperanto Holiday Camp. If we didn't talk to each other, we should have to learn Esperanto. It is a pity that we bore each other so profoundly. On the intellectual plane, I mean.'

'The only plane that interests Coral is the slap-and-tickle plane.'

'Naturally I shall leave Penelope's education in your hands, but you must see that she doesn't pick up any coarse expressions from her mother.'

'Sorry, old man, but five years in the Army—— Don't think that I don't like Coral. I like her very much.'

'Oh, I realised that you liked her very much. The signs are unmistakable.'

'It's only that I don't think that she is the right wife for Raymond. I'm sure she's ruining him.'

'Ah, I hadn't realised that. Financially or morally?'

'Both, I should say . . . What did you mean by Esperanto? Or didn't you?'

'My dear Ruth, I am in the habit of choosing my words. I meant that your family, like every other family, has a language of its own, consisting of unintelligible catch-phrases, favourite but not generally known quotations, obscure allusions, and well-tried but not intrinsically humorous, family jokes. For instance, there was a constant reference last Christmas to somebody or something called Bufty.'

'Pufty.'

'I accept the correction, without admitting that it is in itself elucidatory.'

'It was terribly funny. It was when Raymond was four years old. Let me see, I was six, because it was the day before my birthday, so he would be just short of four. We had taken a house by the sea——'

'Yes, dear, and you all shrieked with laughter, and you have been saying "Pufty" to each other ever since. One needs to have lived in the atmosphere of a family joke to appreciate it properly. Bald narration rarely does it justice. That is the point which I was endeavouring to make.'

'The point being that you are bored stiff at Wheatleys?'

'Let us say rendered uncomfortable by the realisation that I am not there on my own merits, but merely as witness to Penelope's legitimacy; so that when the Vicar's wife says archly to her "Where's Daddy?", you can answer truthfully for her "In the lavatory".'

'Well! Why didn't you tell me all this before I fixed it up? We could have gone to *your* people if you had said so.'

'Nothing would have induced me to say so. You would have found it extremely unpleasant. My mother would have taken you up into her room and shown you countless photographs of myself as a baby, and told you how much, much more beautiful I was than Penelope. Father, unlike yourself, strongly objects to women in slacks, calling constant attention to the place where he particularly disapproves of them. My brother, whom I dislike profoundly, would make love to you and then try to borrow a fiver. My sister and you would loathe each other even more enthusiastically than you and Coral do. It would be an interesting but not a happy Christmas.'

'I don't loathe Coral, and I'm quite sure she doesn't loathe me. I've always tried to help her. If I had had her in my section, I could have done a lot for her.'

'Leaving the question of Coral's higher education for the moment, you now see that I am not a family man, my dear, and that I think family parties are a mistake.'

'In other words, you would rather we spent Christmas here—just the three of us?'

'Yes, Ruth. Or, if you and Penelope liked to go to Wheatleys—just the one of us.'

4

'Then you won't come, Mark?'

'Darling, I've told you, I can't possibly. You know how I'd love to. Oh, Sally, do try to understand.'

'I understand perfectly. I'm going to St Moritz with the Campbells, they've asked me to bring a man with me, I've invited you, and you've turned me down. It's all quite simple, and rather humiliating.'

'Darling, don't be such an idiot. I might have been stuck in an office instead of on my own, and then how could I possibly have come? There's nothing humiliating about asking a man to go out with you, and then finding that he's booked up.'

'Obviously if you had been stuck in an office, I should never have thought of you. But you're perfectly free; and, if you're going to be a writer, I should have thought that the more experience of every kind you got, the better. And there's a good deal of difference between asking a man to go to a dance with you—or having two tickets for Wimbledon or something—and choosing him out of everybody else to spend a fortnight in Switzerland with you, practically alone.'

'Oh God, don't I know? It's wonderful of you. Don't I wish like hell that I could come? You talk as if I were doing it on purpose. I'm just as sick about it as you are, only——'

'I'm not in the least sick about it, don't flatter yourself. There are plenty of other people in the world—Rex would jump at it——'

'Oh lord, not that little twerp?'

'At any rate he isn't tied to his mother's apron-strings, as some people are.'

'I've told you that this has nothing to do with Mother. It's Father.'

'Daddy's little boy.'

'All right, if you care to put it like that. I don't know that it helps.'

'Sorry, forget it. It's just that I simply can't understand you, Mark. You've always pretended to be rather keen about me.'

'Yes, I think you can start with that assumption fairly safely. If this weren't the Ritz Bar, I'd illustrate it for you. What publishers call profusely.'

'All right, you're keen about me. . . . Well, naturally, of course, you're fond of your people——'

'Not naturally, but I am.'

'Yes, and no doubt you'd have quite a good Christmas with them——'

'Well, we'll have a family four-ball one morning, I expect, and I like seeing my niece, she's rather fun, and Father has a new T.V. set—oh, it won't be so bad.'

'Exactly. You're not wildly excited at the prospect?'

'I'm certainly not.'

'Would you enjoy coming to Switzerland with me?'

'Ten thousand times more.'

'One might almost say that you *would* be wildly excited at the prospect?'

'One might. Only wildly is a very tame word.'

'Then why on *earth*——'

'You'd better have another drink, hadn't you, darling? This is where we came in.'

'No, go on, I want to understand. You are of age and your own master. You have the choice of two things, neither of them in any way wrong. And you deliberately choose the "not so bad" one instead of the "wildly exciting" one. I can't make sense of it.'

'Well, try, darling. I'll put it in words, more or less, of one syllable. My people like having all the family round them at Christmas in the old family home. Silly, sentimental, old-fashioned, mid-Victorian, Christmas-number, anything you care to call it. But they *like* it. Raymond was away a couple of years in the war, of course, but Ruth was always stationed in England, and I was at school through most of it, so the war didn't make very much difference. We've always been together at Christmas ever since I can remember. I'd far sooner be in Switzerland with you; I'd far sooner be anywhere with you. When you began about Switzerland this evening, I was just wondering if I dare ask you to spend Christmas with us at Wheatleys. Rather apologetically, because we haven't much to offer you. Well, that's off. You're going to Switzerland. But I can't come with you, because I've told them that I'm coming home. They are expecting me, and it will disappoint them terribly, particularly Father, if I don't come. I'm very fond of them both, and very grateful, because I do think, so far as I'm concerned, that they have been model parents. Well, that's all. *Somebody's* got to be terribly disappointed—me or them. Or as we writers say, I or they. And since I'm doing the choosing, I don't see how I can possibly avoid choosing myself. That's all.'

'I see.'

'You don't. Not in that voice.'

'You didn't think of *my* disappointment, I suppose?'

'You told me not to flatter myself.'

'You needn't. Give her my love, won't you?'

'Who?'

'This other girl, in the country.'

'Sure you won't have another drink?'

'No, thanks. I must ring up Rex. I think Rex, don't you?'

'I think so, from what I've seen of him. Nice curly hair, definitely not Daddy's little boy, and probably in the black market for nylons. Shall we go?'

5

'Good-bye . . . good-bye.'

'Good-bye.'

'Good-bye, Father.'

'Good-bye, my boy. Come again soon.'

'Good-bye, Penelope, bye-bye, darling.'

'Grannie's saying good-bye to you, darling, say "Bye-bye, Grannie." Oh, she said "Gannie"! Did you hear her, Stephen? Yes, darling, that's who she is—Gannie. Good-bye, Mother, I'll send you the pattern.'

'Any time, dear. Good-bye. Good-bye.'

'Good-bye. . .'

'Well—that's over. I think they enjoyed themselves, Helen.'

'Oh, I'm sure they did, darling.'

'Mark looked a bit run down, I thought.'

'He hadn't quite such a good appetite as usual, but I expect it's just that he's in love again.'

'Mark? Nonsense. Working too hard, probably, and not getting enough exercise . . . I think they all liked their presents.'

'Oh, I'm sure they did. Is that the pen Mark gave you?'

'Yes, one of those patent things. Writes five miles or something. Just what I wanted. Wonder how he knew.'

'Oh, well, I expect he knew somehow. Did you like your pipe?'

'Haven't tried it yet, but it looks all right. I expect Ray helped her choose it. She was looking very pretty, I thought. Particularly in that blue thing.'

'Coral? Yes, she's almost too attractive. I hope dear Ray is happy. I wish I could get to know her better. I'm sure she's a nice girl really.'

'Much more friendly this time, I thought, what I saw of her. Next time you go up to London, why not take her out to lunch, and——'

'Yes, I think I will, Gerald, that's a good idea. But don't expect me to go up in a balloon with Stephen, because I just couldn't manage it.'

'Oh, there's more to Stephen than you think. For one thing he's a damned good putter.'

'I daresay, dear. I wouldn't get to know about it in a balloon.'

'I told you, or didn't I, that Mark and I beat them 2 and 1. We were playing pretty well—well, we generally do when we play together—but Ray was right off his drive, and if it hadn't been for Stephen's short game, particularly his putting—though of course that doesn't say that he's easy to live with . . . Ruth was looking as well as ever, I thought. Wonderful health that girl's got. Mark tells me that they think a lot of Stephen in the Treasury. Ruth will be Lady Rawson one day, you'll find. How will you like *that,* Helen?'

'Well, as long as she doesn't expect Jessie to call her Your Ladyship, I shan't mind. I'm just going down to the pillar-box, dear. Can I post anything for you?'

'I'll go, I'll go. Give me your letters.'

'It's quite all right, dear, I shall like the little walk.'

'I'll come with you . . . You know, Helen, much as I like having them all here for Christmas, I must say it's a great relief when they've gone, and we are alone together again.'

The Three Dreams of Mr. Findlay

MR ERNEST FINDLATER, bank manager, 48, married, had two day-dreams of which he was very fond.

The first was of himself and a beautiful native girl (but not too native) lying side by side on the white sands of a Pacific island. He is wearing a hat of palm-leaves which she has woven for him, she a coral necklace which he has strung for her. Otherwise they are in all their naked beauty, Mr Findlater's heightened by a lightly sketched-in six months of tree-climbing, hut-building and so forth before the dream begins. Soon they will plunge into the lagoon ('without hat', he remembers just in time) and swim lazily side by side through the blue translucent waters. Mr Findlater is now a good swimmer. At first he had thought of saving her from a shark somewhere about here, but he soon saw the folly of this. Not only would sharks be a nuisance in the lagoon, but, since she had given herself to him already, there was really no need for one. Back, still lazily, to the beach, and a deep draught of—kvass? kava?—he must look that up, one wants to get the details right—and luscious guavas, tamarinds and pomegranates. And then—love. Or would it be better the other way round: love first and refreshment afterwards? Well, that would be for Lalage to say. He thought of her as Lalage; Hula-hula, his first choice, presenting itself to him later as either a bird or a dance.

The second dream was that he came home from the Exminster Conservative Club one afternoon to find a car outside the gate. As he opens the front door, Bridget comes rushing from the kitchen, tears streaming down her cheeks. 'Oh, sir!' she wails. 'The mistress! The poor mistress!' Firm steps are heard overhead, and Dr Manley's legs are seen coming down the staircase. Arrived in the little hall, Dr Manley puts a kindly hand on Mr Findlater's shoulder. 'You must be brave, Findlater,' he says. 'Death, the Great Reaper. He cometh to one and all. A sudden stroke. I could do nothing.'

It might be thought that one of these dreams was a natural sequel to the other, but this was not so. The two dreams were distinct in Mr Findlater's mind. In the first one Minnie had neither present nor past. Obviously she would have been out of place in person on his island, but he refused to have even the memory of her with him. Just as the dream presupposed six months of rejuvenation to fit his body to lie beside Lalage's, so it may be said to have derived from that glorious day twenty years ago when he decided *not* to ask Minnie to marry him; or, asking, was rejected. He and Lalage were alone in the world; they always had been, they always would be.

Nor must it be thought that Mr Findlater was just a man who hungered for amatory adventures in his real life, and, denied them by a jealous wife, pursued them in dreams. Lalage was no mistress. She stood for all which he had wanted from Minnie, and had never had; sympathy, companionship, appreciation, peace of mind and body, love, happiness, rest. Since Lalage had to be everything which Minnie wasn't, her body must be beautiful, and she must not be ashamed of it; nor scornful of his. So they lay side by side, happy in each other on their island beach, talking as old friends talk. Lalage's English was the prettiest thing imaginable (her father, Mr Findlater sometimes thought, had been a shipwrecked Irishman), and just to lie there and listen to her was to listen to celestial music. There were times in his waking life when Lalage's voice seemed to Mr Findlater her most precious gift of all.

The second dream was also complete and self-contained. Its realisation, if such were to happen, would not lead Mr Findlater straight to the South Seas, in the hope of meeting an actual Lalage. Its realisation would be happiness enough in itself. To be able to have breakfast in bed on Sunday just because he wanted to have breakfast in bed on Sunday; to do his crossword or his Patience of an evening without having it referred to as his 'everlasting

Patience again' or his everlasting crossword; to read what he wanted to read without comment on his childish taste for stories of adventure; to sit and dream without a harsh accompaniment of contemporary scandal; to talk to a charming woman at a party without hearing her disparaged all the way home, without being reminded of his own approaching baldness, greyness, deafness and stiffness in the joints, such as would prevent any charming woman from being interested in him except from pity: Mr Findlater could have gone on for ever like this, recounting the benefits which would follow Dr Manley's delightful announcement that he could do nothing. No need to go to a desert island to look for them. To be free, to be his own master again, was enough.

Now most people would have said that the realisation of Mr Findlater's first dream would have needed a miracle, and that his second dream merely assumed a natural, however unlikely, happening. To him it was otherwise. He could believe more easily in the first dream than in the second. Perhaps this was because the first was fantasy, which creates a living world for itself, while the other was so close to reality that only its realisation could bring it into being. All the facts of life, all his experience of the world, told him that the second dream must remain a dream. Whoever else died, Minnie was imperishable . . . .

And then a third dream began to form itself in Mr Findlater's mind. It was conceived, though he did not know it at the time, in the lavatory of the Exminster Conservative Club; and it was born on that hot, silent afternoon when he came down the hill into the sunken lane, and saw the empty Buick.

2

Mr Findlater was accustomed to lunch at the Club. He was the highly respected manager of the Exminster branch of his Bank; an undistinguished figure of middle height, his lean face clean-shaven and melancholy. He wore, and from his first entry into the Bank had always worn, horn-rimmed spectacles, to enhance his dignity rather than his vision, and he dressed in a short black coat, grey flannel trousers and a bowler hat, thus putting both town and country clients at their ease. He meditated the writing of a history of Exminster, but in spite of the encouragement of his friends and the discouragement of Minnie he had not yet begun it. He found it easier to meditate.

On this particular day Mr Findlater had been called to the lavatory suddenly after lunch, and, as is customary, had bolted the door on himself. Some defect in the bolt made it difficult to release himself later; indeed, for a little while it seemed that he must subdue his dignity to the needs of the Bank, and shout for help. Wondering if it were possible to escape by the window, he opened the lower half of it and looked out. He discovered to his surprise that there was a drop of nearly thirty feet to the ground; and that the angle of the wall in which the window was set cut him off, not only from the basement windows of the Club, but from all outside observation. If he had happened to have with him a rope thirty feet long, he could have escaped to the Bank without anyone being the wiser. As it was, he renewed his attack on the bolt, deciding this time to take it by surprise. A quick but nonchalant pull, and—'There you are!' said Mr Findlater triumphantly. As he hurried out of the Club, he noticed that Rogers, the hall porter, looked up, identified him and crossed his name off the list of members still within. 'Probably the last,' thought Mr Findlater. 'There'll be nobody now till tea-time. What does Rogers do with himself for the next hour or so?'

A few weeks later Mr Findlater found himself again in an unpleasant position. He had gone out by train to discuss some matter of business with an important but temporarily immobile client; had been met in the Rolls, entertained frugally to lunch, and, business done, had been offered the car, a little reluctantly, for the return journey to the station. But it was a fine, summer day, this was a new part of the county to him, and he had protested his eagerness to walk to the station. His host, disregarding the implications of Mr Findlater's bowler hat, gave him a cross-country direction which soon deserted him; within half an hour Mr Findlater knew himself to be completely lost in what seemed to be as deserted a spot as Lalage's island. Trudging on in what he vaguely hoped was the right direction, he came suddenly out of the wild upon a sunken lane. He pushed his way through the hedge and down the bank; and saw, to his great relief, a saloon car twenty yards to his right. It was just in time, for he was beginning to panic. He walked up to it eagerly to ask for further directions, hoping, indeed, that he might even be offered a lift. For he was now tired of this part of the county.

The car was empty. The windows were open, and it was plain that it was not locked; which suggested that the occupants were strolling somewhere not far off. Mr Findlater, therefore, hovered around, listening for sounds or voices. None came. It was one of those still, hot days when the whole countryside seems, in the shimmering light, to be a little unreal. There might be nobody else in the world; the car might be a magic car, it might move off suddenly of its own will, leaving him to wonder if it had ever been there. For the moment, however, it existed. The thought came to him that there should be a map in the flap-pocket of the driver's seat which would give him some idea of his position. A little nervously, after a last look round in the stillness to make sure that he was alone, he opened the door and put his hand in the pocket. There was no map. Instead, he found himself fingering what his detective stories called a gun . . . .

He took it out and looked at it. Like all small bowler-hatted men with a literary taste for adventure, Mr Findlater had always wanted to own a gun. But now there was a new, compelling reason why he should have one. For the moment he couldn't quite remember what it was; he just knew that he had to have one, and that this was his first, and probably his last, chance to get one. Even if the owner of the car came back, as presumably he would, it was unlikely that he would discover his loss until some time later. In any case it was probable that he had no licence for it, and would be unable to report matters to the police. This would be the first time that Mr Findlater had ever stolen anything, but somehow he didn't think of it as stealing. It was obedience to an Inner Voice which said 'Don't argue. Take it and Go', and he took it and went. His sense of direction told him that the car was pointing the way he should have gone, but, fearing to be overtaken, he went the other way for safety. Not surprisingly, it led him to the station.

3

And now Mr Findlater's third dream began; neither fantasy nor mock-reality, but a dream which, at the right moment, would incorporate itself in the real world. He did not tell himself at first that he was going to murder his wife; he just thought that it would be a nice thing to do, and that he might have to do it if nobody would do it for him. Meanwhile it was pleasant to think about it. How, he asked himself, *would* one do it?

Means, motive, opportunity: every murderer had followed those three sign-posts to death: the death of his victim, and, more often than not, the death of himself. One could commit a murder safely, then, if one could conceal those sign-posts. Ah, but that was just what he could do! Consider them for a moment.

The Undiscovered Means: The gun. He had a gun locked up in his safe, which was completely untraceable to him.

The Undiscovered Opportunity: The lavatory window. He hadn't thought it out yet, but he knew, he had always known, that somehow through that window an alibi could be found; so that Rogers would swear that he was in the Club when he was not in the Club.

The Undiscovered Motive: This was easy. All the detective stories made it clear that the police recognised only two motives for the murder of a wife: Money and Another Woman. There had never been any other woman but Lalage; no husband's life could have been more blameless. As for money, there was little enough in any case, and that little could easily be renounced. There was plenty of time.

Time, Mr Findlater saw, was what every murderer lacked, for he never thought of murder save as the last immediate resort. Buy the false beard on Monday and the strychnine on Tuesday; wear the one and dispense the other on Wednesday, and what hope had you of avoiding suspicion? But wait a year after making your purchases before putting them to use, and who is going to trace them to you? Given time, one could do anything. Let us take it easily, allowing ourselves a year from now; a year of preparation, a year in this delightful new dream.

He began that evening.

'You'll excuse my asking, Minnie,' he said, Patience cards spread out in front of him, 'it's entirely your own business, of course, but have you ever made a will?'

'What on earth put that into your head suddenly?'

'Oh, just that I was witnessing a will this afternoon for a lady— we are often asked to at the Bank, you know—and I wondered. So few ladies ever think it necessary.'

'Well, I suppose she had money to leave. I haven't.'

'There are your personal possessions. And I seem to remember your buying some Savings Certificates during the War.'

Minnie made a noise of reluctant agreement; and then added, 'What's the good of a married woman making a will? It all goes to her husband anyhow.'

'Only if she doesn't make a will. You can leave your personal possessions and your money to anybody you like. We have will-forms at the Bank. Morgan would explain it to you.'

'You seem to have arranged it all for me very kindly. Have you any suggestion as to who I leave all my diamond tiaras and mink coats to?'

Mr Findlater smiled to himself at his cleverness, put the black seven on the red eight, and said 'Me.'

'I shall do nothing of the sort! What would *you* want with my things I should be glad to know?'

'Oh, I could always sell them. That brooch your Uncle Herbert gave you—one could get quite a nice little sum for that.'

'Well, of all——'

'The question hardly arises, however, because you are leaving it to your sister Carrie's eldest girl. Or so I have always understood.'

'You have understood correctly.'

'Then doubtless you will say so in your will. Otherwise the brooch will come to me, and I might give it to— ah! the ace at last. Now we can get on.' He got on in silence for a little, and then said casually, 'I had a letter from Robert this morning. Grace goes to school in September. Did I tell you?'

So Minnie made a will a few days later, leaving everything to her sister, except the brooch which went to Mona. If she had had a rattlesnake, she would have left it to Grace. Grace was Mr Findlater's niece.

Motive, like Means, being thus untraceable, there only remained Opportunity. To the leisurely preparation of an alibi Mr Findlater now gave his attention. But still, of course, in an academic spirit.

4

At first Mr Findlater thought of writing down the Pros and Cons of his alibi after the manner of Robinson Crusoe, and then he saw that he must put as little as possible down in writing. What he wanted was an imaginary confederate, an *advocatus diaboli* almost, who would pounce upon the weak points, and so help him to strengthen them. He decided at once that the ideal person for this was Lalage. It was much pleasanter to lie on the beach with Lalage, and talk it over in a lazy, light-hearted way as it came into his head, than put the case seriously before some hard-faced ex-Superintendent of Police. One of the nice things about Lalage was that you didn't have to call the lavatory window the bathroom window, as you would have to do if (supposing such a thing possible) you discussed the matter with Minnie.

MR FINDLATER: Well, that's the rough idea, darling. Now let me have your comments. I mean on the general plan—we'll discuss how to get out of the lavatory window afterwards.

LALAGE: It is the girl's afternoon out, you say?

MR FINDLATER: That's right. It must be, of course. Wednesday.

LALAGE: Then it would be a good idea if you were always in the Club on Wednesday afternoon, not just on the one day.

MR FINDLATER: That's good, darling, that's very good. I'll make a note of that. *(Note 1)*. I must think up some reason. Next?

LALAGE: There must be a back way out of the Club through the kitchens. You want to be sure that nobody could go out that way without being seen.

MR FINDLATER: I never thought of that. Oh, dear!

LALAGE: When is the time you leave?

MR FINDLATER: 3.30. Back by 3.50, I should say. Of course we shall have a rehearsal and time it exactly.

LALAGE: There would be people in the kitchens at 3.30, surely?

MR FINDLATER: Yes, but I must make certain. *(Note 2)*. And also that Rogers doesn't leave his post. *(Note 3)*. This is splendid. Anything else 2

LALAGE *(lazily)*: Not at the moment, darling. Except that I love you.

There was a short interval here, while Mr Findlater forgot his third dream, and went back to his first.

MR FINDLATER *(coming back to business)*: Now then, let's see how we stand. I am known to be always at the Club on Wednesday afternoons. On this particular one Rogers sees me come in for lunch——

LALAGE *(sleepily):* Late for lunch.

MR FINDLATER: What's that?

LALAGE: Always be late for lunch on Wednesdays so that you don't come past Rogers with all the others, and people say how can you notice them all, Rogers, when so many come in together.

MR FINDLATER: Good. *(Note 4)*. Well, Rogers sees me come in, and doesn't see me go out. Oh, but then again, I might have slipped out with the others— that's awkward.

LALAGE: Get Rogers to ring up on the telephone for you at 3. Not every Wednesday, but just now and then, so that it doesn't look as if you were doing it on purpose on this one day.

MR FINDLATER: Darling you're wonderful. *(Note 5)*. Very well, then. I'm in the Club at 3, and Rogers swears that I haven't left by the front, and the people in the kitchen—did I make a note of that? Yes, I did —swear that I didn't leave by the back, and there's no other way out. And it's all quite natural, because I'm there every Wednesday afternoon after the lunchers have gone. Excellent. And now, darling, what about a swim to the reef and back?

So it was that Mr Findlater began at last his *Short History of Exminster*. The Bank closed early on Wednesdays. He had been accustomed to come home for tea, helping Minnie to prepare it in the absence of Bridget; and anything which he had been accustomed to do with Minnie's approval was not easily to be renounced. However, he brought it off. He pleaded the reference library at the Club as his reason for working there; he suggested humbly that Mrs Bryce, who came into Exminster every Wednesday and dropped in to tea, would much prefer to find Minnie alone. This, of course, was obvious. Indeed, it had often been suggested to him, as soon as he had swallowed his first cup, that if he wanted to get on with mowing the lawn, Mrs Bryce (Minnie was sure) would excuse him. Mrs Bryce had a routine for Wednesday which included a hair-set in the morning, followed by lunch with her sister-in-law and a visit to her dead husband's grave. This brought her to Balmoral at precisely 3.45, and put her on the 5.20 omnibus home again. Mr Findlater was getting rather tired of Mrs Bryce, and it was pleasant to think that it was she who would discover the body.

MR FINDLATER: Well, that's all settled. I've attended to all your points, darling, and everything is satisfactory.

LALAGE: You are taking a bag with you every Wednesday to the Club?

MR FINDLATER: I wasn't. Why? So far I have only been making notes for the book.

LALAGE: Darling! What would you do without me——! *There was another short interlude here.*

MR FINDLATER: You were saying something about a bag?

LALAGE: But think on the day of what you will want to carry there. So many things.

MR FINDLATER: Yes, let's think. It's difficult to think of

everything at once. Of course, I shall want the rope and—this is a good idea, Lalage—some towels to prevent the rope marking the cistern-pipe and the windowsill. What else?

LALAGE: Your disguise, of course, darling!

Disguise! Just as Mr Findlater had always wanted to have a gun, so he had always wanted to disguise himself. Of course he must disguise himself! But he would do it cleverly, careful not to overdo it. What was the minimum? As regards clothes, a sports coat and a soft hat, to take the place of the black coat and bowler, with perhaps rather a highly-coloured tie; no more. Face? A false moustache, no spectacles, and pads in the cheeks; this would also disguise the voice if anyone spoke to him. Walk? False heels, which would also add to his height. It was, he remembered from his detective stories, the presence of horn-rimmed spectacles on the mysterious stranger which always suggested disguise to the police. But Mr Find-later would be disguised by the absence of them, which would suggest nothing. His disguise, he told himself, would be simple but impenetrable.

He had to go to London from time to time on business. He bought a large, yellow cavalry moustache (for *Patience,* he explained, humming the Colonel's song), clipped it short and dyed it. At another costumier's he bought heel and cheek pads (*Ruddigore*). He bought a ready-made sports coat and a soft easily-folded hat. When he talked it over with Lalage, they agreed that everything was going splendidly. Until suddenly one night——

LALAGE: Darling!

MR FINDLATER: Yes?

LALAGE: Can you climb a rope?

MR FINDLATER: I imagine that anyone moderately active can go down a rope.

LALAGE: But you have to go up it again.

MR FINDLATER: Oh!

Fortunately, as he had always told himself, there was no hurry. He had bought the rope—'a swing for my little boy, but strong enough to bear his mother too if necessary. Oh, about my weight,

I suppose, the two of them together' —and now he had to learn to climb it. He began by training his muscles in the garden: an eagerness to do all the heavy work which surprised Minnie, and left her uncertain whether to approve or disapprove. There was always plenty of heavy work to be done which she was glad to point out to him, but she hated to think of him keeping fit and strong when she was getting flabby. It was part of her creed for him that he was too old now for any other woman to take an interest in him. However, he went on: morning exercises in the bathroom, digging or cutting down trees in the garden and the little plantation beyond, more exercises at night. Then at a wet week-end, when Minnie had gone to her sister's for a few days, he took off his coat and waistcoat, wrapped himself in his rope, covered it with a macintosh, and went off to Lakeham Woods. He found a suitable tree, climbed it, fastened his rope—(at Lalage's suggestion he had made a study of knots)—and experimented. It was difficult at first; but when he came away he had been down and up, untied and pulled in his rope in two minutes twenty seconds. But it had taken him six months to get there. . . .

And still the planning, the daily and nightly talks with Lalage, went on. This was to be the perfect crime.

5

The perfect crime, like the perfectly produced play, needs a dress rehearsal. On a Wednesday afternoon in June, a week before The Day, a strange man might have been seen in Potters Lane. He was on the tallish side, and walked with a curious forward-thrusting gait, rather like a pre-war débutante. He came to the gate of Balmoral, hesitated a moment, fingered his moustache nervously, and then, with a sudden squaring of the shoulders, walked in. 'Oh, well,' he murmured to himself, but without much conviction, 'I can always say it was a joke.' He rang the bell. 'Coming!' called Minnie, and, a minute later, opened the door.

'You're early, dear, aren't you?' she was saying, and then, 'Oh, I beg your pardon!'

Mr Findlater began to smile apologetically, and then thought that he had better not. He began to take off his hat, and thought that he had better not do that either.

'Er—does Mr Sanders live here?' he asked in a muffled voice.

'Who?'

'Mr Sanders.'

'This is Mr Findlater's house.'

'Oh, I beg your pardon. I must have been misdirected.' He put his hand to his hat again, and turned away.

'There's no—Sanders, did you say?—in Potters Lane. You must have taken the wrong turning.'

'Oh, thank you.'

He went out of the gate and back the way he had come with his curious shuffling walk. As he came out of Potters Lane, he met Mrs Bryce coming in. They passed, ignoring each other. It was pleasant to cut Mrs Bryce. Five minutes later he was back in the lavatory. In another five minutes Mr Findlater might have been seen in the Club library, hard at work on *A Short History of Exminster*.

So that was that. It had been done, it could be done. The only variation necessary was the shooting, and the departure through the plantation at the back, this being not only a quicker but a safer way of return in case anybody heard the shot. Perhaps it would be better to make his approach also from the back, and avoid using his latch-key.

But however successful a dress rehearsal may be, an actor still dreads the first night. Indeed, it is a superstition of the stage that the more smoothly a play goes at the dress rehearsal, the worse the actual performance will be. In the week which followed Mr Findlater had many a talk with Lalage, and always on the same monotonous lines. Indeed, had she not been the angel she was, she must have got very tired of it.

'You see, darling, up to the very last moment I can pretend—I mean I haven't *done* anything yet. It's only just preparation . . . Well, of course, darling, I'm going to, but what I mean is it needn't be next Wednesday. It could be the Wednesday after. No, no, of course, it *will* be next Wednesday, I'm only just saying . . .'

And then, pleadingly:

'It's just a story we've made up, isn't it, Lalage? You and I. Just one of our stories. Say it is, darling. I mean, one doesn't *seriously* murder one's *wife*!'

And then:

'Yes, of course I'm going to. She's detestable. She's ruined my life. My God, I've had twenty years of it, twenty years of hell. Yes, it *is* hell. I daresay it doesn't sound much, just little things day after day, week after week, year after year. But all added together—I doubt if any other man could have stood it as long as I have. Nobody knows what I've been through. Even if I were caught and hanged, it would be worth it. But I shan't be, shall I? We've been too clever for them.'

And so on.

On the Tuesday he came back from the Bank at his usual time. He had made up his mind. He would give Minnie one more chance. If she were the same to-night as she had always been, then to-morrow—— But if she—— His mind thus made up, he put his key to the door and went in.

Bridget came rushing from the kitchen, tears drying on her cheeks.

'Oh, sir,' she wailed, 'the mistress!'

Firm steps were heard overhead, and a pair of legs was seen coming down the staircase. Arrived in the little hall, Dr Manley put a kindly hand on Mr Findlater's shoulder.

'You must be brave, Findlater,' he said; 'you must brace yourself for a great shock. Your dear wife—a sudden stroke. It was all over before I could get here. My poor, dear fellow.'

The River

'The marriage arranged between Mr Nicholas Deans and Miss Rosemary Paton will not now take place.'

I knew them both. I am remembering them now, and that astonishing August morning when I read the announcement in *The Times*, and then read it aloud to Mary, and we stared at each other across the breakfast table.

'Nicky and Roma?' cried Mary. 'Darling, it's crazy! Why, they were here only a month ago, jibbering with love! What on earth does it mean?'

I didn't know. This was in 1937. Perhaps if I had known then, one of us might have done something. We didn't know until two years later, when the Second World War was beginning, and Rosemary had married young Wayne. I am remembering it all now, because at breakfast this morning two paragraphs in the paper caught my eye. The first recorded a posthumous and extremely belated award to an airman who had died very bravely. I had just read this, and had it still in my mind as I turned to the 'Forthcoming Marriages'. At the bottom of the column it said that the marriage arranged between Squadron Leader A and Miss B would not now take place. Nicky fought in the Battle of Britain, rose to be a Squadron Leader with a chest full of medals, and died as bravely as any of them. Somehow it brought it all back. There was Mary across the table, looking not a day older: the same table, the same china. I almost expected to hear her cry 'Nicky and Roma? Darling, it's crazy!'

2

Mary's people had lived at Castle Craddock for hundreds of years. Her father was one of those survivors of the really old families whose founders had somehow been overlooked when baronies were being given out, and who were much too proud to accept titles from upstart Plantagenets and their successors. George Craddock, D.L., J.P. could look any so-called peer in the face, and down his nose at most of them. He became my father-in-law, and I got to know him fairly well. I admired him, liked him, and was rather afraid of him. In the way of wives, Mary used to tell me that he was very fond of me. Well, I wouldn't say that, but he was surprisingly kind to me; particularly when it was broken to him that Mary and I loved each other. Nobody, of course, was good enough for Mary, but he may have thought that at least an unpretentious middle-class professional man was better than an upstart Earl. In any case, Mary could always get round him, even on such an important matter as her marriage.

I was a very young architect in those days, and, leaving out the 'very young', still am. By 1914 George Craddock had reluctantly reached the conclusion that horseless transport had come to stay. Nobody, of course, would want to rush about the country for pleasure in one of those contraptions, but for anybody who lived ten miles from a station they might be useful for shifting luggage, or even guests, from one point to another. So my firm was commissioned to turn an old barn adjoining the stables into a garage, with rooms for a chauffeur above it. My chief went down for the night, made his reconnaissance, and came back to draw up his plans. Then, luckily for me, he fell ill, and it was left to me to see his plans carried out. So, for the first time, I spent a night at Castle Craddock, and met Mary.

We have been married thirty-four years now, and I suppose I am a little more worthy of her than I was; by which I mean that I have done well in my profession, and that nobody could live with Mary for thirty-four years and not be a better man. But I still look across the table at her, and wonder how I dared to ask her to marry me. She was so young, and so old; so innocent, and so wise; so gay, and so serious; so simple, and so precious. I can still remember the agonies I went through when I knew that I was in love with her. I imagined myself telling her; saw her kind, pitying smile; heard old Craddock's ringing laugh; read in *The Morning Post* next week of her engagement to the Duke of This or the Earl of That, and laughed bitterly myself at my own folly. Madness! Still, I suppose I should have had to propose to her anyhow, even without the assistance of Master Nicholas Deans. But I do not know whether, without him, she would have accepted me.

It was the last time I had come down professionally, the last day on which I could pretend that it was necessary for me to be there. There was, as always, company in the house, but on that last morning I had somehow managed to get her alone. We went for a walk. It had rained heavily for a week, but now it was fine and warm again, and if I hadn't been so hopeless I should have been happy. We went down through the pines to the river. Normally it ran gaily and peacefully enough, and in very dry weather an active person could cross it jumping from rock to rock, but now it was a swirling yellow torrent, and only here and there was the top of a boulder momentarily visible in the foam. I told myself that, if only Mary would fall in, I could jump in after her, and we should both be drowned; and perhaps, if she wasn't already in love with somebody else, we should still be together in Heaven, and—well, anyhow, we should still be together. It seemed bad luck on Mary to drown her like this, so I told myself that, if only we had brought one of the puppies with us, and it fell in, then I would jump in and be drowned, and that that was better than the misery which was all I could look forward to for the next fifty years. And I told myself that, if by a miracle the puppy and I came safely to shore, some of Mary's love for the restored puppy would carry over to me, and she might even—well, you see the sort of state I was in. And it was while all this absurd, romantic, heroic, but not really at all heroic nonsense was going through my mind that Master

Nicholas Deans obligingly fell in; and, as near as might be unconsciously, I went in after him. Who wouldn't have done, with the mother shrieking fifty yards upstream, and his girl standing by his side?—particularly if she were already unhooking her skirt, the silly little idiot. I pushed her out of the way and jumped.

It was pure luck that Master Deans and I met, because I couldn't have done anything about it if we hadn't. I grabbed him, and found more than ever that I couldn't do anything about it. I tried to take some small part in events with my left arm, but it hit one of those submerged rocks with a wallop, and that seemed to be that. If it is possible to be extremely happy and extremely angry and extremely frightened at the same time, then that's what I was; or perhaps first one and then the other. Happy because now Mary would never forget me; angry with the river for being so damnably discourteous; and frightened because I was about to die and I didn't know what it was going to be like. I'm afraid that I never thought of Master Deans.

Well, the river took a sudden turn, and we were washed up in a sort of little backwater, and we struggled out. By that time Mary, who could run like Atalanta, was ready for me, while Mrs Deans was still wringing her hands and crying a hundred yards behind. Mary didn't say 'My hero!' or 'Are you hurt?' or 'Is he dead?' she took Master Nicholas Deans from me, turned him upside down, and said:

'You'll find the Craddock Arms down stream by the bridge. Tell them what happened, and ask them to ring up the house. They'll know what to do. Then come back and help. You'd better bring a blanket with you.'

I didn't feel much like running, and I had an idea that I was going to be sick in a moment, but I ran. And then I ran back with the blanket, and a double brandy inside me, feeling like somebody else, and wondering why his left arm looked so silly. Mary, who had been brought up to know everything that a young girl on a desert island, surrounded by wreck-survivors and wild animals, ought to know, was kneeling over Master Deans and pumping air into him in the most professional way. His mother had been sent up the hill where she could see the house, and told to wave to it when help began to come. She would have been a nuisance anywhere else.

'Anything I can do?' I asked.

'Watch me,' panted Mary, 'because you'll have to take over soon.'

'I doubt it,' I said, and passed out.

I had had a fortnight's holiday coming to me; and I spent it at Castle Craddock; the first few days in bed, rather unnecessarily, but I didn't mind because Mary looked after me. It is not quite clear how we became engaged. She said afterwards that it was she who proposed, and that it was when I knocked her down so brutally that she realised that she loved me. I suggested that the moment of revelation came not when I courteously motioned her to one side, but when Mrs Deans, who was a young and pretty widow, flung her arms round my neck and kissed me; and that that husky noise next morning, which she may have thought was a water-pipe, was me proposing to her. She said, 'Well, anyhow, darling, I'm jolly well going to marry you.' I suppose that in the ordinary way we should have seen too much of this Mrs Deans, who had been a complete stranger and now looked like being a friend for life; but the First World War was at hand, and life very soon left the ordinary. Mrs Deans was whirled back to London in a torrent of gratitude; Master Deans, being only two, said nothing of moment; and I married Mary, spent a short but ecstatic honeymoon with her, returned her to her father, and went into the Army.

3

My office was in Bedford Square. We had a flat above it, which I used when I had to, and which Mary and the children used as little as possible, preferring our cottage in Kent. She came up for a night in July 1935, so that we could celebrate the coming-of-age of our engagement— anything for a celebration was our motto.

The always difficult question of whether to dine before the play or sup afterwards, or both, was solved by an invitation to a cocktail party at the Savoy, which fitted in very nicely. It was given by a Mrs Paton, who was a distant cousin of Mary's. I didn't know many of the people there, and was beginning to get a bit bored, when our hostess brought a middle-aged woman up to me, and introduced us. For once I caught the name: Mrs Fellowes.

After we had talked a little, she smiled at me and said, 'You don't recognise me?'

I didn't and said so. I might have added that if I saw her again to-morrow, I shouldn't. She had one of those faces which seem to be about a good deal.

'Well, it was a long time ago that we met, and I've changed my name since then.'

'Your dress too, probably,' I smiled. 'That makes a difference, you know.'

'All the same, I recognised *you*, and you were in pyjamas when I last saw you.'

'Coming out of the bathroom? With sponge?'

'In bed,' she said with an arch smile.

She was obviously enjoying the conversation. I wasn't. Not with her, and on this particular day. I wanted to say, 'Were you bringing my morning tea?' but it would have been rather rude.

I said, 'Sorry, I give it up.'

'I used to be Mrs Deans.'

'That seems to strike a note,' I lied, 'but I'm blessed if I can remember. Mrs Deans,' I murmured to myself, hoping it would come back to me.

'I suppose you're always diving into rivers and saving people's lives?' she said, rather huffed.

'Good Lord! Of course!'

I remembered her. I remembered suddenly that she had kissed me, had come into my bedroom to say good-bye, and that but for her, or the boy—was it a boy? Yes, I was sure it was.

'How is he?' I asked, as if he might still have a bit of a cold. With another flash of memory I got the name. 'Nicholas, I mean.'

95

She beamed at me for remembering the name.

'That's Nicky over there,' she said, nodding towards a young man and a girl standing by the serving-table. 'Would you like to meet him?'

'Very much.' And then I hesitated. 'I say, you haven't told him?'

'He doesn't even know that he fell in. I thought it best not to say anything about it.'

'I'm sure you were right. Let's go on saying nothing about it.'

That was how I met Master Deans again. The girl to whom he was talking was Rosemary Paton. He had just been introduced to her.

4

Mrs Fellowes, fortunately, lived with her new husband somewhere in the North. Nicky was in London, reading for the Bar. He and Roma got engaged one week-end in our cottage. But for Nicky, Mary and I might not have been there, so it was only right that we should have helped him (if we did) to his happiness. We loved Nicky, and I think he loved us; the children adored him. Roma was a very nice girl, but——

It is a funny thing that whenever, at this time, I thought or said or wrote that Roma was a very nice girl, I always went on '*but*——' and then stopped. Because I never discovered what the 'but' was. She was extremely pretty; she was intelligent and could see a joke; she was nice to everybody, and as considerate as a pretty girl is expected to be; she could ride and swim and play golf and lawn-tennis better than most; and I had never heard her say an unkind word about anybody. But—— But what? I couldn't explain, except by saying that something seemed not to be ticking over properly, and I wanted to shake her until it came into play. 'I wanted to shake her.' Was that it? That there didn't seem to be anybody there? Well, that was as near as I could get.

Nicky was tall and dark and eager, with a thin sensitive face, and black hair which kept falling over his left eye and had to be tossed back, and he always seemed to have just discovered, or to be on the point of discovering, whatever exciting thing it was for which he was looking. When two people have been married for over twenty years, their life together, however happy, has a certain regular pitch which can strictly be called monotony. Nicky made a week-end an adventure; not only for himself, but for us. Even the servants—and Mary was always on happy family terms with her staff—used to light up when she told them that Mr Deans was coming.

In the holidays, when the children were at home, we could only manage one guest at a time. It was not until the Easter term of 1937 that Roma and Nicky came down together. They had met again in London a few weeks earlier, and it was obvious at once that they were madly in love with each other. When they came back from a walk on the Sunday afternoon and announced that they had just got engaged, we were a little surprised. In our old-fashioned way we had assumed that they were already engaged; indeed, we shouldn't have been astonished to hear that this was their honeymoon. They had been embarrassingly devoted to each other all the week-end, and embarrassingly unembarrassed in front of us.

Well, we realised that we had lost Nicky for the time being. They came down again at the end of June, and, as far as they were concerned, we might not have been there. In fact, we began to feel a little like an engaged couple ourselves. They were being married in October, and were having a golfing holiday together in August.

They said good-bye to us on the Monday. They wrote their usual charming bread-and-butter letters. And we heard no more of them until that morning when I opened *The Times* and read that the marriage arranged between them would not take place.

'Darling, it's crazy!' cried Mary. 'What on earth does it mean?'

'Some silly quarrel, I suppose.'

'But you don't make a quarrel public in *The Times* one day, and then announce next day that you've made it up.'

That was true. It was obviously more than a temporary quarrel. It was final.

'What does one do?' I asked. 'Write and sympathise? But with which? Presumably one of them wanted it, and one didn't. One is glad and one is sorry.'

'Well, we can't just leave it. I could write to Marjory' —that was Mrs Paton—'but she may not know any more than we do.'

We thought it over.

'I'll write to Nicky,' I said at last, 'and you write to Roma. And we'll just say how sorry we are, and make it clear that if it helps them to confide in somebody, here we are, and, if not, we shall quite understand. That sort of thing.'

So that was what we did. And Roma said politely, 'Thank you very much, but I don't want to talk about it'; and Nicky said, 'It's very decent of you and just like you both, but there's nothing to be said except that I deserve to have lost her, and that it was I who broke it off.'

And what that meant neither of us knew.

5

We didn't see Roma again until April, 1939, when Mary went to her wedding. I made some excuse of business. Whatever had happened, I was on Nicky's side. So was Mary, of course, but Roma was some sort of cousin, and the Craddocks take their relations seriously.

'How did she look?' I asked.

'Radiantly happy, and as pretty as ever.'

'Glad to see you again?'

'I don't think she thought of it as "again". It might have been two years ago, and she was marrying Nicky.'

'H'm!' I said; which meant—well, I don't know what it meant, except that I never understood the girl.

We hadn't seen Nicky. He had gone in madly for flying, had given up the Bar, and had got a job as a test pilot with an aeroplane company in the Midlands. We heard from him from time to time, but he didn't come down to Kent any more. Not for lack of invitations.

And then, a week before war broke out, he invited himself. I drove in to meet him.

'I had to see you all again before the show started,' he said. 'I shall be looking so beautiful in my uniform that you won't recognise me.'

'R.A.F., of course?'

'Yes. How's everybody?'

'Grand. Longing to see you.'

'Martin left school?'

'You mean for good? No, another year, thank God. Elizabeth will want to be a nurse or something, I suppose. What a hell of a business.'

'Oh well, it had to come.'

We had a delightful week-end, almost like old times. We sat up late on Sunday night, after the children had gone to bed. And then quite suddenly he said:

'Let's go down to the garden-house.'

'Won't it be too cold to sit?' said Mary.

'Then get a coat, darling.'

'I think I will too,' I said, 'just in case.'

'As a matter of fact, it's damned hot,' he shouted after us.

We sat out in the still night, one of us on each side of him, my cigarette-end glowing as I drew on it, his face clear cut suddenly in the darkness as he relighted his pipe. We were all silent for a little. Then he gave a long sigh.

'I want to get this off my chest,' he began, 'before——' He left it at that, and went on, 'You two darlings are the only people I could tell it to, and I should like you to know the worst of me.'

'Carry on,' I said. 'It won't be as bad as you think.'

'Pretty bad,' he said.

I felt rather than saw Mary's hand go out and touch his for a moment.

'Well, here it is. I think we told you that we were going to stay with some people in Devonshire—your part of the world, isn't it,

Mary?—we were supposed to be playing golf, they were all mad about it. I drove Roma down. For the first three days and nights it rained without stopping. There we all were, and Roma and I couldn't get alone, and it was general hell. On the fourth morning it suddenly cleared up. Everybody rushed to play golf, but we wanted to get away from them all, so we got into the car and drove off. We fetched up for lunch at a pub called the Craddock Arms. I don't suppose you know it, but——'

'I had a drink there once,' I said.

'Oh, did you? Oh well, then, you'll have seen the river.'

'I have.'

'But not as it was then. It hadn't been like that for more than twenty years, they said at the pub. It was just a raging torrent with waves spouting up on the rocks in mid-stream. We had Duncan with us—you remember Roma's Scottie? He had been sitting at the back, as good as anything, all the way, and we took him along the river to stretch his legs, while they got the lunch ready.'

He stopped. The night was very still. We waited.

'Have you ever frightened yourself with your own imagination? I mean by seeing something which isn't there, so clearly that it is there and you're terrified of it? Off and on all my life I have lain in bed, awake, and seen a river like that, and shuddered with fear, and thought, "My God, fancy falling in!" And there it was. Just as I had imagined it.'

He stopped again to relight his pipe. By the flame of the match Mary and I looked at each other.

'We were walking up stream. Roma had let go of my hand, and was running in front with Duncan, pretending to chase him, and Duncan dodged and fell in. Roma shrieked, "Oh, darling!" All right, now tell me that a sensible person doesn't risk almost certain death for a little dog. Go on. Tell me.'

'He doesn't,' said Mary. 'It's sentimental and idiotic.'

'All right. He doesn't. It's sentimental and idiotic. Human beings are more precious than little dogs, aren't they? Their lives are more valuable. Aren't they? More worth saving?'

'One hopes so,' I said.

'One hopes so. So I did nothing. I just stood there. Damn it, I said calmly to myself, one doesn't risk almost certain death for a little dog. Sensible, that's what I was. Realistic. Not sentimental. Not idiotic. Not——' he paused and added very gently, 'not like Roma.'

Mary gave a gasp. I said, 'Good lord, you mean Roma went in?'

'Whipped off her skirt, and in like a flash. Roma! The girl I loved. Into that raging torrent. Now ask me what I did. Go on!' he shouted. 'Ask me!'

'All right,' I said. 'What did you do?'

'Nothing.' He said it so sadly, so gently, that we hardly heard it. 'Nothing,' he said wonderingly to himself.

Once more there was silence. Once more he put a match to his pipe. Once more Mary and I looked at each other in the flame of it; and she shook her head, meaning 'Not yet'.

'I told myself—I pretended to tell myself that there was nothing I could do. Roma was at least as good a swimmer as I, and I couldn't have helped her. But of course it wasn't that. I was terrified. You've read of people being rooted to the ground in fear. It was like that. I couldn't have jumped for a million pounds. Oh well, that's silly, Roma was worth much more than a million pounds to me. But if I were to have been shot for cowardice the next morning, I couldn't have jumped. There wasn't a muscle in my body over which I had any control. I can't expect you to believe this, but——' He broke off suddenly, shaking his head, as if it were beyond even his own understanding.

'Don't be silly, darling,' said Mary, 'of course we believe you. Tell us what happened to Roma.'

'She caught Duncan up—you know what she's like in the water— and collared him. They were close in shore luckily, where there weren't any rocks and the current wasn't so fast. The river swung round suddenly and they got washed into a little backwater. All danger being over, I became active. I was full of resource. I trotted up stream and fetched her skirt. I trotted down stream with it. And, at the grave risk of wetting the ends of my trousers, I helped them out.'

'*Did* you wet the ends of your trousers?' asked Mary anxiously.

Nicky gave a great laugh, and said, 'Good old Mary, how I do love you two,' and went on with his story, more quickly, more naturally.

'Well, there we all were; Duncan frisking about and shaking himself, Roma wringing the water out of her hair, and I not knowing what on earth to say or do. And then, as soon as she had got into her skirt, she took my hand and said, "Come on, darling, let's run for the inn. I shall have to go to bed while they're drying my clothes, but we can have lunch upstairs if you don't mind my not looking my best in the landlady's nightgown. What fun! Or perhaps it would be nicer if I didn't wear one at all. Don't you think so, darling?" And she gave me a loving look, and squeezed my hand. It was uncanny. It was just as if I had been somewhere else when it happened, and had strolled up and found them on the bank.'

'Poor Nicky. Horrible for you.'

'Yes. Well, it was all like that. Tact. Perfect tact. Not once did she give a hint that anything out of the way had happened, that she had noticed anything, that there was anything for either of us to worry about. With one half of my mind I felt that it was wonderful of her to spare my feelings like this, and with the other half I wished to God she would jeer at me and call me a coward.'

'It was difficult for her,' I said, doing my best for a girl I had never really liked.

'It must have been. But then the whole situation was impossible. There were times in the next few days when I could almost persuade myself that this was my old daydream come back, and that I was imagining it all. And then one morning I heard her talking rubbish to Duncan, and saying, "Did he fall in the river and ask his missis to pull him out?" or something like that. It had happened all right.'

'So you broke it off?'

'Yes. It would always have been between us. Perhaps if we had really had it out—I don't know—but hushed up like that—and anyway a girl can't be expected to marry a coward. Not when she's as brave as Roma. That river —if you could have seen it!

102

No, I couldn't live up to her, she couldn't live down to me. As soon as we got back to London, I wrote.'

Then Mary said an odd thing. Or so I thought at the time.

'Did Roma know what you were talking about in your letter?' she asked.

'Well, you see, I'd been finding it difficult to be as loving as I had been. I always had that moment in my mind. You can't make love when you're thinking of something else all the time. Roma actually thought that I was falling for another girl there. We did have a silly quarrel about that, a girl I'd hardly spoken to. In my letter I just said that, after what had happened, it was obvious that we couldn't be happy together. She may have thought that I meant the quarrel.'

'I'm sure she did,' said Mary. 'How do you feel about Roma now?'

'Do you mean am I still in love with her? Not a bit. I expect it was mostly physical, you know. One gets over that more easily.'

'That's good. Now, Nicky, John has something to tell you. But I think that before he begins I should like to say something about Roma. It's only lately that I have got her clear in my mind, and in any case it wouldn't have done any good talking about it before. You thought that Roma was being tactful—sweetly, unbearably tactful. She wasn't. Tact means considering people's feelings, and Roma has never found it necessary to do that. Rosemary Paton is the supreme egotist. She is the centre of her own stage all the time, and everybody and everything else is just a cue or an audience or a property for her. You didn't exist for her at all when Duncan fell in, except as an audience in the wings. It never went through her head for a moment that you were a coward. You weren't on in the great dog-rescuing scene, so how could you be brave or not brave? And what did it matter to her if you felt this or that off-stage, so long as you were there on your cue, and played your part properly, when the love-scene came on? Roma's whole world is Rosemary Paton—and you are well out of it.'

So that explained Roma; explained that 'but' which used to

103

worry me. I saw it now. She was a dead woman in a dead world of her own.

'I daresay you're right,' said Nicky indifferently. 'That's Roma. But I'm where I was.'

'Well, now John is going to tell you where you were twenty-five years ago. Go on, darling.'

I had known that this was coming, and had been wondering how to deal with it. No friendship between men can survive the knowledge that one has saved the other's life.

'All right,' I said. 'Now listen, Nicky, because this is important, and really quite simple. You say that all your life you have had terrifying visions of a river, that you recognised this as the river you'd always imagined, and that physically and literally you couldn't have gone in whatever the moral compulsion?'

'Yes.'

'Well, it's natural enough. When you were two years old, you did go into that river, at, I should say, that very spot, and the river was pretty much as you saw it more than twenty years later. Terrifying.'

'You're mad!'

'No, it's a fact. And if you like to observe that the world is a very small place, or the arm of coincidence a very long one, you may.'

'How do you know?'

'Your mother talked about it that day we met you.'

He turned to Mary.

'Is this true?'

'Of course, Nicky.'

'Why should my mother talk about it to you?'

Before she could answer, I said:

'Because Mary was there. Your body came to shore in that same backwater. You were dead, Nicky. I don't suppose you knew, but Mary lived at Castle Craddock when she was a girl. She found you there dead, and she restored you to life.'

Mary gave a short hysterical laugh and said, 'Don't be such an idiot, Johnny. Of course he wasn't dead.'

'Who knows?' I said. 'Who knows what happens when the drowned are restored to life?'

Nicky gave a great sigh, squaring his shoulders as if he were easing them of the burden which he had been carrying for two bitter years.

'So you see,' I went on, 'when your mother met Mary again after all that time—well, naturally, when I was introduced to her, she was full of it. We talked of nothing else. And she told me that she had thought it better not to say anything to you; and, like a fool, I said that I was sure she was right. But of course we were desperately wrong. You've had the thing gnawing away inside you all these years, and known nothing about it. So, my dear Nicky, wash out the idea that you are, or were, a coward; or, if you insist, you must give us much better evidence than you have given us to-night.'

There was a long silence this time, a very long silence. It was lighter now, or perhaps I was getting more used to the darkness. I could see Nicky's face. He was looking up into the sky, with that eager look which he always used to have, as if he were on the verge of discovery.

He turned to Mary.

'Did I say thank you nicely at the time,' he said, 'or was I too young?'

'A bit too young, Nicky.'

'Then I'll say it now. Thank you, darling.' He picked up her hand, kissed it, and let it go. 'You'll see. I won't let you down.'

He didn't. He didn't.

Murder at Eleven

Yes, sir, I do read detective-stories. Most policemen will tell you that they don't. They laugh at 'em, and say that they aren't like real life, and that tracking down a murderer isn't a matter of deduction and induction and all the rest of it, which you do by putting your finger-tips together or polishing your horn-rim spectacles, but of solid hard work, over a matter of months maybe. Well, so it is for the most part, I'm not denying it. But why should I want to read books which tell me what I know already? The more detective-stories are unlike the sort of story I'm living, the better I'm pleased. I read 'em for the same reason that you read 'em—to get away from my own life for a bit.

Ever reasoned out why murderers in detective stories are always shooting themselves, or getting killed in a car crash, or falling over a cliff? Ever noticed that? I mean why a story-book murderer hardly ever gets brought to trial? Of course, sometimes it's because he's the heroine's Uncle Joseph, and it spoils the honeymoon if you suddenly wake up and remember that your Uncle Joseph is being hanged that morning. But there's another reason. Proof. All this amateur deducting and inducting is very clever, and I don't say it doesn't find the murderer sometimes; but it doesn't *prove* he's the murderer. Any Police Inspector knows half a dozen murderers he'd like to see with a rope round their necks, but he can't do anything about it. Proof—that's the trouble. I don't mean the sort of proof which convinces a reader who knows anyhow that his favourite detective is always right; I mean the sort of proof which convinces a Jury when the Judge has taken out all the bits which aren't legal evidence, and the prisoner's Counsel has messed up the rest of it.

And that's saying nothing about the witnesses who have let you down. No, it's an easy job being an amateur detective, and knowing that you've only got to point out to the murderer that logically he must have done it, to be sure that he'll confess or commit suicide in the last chapter. It isn't so easy for a country Inspector like me, with a Super and a Chief Constable and a Judge and a Jury to satisfy. Murderers? There're hundreds of 'em walking about alive now, all because they didn't come into detective stories.

All the same, I did know an amateur detective once. Clever he was, he worked it all out, just the way they do in detective-stories. Helped me a lot. But there you are. We were both quite certain who the murderer was, and what could we do? Nothing. I put in everything I knew, all the old solid routine stuff, but I couldn't take the case any further. No proof. Only certainty. I'll tell you about it if you like.

Pelham Place it was called, and a fine place too. Mr Carter who lived there was a great one for birds. He had what they call a Bird Sanctuary in the middle of the park. It was in a wood, and there was a lake in the middle of the wood, fed by a little river, and all sorts of water-birds came there, ousels and kingfishers and so on, and he used to study them and photograph them for a book he was writing about them. I don't know whether it would have been a good book, because he never wrote it. He was killed one day in June, hit on the head with what we call a blunt instrument, and left there. Of course he had a lot of notes and photographs for the book, but it never got finished.

He hadn't made a will, and everything was divided equally between the four nephews, Ambrose and Michael Carter, and John and Peter Whyman. Ambrose, that was the eldest, the one who lived there, wanted to hand the place over to the National Trust, which he said was what his uncle always meant to do, but the others wouldn't agree, so it was sold and they divided up the money. When war came, the Army took it over, and of course that was the end of any sort of bird sanctuary.

Ambrose—that's my amateur detective—looked after the place and helped his uncle with the birds and the book. He said that watching birds wasn't so much different from watching people, and it was the best way of training your powers of observation which he knew, and there was a lot of detective work in it too, and I daresay he was right. It was natural that he should feel more keenly about the place, and want to carry out his uncle's wishes, and equally natural that the other three shouldn't. John and Peter were brothers. John was an actor, mostly out of work, and Peter had just got engaged, he was a barrister but hadn't had any briefs yet, so they both wanted all the money they could get. Michael Carter was Ambrose's cousin, he was in business and doing pretty well, but he had an expensive wife, and money was money. So there it was.

The first I heard of it was from Ambrose, who rang up and said that Mr Henry Carter of Pelham Place had been murdered, and could I send somebody up at once. I couldn't get hold of our doctor, he was on a case somewhere, so I left a message for him, took a sergeant with me and drove off. I don't know why, but I had expected to find the body in the house, sort of taken it for granted, and I was a bit surprised when Mr Ambrose Carter—I'd come across him once or twice, of course—who was waiting for me at the front door, said, 'Round to the left here and take the first fork on the right,' to the driver, and got into the car. And then he said, 'Sorry, Inspector, hope you don't mind my giving orders, it's in Sanctuary Wood. We can get a bit nearer to it this way.' Seemed to have his wits about him, which is what I like.

Well, this is what had happened. Mr Carter had gone out to his sanctuary at about ten in the morning the day before. He generally spent the whole day there and came back in time for dinner, but every now and then he'd stay the night, so as to be ready for them at the first light, so when he didn't turn up the night before nobody missed him.

'Where did he sleep?' I asked.

'There's a hut there. You'll see.'

'Food?'

'Yes, and a spirit lamp and all that. It's quite comfortable. I've spent a night there more than once.'

'So nobody thought anything of it when he wasn't there at dinner?'

'Well, there was comment, naturally, but we were just a family party, and most of us knew what Uncle Henry was like.'

'Then when did you get anxious—or didn't you?'

'He would have been back in the morning for a bath and what little breakfast he had, he always was. John, my cousin, and I went to look for him. We thought perhaps he'd been taken ill. John's there now, not that there was the slightest chance of anybody interfering with—with the body. Nobody ever goes there. It's complete sanctuary.'

If that was right, then it was a family job. So I'd better give you an idea of the family as I meet them. Ambrose and John both had what I call actors' faces though they weren't a bit alike. John Whyman was tall and dark and handsome with the sort of Irving face, you know what I mean? About thirty and a bit cynical-looking. Ambrose Carter, a little older, had one of those round blank comedian's faces which can take on any expression, d'you know the sort? Medium height. Might be fat one day.

He stopped the car and we walked a short way across the park to a wood. The lake in the middle of the wood— well, it was a large pond, really, I suppose—was as lovely a thing as I've seen, and the trees—but we'll skip all that or I shall be all night talking. John Whyman was sitting on a log, smoking a cigarette, and he looked at his watch as we came up and said 'A whole bloody hour,' and Ambrose said, 'Sorry, John, couldn't have been quicker, this is Inspector Wills.' He hadn't seen anybody or anything, of course, and I sent him off in the car with Sergeant Hussey, and told Hussey to wait at the house for the doctor and bring him back. And I wrote out a message for him to send, because I could see that we would want more help. And then Ambrose and I looked at the body.

'Fond of him?' I said.

'Enough not to kill him, do you mean?' he said, looking at me rather comical.

'I didn't mean that, sir, at all,' I said, and it's true, I didn't.

'Sorry, Inspector. And the answer is that we got on very well together. I liked my job, but I can't say that I either liked or disliked him. He was a little—inhuman. More interested in birds than men, and had never had any great affection for anybody, I should say.'

'I know the sort,' I said.

Mr Carter lay on his back. His head and his right wrist were broken, as if he'd put his arm up to defend himself from the first blow, and been killed by the next. It looked as if he'd been dead for some time.

'When was he last seen alive?' I asked.

'About half past nine yesterday morning,' said Ambrose.

'Well, he wasn't alive more than two or three hours after that, I should say, but we'll know more when the doctor comes.'

'Meanwhile, what about his watch, that ought to tell us something.'

I bent down to look at his wrist. The watch had been badly smashed but I could see the time. Eleven o'clock. Murder at eleven, I said to myself. Good title for a detective story.

'Hallo, that's funny,' said Ambrose. T could have sworn——' He stopped suddenly.

'What?' I asked.

'He wore his watch on his left wrist,' he said, a little lamely. It sounded as if it wasn't what he'd been going to say.

'Where was it when you and Mr Whyman first saw him?'

'Where it is now, I suppose,' he said, staring.

'You didn't notice particularly?'

'I noticed that his wrist and his watch were smashed, without paying much attention to it. Subconsciously I assumed it was his left wrist, as that's where you keep a watch. That's why I was surprised.'

'You're certain that Mr Carter did?'

'Absolutely. Look, you can see the strap-mark on his left wrist.'

It's true, you could. I should have come to it in time, but he was quicker. Bird-watching.

He walked round the body, and looked down from behind it. Then he laughed softly to himself.

'What's the joke, sir?'

'Well, well, well,' he was saying. I went over to him and looked too. The watch was the wrong way round.

'You see what happened, Inspector? The murderer broke Uncle Henry's wrist before he managed to kill him. Then he changed the watch to the broken wrist, and broke it too. So now you know that the murder took place at precisely eleven o'clock. Which you wouldn't have known otherwise.'

'Looks like it,' I said.

'Like tying another man's tie for him. More difficult than you think. You're looking at the watch the other way round. What's right for you is wrong for him.'

'What it comes to,' I said slowly, 'is that he wanted us to put the murder at his own chosen time.' I wasn't going to be hurried.

'Right.'

'Which means that it *didn't* take place at eleven.'

'Right. Which means—what, Inspector?'

'Which means,' I said, rather proud at seeing it, 'that the murderer probably has an alibi for eleven.'

'Probably?' he said, surprised like. 'Certainly; or why alter the watch? Well, we know *something* about him.' 'But that's all we do know. We don't know what time he hasn't got an alibi for. The time of the murder.'

'Oh, I wouldn't say that,' he said rather airily. You know what I mean—rather sure of himself.

The ground was dry and hard. No footprints or anything like that. I had a couple of men coming, and they could look for the weapon, but they wouldn't find it, because it was probably in the middle of the lake. As soon as the doctor came I wanted to get back to the house, and ask a few questions. Meanwhile I might as well listen to Mr Ambrose, if he fancied himself as Sherlock Holmes, because he seemed to have ideas, and good ones too. We sat down on a log together and smoked.

'Let's have it, sir,' I said.

'Have what?'

'What you've got up your sleeve, about the time of the murder.'

'Nothing up my sleeve, Inspector, I assure you. Your guess is as good as mine.'

'I haven't started guessing yet,' I said. 'You go first.'

'D'you mean it? Good!' He beamed at me. 'First of all, what would you say the limits are, I mean from the condition of the body?'

'We shall have to wait for Dr Hicks to tell us that. And he'll make 'em pretty wide. May be six hours or so.'

'As much as that? Oh well, let's see what we can do. Now the first thing—— Oh!' He stopped suddenly, and looked uncomfortable.

'Yes, sir?' I said.

'I was forgetting. Of course, that's the first thing to be settled.' He was talking to himself rather than to me, and I waited a little, and then said, 'What is?'

'Where are you looking for your murderer, Inspector?'

'Haven't begun to look yet, sir.'

'Inside the house or outside?'

'I shall want to see everybody inside, of course. And I daresay a lot of people outside too. Any reason yourself, sir, for thinking it was one or the other?'

'The best of all reasons for thinking it was outside.'

'You mean the best of all reasons for hoping it was outside?'

He laughed and said, 'I suppose I do,' and then to himself, 'I suppose that's all I mean, dammit.'

'I should like you to be frank with me,' I said. 'A murderer's a murderer, even if he's a relation.'

'That's true.' He threw his cigarette-end away, and lit another. 'I'll give you both sides,' he said. 'A tramp or a trespasser, an outsider of some kind, comes whistling through the wood, knocking at the undergrowth with the stick he carries, making the hell of a row, and disturbing all the birds. My uncle rushes out at him furiously—as he certainly would—and asks him what the devil he thinks he's doing. There's a fight, the tramp hits him in self-defence, loses his head, and hits him again. Easy.'

'Except for the watch,' I said.

'Exactly, Inspector, you've got it. Except for the watch. In the

112

first place, a tramp wouldn't think of it; in the second place, he'd have a long way to go for an alibi, and a tramp's alibi isn't much good anyway; and in the third place, he wouldn't dare to put the watch on, in case the body was found before the false time was reached, or put it back in case Uncle Henry had been seen alive afterwards.'

'Doesn't that apply to any murderer who fakes the time?' I asked.

'Yes. Except in special circumstances.'

'And those are——?'

'That you know that the murdered man is going to remain in a certain place for a certain time, and, dead or alive, will be visited by nobody.'

'Which was true in this case, and which everybody in the house knew?'

'Yes,' he said, rather reluctantly.

'And, I suppose, the outside men, gardeners and gamekeepers and so on—they would know too?'

'That's true,' he said, brightening up. 'Oh, well, then, just as a bit of theorising, here you are. If you murdered a man at three, and were altering his watch to two or four, which would you choose.'

'Which would you, sir?' I asked.

'Two o'clock, obviously.'

'I don't see the obviously.'

'Well, if I make it two o'clock, it's because I've already got an alibi for two. But if I make it four, it's because I hope to get an alibi for four; and I can't be absolutely certain that I shall. Something might go wrong. I might be with somebody then, but his memory might be bad, or he mightn't have a watch, or he might be a notorious liar. The other way I have made certain of a perfect alibi first, and I put *back* the watch to a time when I can prove I was elsewhere. Even if it is an unplanned murder, there's such a time somewhere.'

Well, that was true enough. Perhaps I should have thought of it, perhaps I shouldn't, I don't know.

'All right then,' he went on. 'The murder took place *after* eleven. How long after? If it were very soon after he couldn't have an alibi for eleven which was watertight. He's got to allow a margin for watches being wrong, and another for his distance from the place of the alibi— in this case, the house, presumably; a good twenty minutes away, if he walked, for he would hardly dare to leave a car about. I think that one's feeling would be for a good safe margin of an hour. You've got your alibi for eleven and a bit after, you kill at twelve, and you put the watch back to eleven.'

'Then why not kill at one or two or three? Still safer by your reckoning.'

'Lunch,' he said. Just like that.

'Does a murderer let his lunch interfere with his plans?' I laughed, sort of sarcastically.

'Not *his* lunch, the dead man's. You can tell, can't you, when a dead man had his last meal?'

'That's right, sir, stupid of me.'

'Uncle Henry would have his at any time between twelve-thirty and one-thirty, and what's the good of pretending he died at eleven, if he'd just finished his lunch? No, Inspector, the absolute limits for the time of death are eleven-thirty to twelve-thirty, and the nearer to twelve the better.'

Well, that was clever, it really was, and I couldn't see anything against it.

'All right, sir,' I said. 'He was killed at twelve. That means that the murderer has no alibi at all for twelve and a watertight one for eleven.'

'As you say, Inspector.'

'In that case, sir, I will ask you where *you* were at eleven and twelve.'

He gave a great shout of laughter.

'I knew you would,' he said, twinkling at me. 'I felt it coming.'

'Nothing meant, sir, of course, but we have to know these things. Same with everybody at the house.'

'Of course. Well, let's think. Times a bit vague; general plan—I walked over to Weston to lunch with some friends. Name given on demand. I left the house a bit after ten, and went over to the garage; talked to a chauffeur and a gardener or two till ten-thirty, and got there, I suppose, at twelve-thirty. It's four miles, isn't it, through the fields, but it was a hot day, and why hurry?'

'Why not take the car, sir? I suppose there was a car available?'

'Mrs Michael wanted to go into town to do some shopping. Besides,' he patted his stomach and looked at mine, 'walking's good for the figure.'

'Meet anybody?'

'Not to remember or identify.'

'Did the others know you were going?' I asked.

'We discussed plans a bit at breakfast. Michael was— oh, but you'll prefer to ask them yourself. Sorry.'

I thought that I might as well know what they had planned to do, even if they didn't do it, or pretended they hadn't. So I told him to go on.

'Michael always brings down masses of papers with him, he's the sort of man who works in the train. I told him he could have my room, and I'd send him in a drink later, and he told his wife that he'd be busy all morning. Peter and his girl—well, you know what the plans of a newly-engaged couple are, Inspector. As long as they are together, they don't mind where they are. I wanted to fix John up for golf, he's always very keen, but an agent or a manager or somebody was ringing him up at eleven, and that would have made it rather late. So he said that, as soon as his call had come through, and he'd done his business, he'd take an iron out in the park and knock round a bit. I don't know if he did, or what he did, or, in fact, what any of them did, but that's what was said at breakfast.'

He got up suddenly, as if he had an idea, and I asked him what it was, because I'd had a sudden idea too.

'His notes,' he said. 'What idiots we are!'

'I was just going to ask you,' I said, and I was, because I thought if he was watching a couple of birds nesting or something he'd make a note of the times when things happened, or anyhow make a note of the time of any photograph he'd taken. That hidey-hole!

You wouldn't have known it wasn't a great beech trunk with bushes all round, and inside a regular home from home. And there was his diary, and the last entry was 10.27! 'What d'you know about that?' I said to Mr Ambrose.

'It's funny,' he said, picking up the diary and turning the pages backwards and forwards. 'After all our clever theorising, too. He would hardly go an hour and a half without an entry or a photograph. Hallo!'

'What?'

'Last entry comes at the bottom of the page. Co-incidence?'

'You mean a page might have been torn out? A page going on to 12 o'clock?'

'Yes.'

'If so, the corresponding page would be loose.'

We looked. There was no loose page, but the corresponding page way back in March was missing. We knew, because an entry broke off in the middle and never went on. Well, it all fitted in, and Mr Ambrose looked rather pleased with himself again.

Well, that was my amateur detective, and very good too, I thought; and now I'll tell you what the professionals got. Mr Carter's last meal was breakfast, and, putting his lunchtime at 12.30, he was killed between 9.45 and 12.30. So our guess at 12 was probably right. But when I came to alibis—and remember, the murderer had to have one for 11, but not for 12—things began to go a bit wrong. There was a woodman called Rogers who had no alibi at all, and the other employed men gave each other alibis for the whole morning. Mr Michael Carter was shut up in Mr Ambrose's study all the time, or so he said. He was a solid, bossy sort of man, looked older than Ambrose, though he wasn't.

'Nobody came in that you can remember?'

'A maid brought me a whisky and soda some time in the course of the morning. I hadn't ordered it, but I drank it.'

'When would that be, sir?'

'She might know; I don't.' Much too busy a man to notice such trifles, he seemed to be saying.

Doris, the maid, confirmed this, but was uncertain of the time.

'It was his elevenses as you might say, sir, only Hilda sitting down on a queen wasp and naturally having to go upstairs to put something on and me helping her and then taking it in myself, well it all made it late like.'

Mr Peter and Miss Mayfield, that was his girl, gave each other complete alibis, as did the chauffeur and Mrs Michael. Of course you'll say that Mr Peter's real alibi, for 12 o'clock, being only confirmed by a girl in love with him, wasn't very satisfactory. But how I looked at it, if the girl was going to give him an alibi anyhow, all that business of changing the hands of the watch to 11, and then smashing it, was pointless. Any time was alibi-time for him.

Mr John Whyman was the one I was most disappointed in. His call had come through at 10.30—not 11, as he had expected and I had hoped; it was over by 10.35; and he took an iron and half a dozen golf balls, and went off into the park. All of which was confirmed by the Post Office and Mrs Michael.

So there we were, and, after all our checking up, the possibilities came down to these:

1. Michael Carter, assuming his drink had come in at 11.10, as he would have known; which gave him an alibi for 11 o'clock in the wood; and no alibi for 12.

2. Rogers; but only if John Whyman had altered the watch when left alone with the body, and had torn out the page of the diary. Why should he do this? Because he was afraid he might be suspected of the murder, being the hardest-up of the nephews, and having discussed with Ambrose the possibility of getting help from his uncle.

3. Any tramp, with John Whyman assisting again. But this was very unlikely, as the wood was in the middle of a private park, a long way from the road.

In the last two cases why didn't John make the time 10.30, when he had an alibi, instead of 11 when he hadn't?

No reason. So you can take out 2 and 3, and that leaves Michael Carter.

And then I'm blessed if that wretched little Doris didn't come and say that what with one thing and another, and talking it over with Hilda like, and not noticing the time Hilda making such a fuss and all, it was 12 o'clock before she took in the whisky. So Mr Michael Carter was out too—and nobody did it.

I had a good think about it that night. I lay in my big chair, and put a pipe on and a drink handy, and another chair for my feet. Because the Super was wanting to take a hand, and I thought I should like to tell him who'd done it before he got all the credit for himself, or called in Scotland Yard.

The first thing I thought about was the watch.

Now it couldn't be clearer than it was that the murderer had done some funny business with that watch so as to fool us about the time. Look at what we had. The mark on the left wrist showing where it was usually worn; the fact that it was upside down, showing that it was put on the other wrist by somebody else; and the page torn from the diary, showing that the real time of death was being hidden from us. What could be clearer than that? 'Nothing,'

I said to myself . . . and then found myself saying 'Nothing' again in a wondering sort of voice, and going on, 'Nothing. Absolutely nothing. The murderer *couldn't* have made it clearer!'

Silly of me, wasn't it, not to have seen it before? Why should the murderer want to make it so clear to us that 11 o'clock was the wrong time, unless it was because 11 o'clock was the right time? You see, if he had broken the watch in the ordinary way on the left wrist, then, whatever time he'd put the hands at, he couldn't be sure we'd accept it. Because everybody knows that the hands of a watch or clock can be altered to suit a murderer's plan. So he did a double bluff. He made us think that he had to get the watch on the right wrist because the wrist was already broken, and he let us think that he hadn't noticed the clues he was leaving behind. In fact, the murder took place at 11, and this was the murderer's clever way of making us think that it didn't.

Mr Michael Whyman, then, could have done it. He had no alibi for 11. Everybody was out of the house by 10.35, and he was alone until 12 when Doris brought in the drink. I took my feet down, and told myself that I had solved the case . . . and then I put my feet up again and told myself that I hadn't. Because Ambrose and John could have done it equally well. Neither of them had an alibi for 11. So I had a drink and lit a fresh pipe, and went on thinking.

Motive and opportunity made it pretty certain that one of the four nephews did it. If the one who did it was trying to make us think that the murderer had an alibi for 11, wouldn't he make sure that one at least of the other three had such an alibi? Only so could he feel safe. Well, what about it? Did Michael know where Ambrose was at 11? No. Ambrose might have been anywhere. So might John. Did John know where the others were? No. He didn't know where Ambrose was, and even if he knew that Michael was in Ambrose's office, he wouldn't know if Michael could prove it. Did Ambrose—and at that I shot out of my chair, banged my fist into my palm, and shouted 'Ambrose!'

He had ordered a drink to be sent in to Michael at 11. That was to be Michael's alibi. John, he knew, had a telephone call coming in at 11; that would be John's. It wasn't his fault that both alibis failed him. Ambrose! The amateur detective who had led me on, who had pointed out the mark on the left wrist, and the upside-down watch, and the missing page of the diary; who was taking no risks with a stupid country policeman, but handing it all to him on a plate. Ambrose, who had asked all of them their plans at breakfast and known where everybody would be. Ambrose, who had so casually let me know that two of his cousins had an alibi for 11. Ambrose, who had proved so convincingly that the murder took place at 12, when neither cousin would have an alibi! Ambrose!

Well, there you are, sir. If he hadn't been so clever, if he hadn't done so much amateur detecting in the wood, I shouldn't have tumbled to it. Helped me a lot, he did. There didn't seem any way of getting legal proof, and we never did prove it. But, as I said at the beginning, we both knew who'd done it.

A Rattling Good Yarn

Most people have heard of Michael Hartigan. It is a well-known name behind the counter, where faces light up when he gives it, and voices say shyly, 'I read your last book, Mr Hartigan,' before adding for the record, 'Then I'll see that that goes off at once, Mr Hartigan.' Mr Hartigan likes this. He likes it all: the recognition, the letters, the invitations, the speeches, the press paragraphs, and, of course, the money. Who wouldn't?

Michael Hartigan writes the Lord Harry books. His publishers print a first edition of 50,000 copies, if they have the paper, and sell it before publication; and there are, of course, serial rights, film rights, radio rights and all the rest of it. Even so, there may be superior persons in Bloomsbury and the backwaters of our older Universities who have never heard of Lord Harry; it is also possible that, as the result of insomnia, shipwreck or other Act of God, one or two of them may be temporarily among my own readers. For their benefit some introduction to Mr Michael Hartigan's hero seems necessary.

Lord Henry Wayne (only called Lord Wayne alternatively in the first book, which has now been withdrawn) was the son of the Duke of Scarborough. He was amateur heavyweight champion in the year when he won the Grand National, besides scoring a century against Oxford. I fancy he won the mile too. I think I remember some mention of it in the first Lord Harry book, at a time when the Wambesi head-hunters seemed to be gaining on him; but, as I say, this one is now out of print. One way and another it had given Hartigan a good deal of trouble. Not foreseeing the future, Lord Harry had pledged himself to Estelle da Suiza, the lovely girl whom he had rescued from the Wambesis when she was on the point of being sacrificed to the Sacred Crocodile. They were married a little later in the Brompton Road. At this time Hartigan was employed in a bank, and there was no immediate thought of a second book. But the acceptance of the first, and its subsequent sales, were sufficiently encouraging for him to try again. It seemed a pity to waste such a well-equipped hero, and almost inevitable that his visit to the Bagoura Hinterland should lead to the rescue of the beautiful Maddalena Ramona as she was being pegged down to an ants' nest. Estelle, meanwhile, was on a visit to her mother at Harrogate; for naturally one wouldn't want one's wife around when rescuing. Unfortunately a similar situation arose in the next six books, in the course of which Estelle went four more times to her mother at Harrogate, and twice to a nursing-home in Portland Place. This proved very helpful, but Lord Harry's style was still a little cramped. So it was that in the ninth book Michael Hartigan took a fateful decision. The poisoned chocolates ('from an admirer') which had been sent to Lord Harry by his old enemy the Ace of Spades, were eaten by the lovely Estelle. The inevitable end came as a relief to the public (who thought that she was seeing too much of her mother), and gave Lord Harry a freedom of expression which he had not hitherto enjoyed. Now he could clasp one lovely heroine after another to his breast, so long as nothing was said about marriage.

Michael Hartigan was a good business man. His early training had given him an insight into the economic laws which govern industry, and he understood why he grew richer and richer as his books became more and more popular. What he didn't see was why his publishers should. John

Smith wrote a bad book, and they made £10 out of it. Michael Hartigan wrote a good one, and they made £10,000. Why? What had *they* done? Nothing. There was no justice in it. A stickler for justice at this time, he acquired a controlling interest in a publishing firm, and became, in effect, his own publisher. This made things much fairer. Now the man who was earning the money was the one who was receiving it.

He received so much that with the publication of his twelfth book he was living in a large flat in Park Lane and employing two secretaries. But he had no illusions about himself. This was what his friends liked in him.

On a certain afternoon in December, Miss Fairlawn, the one he didn't take out to lunch, buzzed through to what she called his inner sanctum to say that a——

'Just a moment,' said Michael. 'With one bound Lord Harry reached the stake to which the half-fainting Natalie was bound, damn, tied. A quick slash of his knife—no——As the oncoming savages—no——The astonishment of the High Priest at this sudden apparition gave him a moment's quarter—grace—dammit, what's the word— breathing-space. Taking full advantage of it he—no— with a quick flick—flash—hasty flick—with a—hell, who cares?' He switched off the dictaphone. 'Well, Miss Fairlawn, what is it? And remember that savages are oncoming all the time, and we mustn't keep Natalie waiting.'

'Oh, I'm sorry, Mr Hartigan. There's a gentleman here who wants to see you.'

'Did you tell him that I didn't want to see *him*?'

'Yes, but—it's all very peculiar.'

'Who is he, anyhow? Press or public?'

'That's what's so peculiar. He says—really, Mr Hartigan, I don't know what to make of it—he says he's Michael Hartigan.'

'You mean he said *I* was? He's right. I am.'

'No, no, that's what *I* said, and *he* said *he* was.'

'Crackers,' said Mr Michael Hartigan after a little thought. 'Does he look crackers?'

'Well, no. He's very young.'

'That means nothing. You can start at any age. You can be born crackers, if it comes to that. Is he listening to all this?'

'Oh no, he's in the lobby. I really think you should see him, Mr Hartigan.'

'Oh, well, if you think so.'

Mr Hartigan brushed his hair, filled and lit the pipe with which he received visitors, puffed out a cloud of smoke, and called 'Come in!' To his surprise a small, unattractive boy in spectacles, clutching a dirty bowler hat, edged through the door.

'Well, young man,' said Michael genially, 'what's all this in aid of? Sit down, make yourself comfortable. My time is your time.'

The visitor sat nervously down.

'I understand,' he said gruffly—'that is, I have been informed, that you write books under the——'

'Just a moment,' said Michael. 'Quite apart from everything else, hasn't your *voice* cracked rather early?'

'What do you mean? I'm eighteen and a quarter.'

'Mr dear Sir, I do beg your pardon. In that case you must have a cigarette. There's a box at your elbow.'

'Er, I—thank—I think—er, no. *No!*'

'Just as you like. Or don't like. Well, now tell me all.'

'What I want to know is are you the man who writes these ghastly books under the name of Michael Hartigan?'

'Or should it be "over" the name? I never know. It doesn't matter, of course. Yes, Mr—er—I am. I gather, sadly, that you are not one of my admirers. By the way, I'm afraid I didn't get *your* name.'

'Michael Hartigan.'

'No, no, that's *my* name. You had all this out with my secretary. We don't want to get wound up about it again. What do they call you at school? Are you still at school, by the way?'

'Er, I—no—I mean, yes.'

'Surely there can't be any doubt in your mind? It's the sort of thing one usually knows so well. Well, what do your friends there call you?'

'Er—Scruffy.' It came out unwillingly.

'An excellent name,' said Michael kindly. 'With your permission, and so that we shall know which one of us is talking, I shall call you Scruffy. Now then, Scruffy, what's the trouble?'

'I want to know if your name is really Michael Hartigan.'

'It is.'

'I don't believe it.'

Michael shook his head sadly. 'When you are an old man, Scruffy, sitting in your bath-chair at Eastbourne, you will regret this.'

'*I'm* Michael Hartigan!'

'Are you sure?'

'Of course I am. Look at that!' He held out his bowler hat. 'Look inside!'

A little reluctantly Michael looked inside, and read on the dirty lining, 'M. R. Hartigan, 256.'

'My dear Hartigan,' he said, 'this is indeed a moment in our lives.' He got up, shook hands solemnly with his visitor and sat down again. 'I shall dedicate my next book to you. "To Michael Hartigan, in admiration and friendship". That'll make the critics think a bit—if,' he added, 'they ever do think.'

'The chaps all believe that you're my father.'

'I hope not,' said Michael, considerably alarmed by this. 'Can't you tell them that I am much too young, much too careful, and much too—well, tell them. Or couldn't your father come down one day and watch you rally the School forwards in the second half, and then you could introduce him?'

'Good lord, I don't play rugger now I'm in the Sixth. Allow me a little self-respect.'

'The things I would allow you, Mr Hartigan, you wouldn't believe. Well, you now have my permission to return to your school friends and tell them that you are *not* my son. Was that what you wanted?'

'What I want is that you should stop using my name. I'm going up to Oxford with a schol. next autumn, and I'm going to be a writer, and how can I write when you've bagged my name?'

'You must do what I seem to have done, Scruffy. Bag somebody else's.'

'There you are!' said Scruffy triumphantly. 'I knew it wasn't your real name. You've got no right to it at all.'

'I assure you I have every right. Deed poll, and all that.'

'If you had to write all this frightful tripe, why couldn't you have stuck to your own name, instead of ruining mine?'

'Oh, believe me, I did want to. For months I had been imagining well-groomed men saying to delicately nurtured women across the dinner-table, "*Have* you read 'The Priestess of the Crocodiles'?"

For months I had imagined bearded members of the Athenaeum Club saying to each other across the billiard table, "Who *is* this Thomas Hardy everybody's talking about?" For months——'

'Is *your* name Thomas Hardy?'

'Was, Scruffy, was. But I bore no grudge against the other Mr Hardy for that. *I* didn't burst into his flat and ask him what the devil he meant by it. *I* didn't whine that he had ruined my literary career by making my name a household word. No, I just sat down at the instigation of my publisher, and thought of Michael Hartigan. So my advice to you, Scruffy, is to pull up your socks—or, of course, pull down what seem to be your pants, I don't mind which—and do the same.'

'It's pretty good cheek, you know,' said Scruffy, with dignity, 'to assume that the cases are parallel. Thomas Hardy, despite his old-fashioned attitude to the novel and his lack of style, was at least a conscientious writer with some knowledge of agricultural matters; whereas——'

'Keep the rest of your fascinating essay for the school Literary Society,' said Michael, getting up. 'Here is your hat. What does "R" stand for?'

'Russell,' muttered Scruffy unwillingly. He didn't know why he said it, when he wanted to say, 'What the hell's it got to do with you?'

'Then you can write your interesting masterpieces under the name of Russell Hartigan. I shan't object. And now,' said Michael, 'rustle off.'

He opened the door.

2

This was the only meeting between the two Michael Hartigans, and Scruffy never forgot it, nor forgave the other his share in it.

Scruffy went through life neither forgetting nor forgiving. He hated almost everybody because almost everybody exposed him in some way. He hated tall people because he was short, good-looking

125

people because he knew himself to be ugly. He despised games because he had never been able to play them; he was contemptuous of good manners because his own manners were so graceless; he scorned pretty girls because he felt that he was an object of scorn to them. Even though he was clever, and was at times assured of it, he hated the more clever for his moments of doubt, and the equally clever for his inability to look down on them. The whole world was in a conspiracy against him. Whatever anybody else did, it was done with the idea of showing up M. R. Hartigan.

So now he hated Michael for his good humour, his ease of manner, his obvious attraction for women (women, ha!); for the absence of all the pomposity, stupidity and conceit which had been imagined for him. Even if the other had exhibited these undesirable qualities, Scruffy would still have hated him for his success, and for his lack of shame in it. And this was Michael Hartigan, the only Michael Hartigan whom the world would now know! Scruffy's righteous indignation accompanied him to Oxford in the autumn.

At Oxford he wrote for the undergraduate papers, contemptuous little articles such as undergraduates love. Whether by pulling up his socks or (as suggested) pulling down his pants, he managed to think of a new name for himself: Gryce. As Russell Gryce he had a small circle of admirers, who looked forward to his triumphant descent on London. His father, a hardware manufacturer, who thought little of writers but never ceased to wonder how they did it, said that he would stake his son for two years in London, and if he wasn't earning a living by then he would have to come into the hardware business. Scruffy left Oxford, settled in London and changed his name by deed poll to Gryce. This annoyed his father considerably, but his word was his bond, and what he had said he wouldn't go back on.

'But if you think I'm going to address my letters to him "Russell Gryce Esquire"——'

'I'll address them, dear,' said his wife. 'Besides, you know you never do write.'

Scruffy began with a novel of Oxford life. It was to be the first real novel of Oxford life, but publishers didn't think so. He wrote an entirely original play, released from the old-fashioned strait-jacket of plot and counterplot. It was thought by managers to owe something to Tchekov. This annoyed Scruffy almost as much as it would have annoyed Tchekov. He wrote many other things, but was seldom rewarded. His contempt for the theatre and the publishing world was now extreme. He saw no future for himself save as a critic.

It was when the two years were nearly over, and he was still far from earning a living, that he came across Archibald Butters again. Archie was a round-faced, beaming, hospitable youth, a contemporary at Oxford, who had sat at Scruffy's feet imbibing culture. He had admitted apologetically that he knew nothing about literature and all that, but knew what he liked; in which respect he differed from Scruffy, who knew a great deal about it, but was never sure of liking anything until it had been rejected by the public. At first he was Scruffy's only friend and admirer; but as Russell Gryce got better known, Archibald Butters was a little overlooked, although it was always a pleasure to have a free meal in his hospitable rooms. Meeting him now, Scruffy found himself hoping that another free meal would be offered him; perhaps even a succession, such as might postpone the hardware business for a few days longer.

'Scruffy, old man!'

'Hallo, Archie.'

'I say, you're just the man I wanted! I've been trying to find you in the telephone book.'

'You wouldn't find me in the book. I've changed my name, you know.'

'I didn't. What? Why? Been left money?'

'Russell Gryce.'

'Oh, of course. Well, that's lucky, because it's really Russell Gryce I wanted to see. Because, old man, it's the most wonderful thing. The old governor died last June— well, of course, that wasn't so good, but it *was* last June —and it turned out he was practically a millionaire. Well, not quite that, but anyway I've got a nice whack of it, and I'm going to start a paper—literary monthly, like we always said we would, remember?—and I simply must have *you*.

Look, let's go and have a drink, and I'll tell you all about it, and then we could go and have dinner somewhere, and you can tell *me*. Old boy, we'll wake them up. Gosh, I *am* glad to have run into you like this!'

3

That was how the 'advanced literary monthly' *Asymptote* was born. Scruffy had naturally supposed that he was to be Editor, with a satellite Butters making seasonal appearances, cheque-book in hand, admiration on lips. In this he was to be disappointed. Archie had grown up since Oxford days. He now knew everything about literature and all that; and, with a cheerful certainty which he had only exhibited at Oxford when talking about food, he gave Scruffy the benefit of it.

He spoke of Gertrude Stein ('and I'm sure you agree with me, old man') as pathetically old-world, 'though, mind you, I'm not saying not all right for prep schools still.' He dismissed E. E. Cummings, 'the modern Longfellow' as a poet who left nothing to the imagination, 'drawing-room ballad stuff, old boy, we must do better than that.'

'I've got Brant as Editor, bit of luck there, and Speranza —you know him, of course, the man who invented Indifferentialism—as assistant. Brant wants a monthly review of novels, we must keep in touch with the lower orders, he says, and I said I knew just the man. That's you, old boy. Fifteen pounds a month, I thought, for an article of about 2,000 words, and of course you'll have the pick of the books, and sell as many as you like. Ought to be a good thing. We thought you might call it 'The Sheep and the Goats'. See the idea? Give the goats hell, same as you did at Oxford and do what you can for the real writers. They'll most of them be writing for us, of course, but one can't let personal considerations stand in the way.'

Scruffy's mind was in confusion. He was bewildered by the extraordinary change in Archibald Butters; a change the more remarkable because it seemed to have had no effect on his personality. He was the same cheerful, friendly soul as before, but with a new set of values and a new assurance, which he wore like a new and well-fitting suit of clothes; something which, with money in his pocket, he had decided to buy.

Scruffy was also confused by the strange mixture of powder and jam which he was being asked to swallow. Somebody was wanted to 'keep in touch with the lower orders', and they had immediately thought of *him*! As against this, his Oxford articles were still remembered, and the hardware business could now be forgotten. He wanted to hate Archie for his money, his mental growth, his new self-confidence and, most of all, his patronage; but the presence of a bottle of Burgundy inside him, and the promise of security ahead of him, left his hatred unstabilised. He told himself that once on the review, in whatever capacity, he would put Archie in his proper place.

Asymptote was undoubtedly advanced, but with a month's rest between numbers its readers were able to keep up with it. A long poem consisting almost entirely of punctuation marks raised '!'s' and '?'s' from one or two foolish correspondents . . . until the Editor reminded them that Browning was thought unintelligible when he first began to write. Puzzled (S.W.7), who had forgotten about this, was reassured. Art (and it made all the difference to Anxious at Ponders End) could not stand still. Under the guidance of *Asymptote* it advanced at the double.

Whatever of humiliation Scruffy had considered himself entitled to feel at that inaugural meeting, he soon lost when he began to write his monthly article. He had objected to the title 'The Sheep and The Goats' on the ground that the distinction between them was not sufficiently marked for what would mainly be a non-agricultural public, some of whom might prefer goats. Moreover, as an attribute of advanced fiction, would not 'sheeplike' raise less interesting anticipations than 'goatish'? If all one's goats were sheep, following the old trail, and one's sheep exhibited goat-like tendencies, what then? This being agreed, the final decision was for 'Gold and Tinsel'.

In his new position Scruffy justified the good opinion of himself which he had struggled so hard to hold. If a magazine which scarcely anybody saw can be said to have a feature, 'Gold and Tinsel' became the feature of *Asymptote*. The few subscribers enjoyed it because the writer was so obviously enjoying it. At last he had a platform from which he could get back at the world. Everything and everybody that he hated could be dragged in somewhere, and held up to contempt. Most of all, and in almost every number, the man who had robbed him of his birthright: Michael Hartigan.

'This month we propose to review one novel only: "Lord Harry to the Rescue." It will be asked "Have we then, nothing on the other side to show our readers, no gold to match the tinsel?" The answer is that when a Hartigan book appears on the bookstall, all else seems shining gold; so that we dare not estimate, we cannot estimate rightly, the true worth of any other.'

This was the beginning of the only full-length review which Michael ever had. One would have supposed that Scruffy could have worked off his hatred in 2,000 words, or at least kept what was over for the next Lord Harry book. But Michael had become his King Charles' head, a head for which a place could always be found.

'Severely as we have castigated him, let not Mr Sprott suppose that we place him among the Hartigans of the bookshops. We would not so insult him; we would not so betray our sense of literary values. All we ask of Mr Sprott is that he should abandon creative writing in favour of some other activity.' That did for Mr Sprott *and* Mr Hartigan. 'Although we have considered "Chased Bodies" to be worthy of inclusion in our Gold section, Mr Firkin must not be complacent. One can be illiterate, and yet above a Hartigan; one can be a writer of near-genius, and yet below a Proust. Mr Firkin has still something to learn.'

All this was good reading for Anxious and Puzzled, if not for Michael Hartigan. It was good reading for those non-subscribers who picked up *Asymptote* in their clubs and found in 'Gold and Tinsel' the only matters which they could understand. And it was a great day for Scruffy himself when a publisher's advertisement attributed to Russell Gryce the opinion that 'Dead Grass' was a novel which nobody interested in modern fiction could afford to leave unread. It was a greater day still when another publisher boasted of one of his more unsaleable books that it 'bore the hall-mark of *Asymptote*'s gold standard'.

As the result of this public recognition Scruffy saw himself suddenly as not only the blaster but the maker of reputations. It would be for 'Gold and Tinsel' to herald a still newer and more sideways approach to creative fiction than had yet been seen; it would be for Russell Gryce to place the laurel wreath firmly on the brow of whomever he chose as the new Master.

He chose J. Frisby Withers, author of 'Metronomic Beat.' Mr Withers had written three other novels, each of them more disordered than the one before. To the old-fashioned reader they suggested an almost illegible, much corrected, first pencil draft, which had been pulled together with a '*stet* everything', and handed over to a typist whose six easy lessons had not taken her up to capital letters and punctuation marks. The result was chaos and old night, but very impressive. In fact, it was Russell Gryce's considered opinion that 'Metronomic Beat' was the most profoundly impressive contribution to creative fiction in our time.

4

One would not have expected Michael Hartigan to be an original subscriber to *Asymptote*, and in fact he was not. But he subscribed to a press-cutting agency. Miss Fairlawn read all the cuttings which came in, destroyed the unflattering ones, and passed on the others. She came into the inner sanctum one morning, put a bunch of them on Michael's desk, and stood hesitating.

'And then there's this one, Mr Hartigan,' she said, holding it up. 'Good?'

'By no means, Mr Hartigan.'

'Then I don't want to see it. Why should I?'

'Well, I think it's libellous, Mr Hartigan. I thought you might want to do something about it. It's—it's disgraceful! People oughtn't to be allowed to write such things!'

'As bad as that? Let's have a look.' He took it, said 'Oh, one of *those* papers,' and began to read. Miss Fair-lawn watched him anxiously, tears in her eyes, muttering 'Abominable' to herself.

'We must face it bravely,' said Michael, putting down the cutting. 'Russell Gryce doesn't care for us. Who is he? Ever heard of him?'

'Never!' cried Miss Fairlawn indignantly.

'Probably I missed a catch off his bowling at school, or did him out of the Divinity prize. These things rankle.'

'Do you want me to do anything about it, Mr Hartigan?'

'Such as?'

'Making an appointment with your solicitors, so that you could bring an action against him.'

'I'd sooner kick him and be fined forty bob. Much cheaper and much more pleasurable. Well, we'll see. Meanwhile, let me have every cutting by this fellow. In fact, I think it would be a good idea to take in his damned rag, what's it called, *Asymptote*. Will you do that?'

'Very well, Mr Hartigan.'

So for six months Michael read *Asymptote*, and comforted himself with the thought that nobody else read it. And more and more he wondered about Russell Gryce, and damned his soul. Then one day, at what was called a Literary Lunch, he saw the hated name on the table plan; located the seat; and knew that somewhere he had seen that face before. All through the meal and the first speech he was searching his memory, but in vain. Suddenly he banged the table, and cried *'Scruffy!'* Luckily the speaker was just sitting down, and it passed as an Italian expression of enthusiasm.

Scruffy!

Michael went back to his flat, still murmuring 'Scruffy' to himself. The new number of *Asymptote* was in, and J. Frisby Withers was making his bow to posterity. What Russell Gryce had not realised was that Alstons Ltd, who had recently assimilated the Daffodil Press and so become the publishers of 'Metronomic Beat,' were also the publishers of the Lord Harry books. Michael, being in effect Alstons Ltd, realised it at once. He began to smile gently. He went on smiling to himself for quite a long time.

The meaning of the smile was not immediately clear to Scruffy. A chaste little advertisement of 'Metronomic Beat' quoted *Asymptote*. 'Russell Gryce, the well-known critic writes . . .' and Scruffy read it, and looked modestly down his nose. This was fame.

But next week there was another advertisement.

Messrs Alstons Ltd have the honour to announce
TWO NEW BOOKS.

LORD HARRY AT BAY by Michael Hartigan,
METRONOMIC BEAT by J. Frisby Withers.

RUSSELL GRYCE, the famous critic of *Asymptote*,
calls this 'the most profoundly impressive
contribution to creative fiction in our time.'

A protective circle round the advertisement made it clear that this was Messrs Alstons' only contribution to creative fiction that week, and one gathered that Mr Gryce thought it impressive.

Scruffy didn't like it. The Editor of *Asymptote* didn't like it. Even Archie Butters didn't like it. In a dignified letter to the publishers the Editor pointed out that the advertisement was misleading. Alstons Ltd expressed surprise. They could not believe that any intelligent reader of *Asymptote* had been misled; but rather than mislead even one person they would withdraw the advertisement in its present form. They withdrew it a fortnight later.

Michael had an uncle, who was the Bishop of St. Bees. The Bishop was a kindly man, and when his nephew sent him a book to read ('which my firm has just published, I wonder what you will think of it') he did his best. In the following weeks the advertisement took a new form.

METRONOMIC BEAT
By
J. Frisby Withers

RUSSELL GRYCE, the famous critic, writes:
'Profoundly impressive.'
THE BISHOP OF ST. BEES writes:
'Undoubtedly clever.'

The Bishop had written a good deal more, beginning with 'but'; space, however, was limited.

At this period the money which Michael earned, whether as author or publisher, meant very much less to him than it did to the Chancellor of the Exchequer. Anything on the debit side of the account was so much off income-tax; and if 'annoying Scruffy' could be counted as legitimate expenses, it was a much cheaper amusement than buying a new car. But, as it happened, the money was beginning to come back. Continuous advertisement was so swelling the sales of 'Metronomic Beat' that it justified (or nearly) the next announcement.

> 'It is reassuring to find that the literary taste of a critic like Russell Gryce is at one with that of the general public; it is good to know that a popular best-seller can win the approval of such an eclectic review as *Asymptote*. Such has been the fortunate destiny of "Metronomic Beat," whose fifth large edition is announced today. It was this book that Mr Russell Gryce, the famous critic of *Asymptote*, speaking for the average man, proclaimed "the most impressive contribution to creative fiction on our time".'

Michael was enjoying himself, almost as much as Scruffy had once enjoyed himself. If there were times when he felt sorry for Scruffy, he read again the review of 'Lord Harry to the Rescue', and hardened his heart. Nobody should be allowed to get away with that sort of thing.

Scruffy was not enjoying himself. When he went in now to the

office of *Asymptote*, the Editor gave him a cold nod, Speranza said
'Oh—you?' and turned away, and even Archie made an excuse for
leaving him—'Just a moment, old man'—and never came back.
They all seemed to be telling him that it was not *Asymptote's*
business to boom best-sellers, not their business to ally themselves
with Bishops. He dreaded to look at the Sunday papers now. What
new indignity was waiting for him?

Next Sunday he knew.

THE POPULAR TASTE

METRONOMIC BEAT (8th Edn)
MR RUSSELL GRYCE, the popular critic, writes:
'The most impressive contribution to creative
fiction of our time'.

MR MICHAEL HARTIGAN, the popular author, writes:
'A rattling good yarn'.

'And if that doesn't do it,' said Michael to the admiring Miss
Fairlawn a week later, 'nothing will.'

But it did. Russell Gryce, the popular critic, was already in the
train, on his way to the hardware business.

Portrait of Lydia

Arthur Carstairs was born in London in 1917, to the sound of one of those air-raids which have seemed so small an affair since, but which were so terrifying then. His mother was continuously frightened anyhow, for her husband was a subaltern in Flanders, soon to be killed. Mrs Carstairs and her baby retired to a cottage on the outskirts of the country-town of Kingsfield, and lived as best they could on what little money there was. When he was old enough, Arthur went as a day-boy to Kingsfield Grammar School. Not surprisingly he grew up a quiet, rather shy, industrious boy, with none of the vices and few of the picturesque virtues, clinging to his mother, more from a sense of duty than because he desired no other companionship. When she died on his twentieth birthday, he had never kissed a girl, nor climbed a mountain, nor swum in the sea, nor spent a night in the open, and all the adventures he had had were adventures of the mind, romantic, exciting, but, as he well knew, not for him. Mr Margate, one of Kingsfield's three solicitors, and a good friend of his mother's, had given him his articles, and had promised him a post in the office when he had passed his finals. It seemed to him now at twenty-one that he would remain in Kingsfield for ever, a commonplace lawyer whom the world passed by. Perhaps, he thought sometimes, it would be better if he tried for a job in London when he was qualified. In London adventure waited on the doorstep, as his reading of Stevenson assured him. In London jewelled hands beckoned to you from broughams . . . .

On his mother's death her cottage had been sold, and he lived now in lodgings close to Mr Margate's office. Occasionally after dinner he would go round to the Cap and Bells and have a glass of beer; not because he liked beer, nor the atmosphere of public houses, but because he felt that in this way he was seeing life. He was a nice-looking boy, with an earnest, innocent face which appealed to ageing barmaids; who called him 'Ducks', as if they really meant it, and made him feel a man. And a rather highly-coloured sporting gentleman called Platt, who frequented the Cap and Bells, had made friends with him one night over a double cherry-brandy, and had received, as one man of the world from another, all Arthur's confidences. This encouraged him to think more hopefully of the future. He told himself that, when he had passed his finals, he would open out a little more, spending at least three evenings a week at the Cap and Bells. He might even learn to play billiards, which Platt had offered to teach him. His own game was chess; but an offer to teach Platt chess had been unacknowledged at the time, and not repeated. Presumably, in the noisy environment of the Public Bar Platt had not heard.

On this January evening in 1939 Arthur had just finished dinner and was sitting over his books, when his landlady put her head in at the door and said suspiciously, 'There's a lady to see you.'

He looked up with a start, trying to make sense of it, and then asked nervously, 'Who is it?' He had the absurd idea that Doris the barmaid had come to fetch him, and that Mrs Heavitree didn't approve of her.

'Didn't give a name. Said she wanted to see you professionally.'

'Oh! Oh well, you see, the office is closed, and she may have gone round to Mr Margate's house, and he may be out, and she may have been sent——' He broke off, thinking ashamedly, 'Why am I such a coward, why am I apologising for what is none of her business?' and said firmly, looking as much like a solicitor as he could, 'Show her up, please, Mrs Heavitree.' As she closed the door, he hurried into his bedroom and brushed his hair. A pity that the remains of a rice pudding were on the table, but if she were a nice old lady they could laugh it off together.

There was a knock at the door. He called 'Come in!' and she came in.

Arthur stood up to receive her. He had been preparing to say 'Good evening, Mrs—er—won't you sit down and tell me what I can do for you?' What he did say was 'Good lord!'

She was young, she was lovely, she was everything which he had hoped that a girl might be, she was the girl of his dreams. He stood gaping at her.

She had a low, deep voice, wonderfully sweet. She said, 'Do forgive me, Mr Carstairs, for coming at this time,' and he pulled himself together and said, 'Not at all, sit down, won't you?' Apologies for the springs of the arm-chair and the death-throes of the rice pudding rose to his lips, but her pretty, 'Thank you,' and the smile she gave him left him speechless. He told himself that, as once or twice before, he had fallen asleep over his books, and presently would wake.

'Mr Carstairs,' she said, 'you are a solicitor, are you not?'

'Well—er,' he said, 'yes, and—er—no, I mean I shall be —I hope—in a short time, as soon as I have passed my final examination, but actually I'm not yet qualified. Does it matter?' he added anxiously.

'Oh dear!' she said. 'I thought you were a solicitor.'

'Well, I am in a way. What it comes to is that I could give you my advice, my help, unprofessionally, I mean without payment—but then,' he hurried on, 'of course I shouldn't want that anyhow, I mean——'

She smiled and said, 'You mean I could thank you without offending your legal etiquette?'

'Yes, of course, I mean—er—well, perhaps you had better tell me what it is. I expect it will be all right.'

'It's a question of a will. Must you have a qualified solicitor to write a will for you?'

This was easy.

'Anybody can write a will. People generally employ a solicitor so as to be sure of covering all the ground, and the solicitor employs a special legal language so as to be sure of doing this. But anybody can write in plain English on a piece of paper "I leave my gold cigarette-case to John Smith," and if it's properly signed and witnessed, John Smith gets it.'

She smiled at him delightedly and said, 'Then there you are! You read this will which my father has made, you assure him as a friend that it is legally correct, it is signed and witnessed, and then we thank you, we show our gratitude'—she held him for an endless moment with her wonderful eyes—'in any way you wish. So long, of course, as it does not include six-and-eightpence.'

She laughed as she ended, and her laughter was divine music to him. Nobody had ever laughed like that.

'That's right,' he said, laughing too.

'Then you will come with me?'

'Of course, if you really——'

'To Norton St. Giles?'

He nearly said, 'To the ends of the earth!' but stopped himself just in time.

'Norton St. Giles? I don't think I——'

'It's a village about twenty-five miles from here. We're a little way out of it. The Old Barn.'

'Twenty-five miles! I say! But I don't understand.' He frowned at her, trying to remember that he was nearly a solicitor. 'It doesn't make sense.'

She rose from the broken chair as if it were a throne, and held out her hand to him.

'Nevertheless, because I ask you, you will come— Arthur?'

He was on his feet, taking her hand in his, saying huskily that he would come, seeing the squalid room as it would be if she left him alone in it, romance and beauty gone from his life for ever. All the same, it didn't make sense. Perhaps that was what was so attractive about it.

She pressed his hand, thanking him with her eyes, and, surprisingly, sat down again. She smiled at him, and said, 'I knew I could be sure of you. So now let's make sense of it.'

He pushed his books further out of the way, and leant forward, chin on hands, watching her eagerly.

'My name is Lydia Clyde. My father and I live alone together.

I am all that he has left in the world, and I am devoted to him. He is, I am afraid, a sick man.' She put her hand to her left breast. 'He may die at any moment, the doctors tell us; but he and I'—she gave a confident little laugh—'we don't believe the doctors. And yet sometimes —do you understand?—we do believe. For weeks now he has been insisting that he must make a will, so as to leave me provided for. You know how it is; one puts off doing a tiling for years, telling oneself that there is no hurry, and then, when one suddenly decides to do it, every wasted minute seems of importance. So I arranged with a London friend of ours, a lawyer, to come down for a night. I would meet him at the junction, for we are many miles from a station. But he is not there! So I ring up my father, and I learn that our friend has telegraphed to say that he is prevented from coming. My father implores me to find some other lawyer and bring him back with me. He dare not put it off any longer. Foolish, unreasonable, I know, he may live for twenty years yet, but'—she shrugged her shoulders—'sick men *are* unreasonable. And I cannot have him worrying. So——' she broke off, and looked at him gratefully '—you!'

'Yes, but how——'

'You have met a man, Roger Platt, at—the Cap and Bells, is it?'

'Is he a friend of yours?' he asked, surprised.

'We have known him a long time, but that is not to say that he is a man I approve of altogether. Poor Roger! He is not'—she smiled at him confidingly—'our sort. But he has spoken to me of you. He has a great admiration for you, did you know? So, when I was so badly in need of a friend, a friend who was also a lawyer, but a friend who was young enough not to mind doing an unusual thing, I remembered suddenly what he had said of you. You will come? I have my car outside.'

'Of course,' said Arthur, flattered to think that he had made such an impression. But he looked at her in a puzzled way, for there was still something which didn't make sense.

'What is it?' she asked, suddenly alarmed.

'Your father——'

'Yes?'

'You are his only child. Then why the urgent need for a will? Everything will be yours anyhow.'

She gave him the most pathetic look which he had ever received from a human being. She turned away from him, and her lovely head drooped upon her shoulder. 'Don't you understand?' she whispered.

To show that he was a man of the world and practically a qualified solicitor he said quickly that he did, of course he did, but—and stopped, hoping that she would explain.

'I didn't want to tell you,' she murmured, 'I wanted to keep my poor little secret. But I cannot have secrets from my friend. You see, Arthur, I am his daughter, but—oh, must I say it?' She looked forlornly at him.

'Oh!' Now he understood. 'You mean—he never married your mother?'

She bowed her head.

He got up, saying, 'I'm a fool, forgive me. I'll just get my coat.' As he went into his bedroom she looked at her watch. It was 7.47.

They said little on the way. As they wound out of the half-lit streets into the deep blackness of the country lanes she asked him if he were ever frightened in a car, and he said 'Not with you.' She gave him her hand for a moment, saying simply, 'I am a good driver and the roads will be empty.' He was too happy to be frightened. Once or twice his heart turned over, but her reassuring smile, her little apology, brought forgetfulness. They flashed through a village and she said, 'Barton Langley, half-way,' and he looked at his watch to find that it was only just after eight. Twelve-and-a-half miles, that was fifty miles an hour! Fifty miles an hour on a pitch-black night with a lovely girl, this, he told himself, was life. He closed his eyes happily, and went into a dream . . .

'There! Thirty-three minutes. That's as good as I've ever done at night. Come along!'

She switched off the engine, took his hand, and drew him after her. She opened the front door into darkness, saying, 'The lights went this evening, you must keep hold of me,' and he was glad to be still holding her hand. They went into a room on the left.

It was a man's room, lit now by many candles; plainly furnished with a couple of comfortable chairs and a sofa, all in green linen covers on which were brightly coloured patchwork cushions. At a gate-legged table with a check tablecloth, an elderly man was playing Patience. He rose, sweeping the cards together, as Lydia said, 'Darling, this is Mr Carstairs, who has very kindly come to help us.'

Mr Clyde bowed low from behind the table, saying, 'Mr Carstairs, I am your most obliged, humble servant.' He was an oddly old-fashioned figure, thought Arthur, in his black velvet jacket and black stock, with an eyeglass, dependent from a black ribbon, now in his eye. He had a long, pale rather melancholy face in a setting of crinkly, silver hair, but his eyes shone alertly, and his hand, as he held it out, did not tremble. After all, thought Arthur, why should Lydia's father be more than fifty? It's only the hair which makes him seem old.

'I'll get the drinks,' said Lydia. 'Have you got the will there, Father? We mustn't keep Mr Carstairs.' She took a candle and went out. Arthur turned to watch her go, saw the picture on the wall, and gave a gasp of astonishment. Mr Clyde, fumbling among some papers on his table, presumably for the will, said, 'Ah, you have seen my Corot.'

Arthur was surprised, for he did not associate Corot with nudes, and it was certainly difficult to associate him with this particular one. She sat on a rock, her crossed feet just in the water, and she was leaning back on her hands, looking up into the sunlight, her eyes bright with the joy of living. She was so real, he felt, that if he called to her she would look down and smile at him, and say, 'Ah! there you are!' happy to have found him; as Lydia was happy to have found him such a little while ago. For the face was the face of Lydia; alive; unmistakable.

He looked quickly away, and saw what he supposed was the Corot on the other wall. Pale, delicate fantasy, a dream world, an eggshell world which broke at a touch, insubstantial faeryland which somehow made the other picture doubly alive, filling the room with Lydia.

'It's lovely,' stammered Arthur, and the old man chuckled to himself.

And now Arthur was to be startled into admiration again, for on a small table in the window a chess-board was laid out, with the most elaborately carved red and white ivory men which he had ever seen. The knights were real knights, the bishops real bishops; to sit down behind them would be to fight a battle, not to play a game. He wondered how long it would take to get used to them; whether it would upset one's game not to have the familiar pieces under one's hand. He longed to try.

Lydia came back with a tray. Arthur felt shy of her suddenly. He wanted to look at the picture again, and then at her. He was afraid to look at either, to look at the picture under her eyes, or to look at her with the secret of the picture showing in his own eyes.

'I must have left it in the other room,' said Mr Clyde, coming from behind his table. 'No, no, Lydia,' he cried testily, 'I am *not* dying. I *can* walk into the other room. I am *not* going upstairs.' He took a candle and went out.

She felt his uncomfortableness. She took his hand and deliberately turned him round to the picture. They looked at it together.

'Are you shocked?' she asked gently.

He blushed and said, 'It's too beautiful for that—I've never—it's just beauty. Oh, Lydia!'

'I was a model before my father found me again. It was either that or—the other tiling. You don't despise me?'

'No, no, no!'

'I think it is only a few special people who recognise me. To most it is just'—she shrugged—'Aurora or June Morning or Sea Maiden. But you are different. I knew —didn't I say so?—that I could have no secrets from you.' She pressed his hand and left it as the old man came back.

'Now, Mr Carstairs, here you are. It's quite short, as you see, and I don't want any nonsense about messuages and hereditaments, because I haven't got any. These ridiculous doctors order me from one place to another, and my life is lived, you might say, in short leases.'

Arthur read the will and said: 'It seems all right. I see you just say "my daughter Lydia". I think——'

'Exactly. As you notice, I've left a space there.'

'Well, legally—er—it's a question of—I mean——'

'I've told him, Father,' said Lydia.

'Then what are you stammering about, young man? Go ahead.'

'Well, is her name Clyde?'

'Yes. She took it by deed poll as soon as—well, some years ago.'

'That's good. Any other Christian name?'

'Lydia Rosaline,' said Lydia.——

'Then I should say "my daughter Lydia Rosaline Clyde, who is now living with me", and I don't see how there could be any doubt.'

'That's what I want. Thank you.' He sat down and began to write.

'We shall need another witness, of course,' said Arthur.

'We only want two, don't we?' said Lydia. 'You and me. Why, what's the matter?'

It was absurd that anybody shouldn't know what he knew so well. He smiled at her as he would have smiled at a child, and said, 'A witness can't benefit from a will, you know. We need some other independent person. A servant will do.'

'Father, did *you* know that?'

'I take no interest in the artificialities of the Law,' said Mr Clyde grandly. 'I leave them to this young man.'

'But we have no servant here!' cried Lydia. 'A woman comes in, but she is ill and hasn't been coming this week— what are we to do?'

'One of your neighbours?'

'We hardly know them. Father's health—Oh, if I'd only known, we could have brought Roger with us!'

'Then as you didn't,' said Mr Clyde, 'may I suggest that the simplest thing would be to go and fetch him now?'

'But Father!' She looked at her watch. 'Half past eight, I couldn't

144

be back before 9.40, say, and to keep Mr Carstairs waiting about all that time——'

'You'll keep him waiting about much longer, if you're going round from one strange house to another trying to persuade somebody to come out on a damned cold night, and probably getting nobody in the end. Don't you worry about Mr Carstairs, I'll look after him. You play chess, Mr Carstairs?'

'Yes, rather, I—er——'

'Well, if you'd like a game——'

'Oh, I say, I'd love it!'

'There you are, my dear, you aren't the only attraction in this house. Now then, don't waste any more time, off you go.'

'Well, if you really don't mind—Arthur?'

'It's quite all right—Lydia!'

'You're very sweet.' She gave him a warm loving smile, glanced up at her picture, and said in a low voice, 'I shall be watching over you. Look at me sometimes.' She pressed his hands. Mr Clyde busied himself with the chessmen.

It was a curious game which they played. The strangeness of the pieces; the insistent presence of Lydia; the urge to look at her which made it so difficult to concentrate on the board; a sort of nightmare feeling that he could not escape from his opponent, that every move was a foolish move to which the counter was inevitable and should have been foreseen—and then, unable to be resisted any longer, Lydia, beautiful, desirable, filling the room. The game came to an end with the noise of wheels on the gravel, so completely was it in the other man's control.

'9.35!' cried Lydia gaily. 'I beat our record, Arthur.'

'I should say she did,' said Platt. 'Evening, Carstairs. I'm all of a tremble still.'

Arthur nodded to him; as the family solicitor might nod to some rather undesirable member of the family with whom he had a business appointment.

'It's good of you to come, my boy,' said Mr Clyde. 'Now then, Mr Carstairs, tell us what we have to do.'

'Lead me to the dotted line,' said Platt, taking out his pen, 'and watch me spell my name. You'll be surprised.'

The will was signed 'Philip Clyde', and witnessed.

'Exhausting,' said Platt, putting his pen away. 'I must have a drink, Lyd.'

'Only a small one, darling, you're going to drive us back.'

'That's nice.'

'And you'll take forty-five minutes exactly.'

'When they tell you, Carstairs, don't argue, just do it.'

'Arthur?' She looked at him, decanter poised over glass.

'Just a very little,' he said nervously. He had never drunk whiskey before.

'There! And a very small one for me. I like driving fast, but I don't like being driven fast. We'll sit comfortably together at the back without hitting the roof. Through Barton Langley, Roger, it's the better way.'

'Oh, right.'

The moon had risen, relieving the blackness a little. Arthur and Lydia sat in silence together, a rug wrapped round them, clasping hands beneath. He saw nothing but her face beside him, her picture on the wall, and a magic future in which, somewhere, somehow, they were together for always. . . .

'The Cap and Bells,' said Platt, as the car came to rest, 'and that's that, as far as I'm concerned. Lyd, you can take Carstairs home. And a very good night to you both.'

'Thank you for everything, darling, ever so much.'

He got out of the car, waved to them, and went inside. She moved into the driver's seat, and Arthur sat next to her. It was only a few hundred yards to his lodging. The street was empty. She turned to him, holding out her arms. He clung to her, kissing her cheeks clumsily, whispering, 'Oh, darling! Oh, Lydia!' She guided his mouth to her own. He had never known such ecstasy. Oh, to die like this in her arms, his soul drawn slowly through his lips to rest in hers!

He was almost suffocating when she released him. She said smilingly, 'Better than six and eightpence?' and then, 'Darling, you must go.' She reached across him and opened the door on his side. 'Quick.'

'I shall see you again—soon?'

'I expect so,' she smiled. 'In a day or two. Goodbye, darling, and thank you a thousand times. You can't think what a help you have been.'

He was out on the pavement; she had pulled the door shut, kissed her hand and was gone. He stumbled up the stairs to his sordid little room. It was 10.30. Just three short hours, and he had experienced a new world. He undressed. He lay in bed in the dark, seeing her picture on the wall.

That was Tuesday. On the Thursday morning he was summoned to Mr Margate's room. Vaguely apprehensive, feeling, as he had felt ever since, that he had done something unprofessional on that evening and was to be reprimanded, he went in. There was another man there. Mr Margate said, 'Oh, good morning, Arthur. This is Inspector Wells. I'll leave you to him. Answer his questions and help him in any way you can.' Completely bewildered, a little alarmed at contact with the police, yet relieved that his conduct as a solicitor was not to be impeached, Arthur waited. The Inspector sat negligently on the corner of Mr Margate's desk, one leg swinging. He was a stocky, pleasant-looking man with a gentle, rather tired voice.

'Just a few questions,' he murmured. 'Nothing much.' He smiled in a friendly way and added, 'I can hardly ask you to sit down in your own office, but you'd be more comfortable.'

Arthur sat down.

'Never mind for the moment why I'm asking these questions. If you do happen to guess, well, you're a lawyer and can keep a confidence. That right?'

'Of course.'

'Know a man called Platt? Roger Platt?'

'I've met him once or twice.'

'When did you last see him?'

'Tuesday night.'

'Where? At what time?'

'At about 10.30, going into the Cap and Bells.'

The Inspector was silent for a little, swinging his leg, and then said, 'I'm trying to confirm his account of himself on Tuesday evening. It involves, among other people, some friends of his called Clyde, who live at Norton St. Giles, and yourself. Now give me *your* account.'

Arthur gave it. The Inspector smiled and said, 'I gather that the lady is not ill-looking.' Arthur blushed and said, 'Yes, I mean No.'

'All the same, if you can drive fifty miles on a dark winter's night for a lady, you can drive fifty miles for a mere policeman on a nice sunny morning. Can't you?'

Arthur couldn't keep the excitement out of his eyes and voice as he asked, 'Do you mean you want me to come with you to Norton St. Giles—now?'

'That's the idea. I gather that it finds favour with you.'

Arthur blushed again and said defensively, 'Well, it's better than stuffing in an office.'

'No doubt. Now just a word before we start. You would, of course, vouch for the honesty and integrity of your friends the Clydes?'

'Of course!'

'Although you only met them on Tuesday. Well, I'm not saying you're wrong. But would you also vouch for Mr Roger Platt?'

'N-no,' said Arthur. 'I suppose I wouldn't.'

'You wouldn't—and I'm not saying you're right. You see, the police can't come to these quick decisions. To the police every man might be a liar, and every woman is one. I don't feel bound to accept the Clydes' word, nor Platt's, nor yours. But if you all agree on something, then it's probably the truth. You've told me that Platt was in a certain place at 9.35 on Tuesday night in the company of yourself and Mr and Miss Clyde. If he was there, then he can't have been thirty-five miles away at 9.15—in which case I've no more interest in him. So, with your permission, we'll just make sure that you're speaking the truth, and that that's where you were yourself at 9.35. No offence?'

'Of course not.'

'Right. Then let's go. I've warned them that we're coming.'

They went out to the police-car. A constable-driver was studying a map.

'Found the way, Lewis?'

'There seems to be two ways, sir. I don't know that there's much choice.'

'Perhaps Mr Carstairs can tell us.'

Arthur was about to explain that it was much too dark to see anything, when he remembered. 'We go through Barton Langley,' he said, with the assurance of one who always did.

'That's right,' said Lewis. 'I thought that looked the better way.'

'All right, then. Step on it.'

It was like coming home to be in that room again; to see the picture, the two pictures, and the great chessmen under the window, and old Mr Clyde with his Patience spread out on the chequered table-cloth, and now, making her even dearer, Lydia in a chair before the fire busy with her needle. 'I've brought a friend of yours with me,' the Inspector had said, and her eyes had lit up, and she had cried 'Oh, how nice!' and held out a hand to him, and the old man had chuckled and said, 'Hallo, boy, come for your revenge?' The Inspector had managed it all very tactfully, leaving Lydia a little bewildered, a little anxious for Roger, and the old man cynically amused.

'Yes, you want to keep your eye on that gentleman, Inspector. Reckless young devil. You never know what he'll be up to next. What's he done now? Didn't run over anybody, did he, when he drove Mr Carstairs back?'

'Of course he didn't, darling. I don't know what it's all about.'

'Just a matter of confirmation, Miss Clyde,' said the Inspector vaguely. 'You know how it is, one friend recommends a book, and you say "Really?" Another friend recommends it, and you say "Oh, I must get it". Then a third friend recommends it, and you really do get it. Same with evidence.'

Now he was saying good-bye to Lydia. Now he was saying good-bye to the other Lydia, the Lydia of the picture—oh, Lydia,

149

my lovely!—and then he was in the car, and perhaps would never see her again.

'And that's where you were at 9.35 on Tuesday night, Mr Carstairs?'

'Yes.'

'Playing chess with Mr Clyde when Miss Clyde came back with Platt?'

'Yes.'

'Certain?'

'Yes.'

'Good enough,' said Inspector Wells regretfully, and began to talk about football.

Six years later Arthur was in Cairo. He had been half round the world; he had kissed girls of many nationalities; he had climbed mountains, swum in strange seas and spent more nights under the stars than he could count. He had seen life and he had seen death. Now he was in Cairo, having what he called a spot of leave.

A hand came on his shoulder and turned him round. He saw a pleasant-looking middle-aged man in captain's uniform.

'Carstairs, surely?' said the other. 'Though it's a long time since we met.'

'I'm afraid,' began Arthur, looking at the man again, and went on, 'Yes, but I do know your face, only—I'm sorry— I can't for the moment——'

'I used to be Inspector Wells. Field Security now. Same job really.'

'Of course! Nice to meet you again. Are you dug in here? I'm just on leave.'

'Then you must let me give you a drink. Groppi's suit you?'

'Anything you say. It's your home town.'

They sat out at a little table with their drinks, each of them, because he was in the company of someone who knew his own particular corner of England, stirred by a vague feeling of happiness.

'Did you ever see your friends the Clydes again?' asked Wells, after they had exchanged immediate news about themselves.

'No,' said Arthur shortly. He could still feel ashamed of his utter surrender to that revelation of Lydia; still remember with contempt the feverish anxiety in which he had waited for some message from her, had written to her imploringly and reckoned the hours by the deliveries of a postman who never came, had hired a bicycle at last and ridden out one Sunday to find the house in possession of new tenants who could give him no forwarding address. And although five years in the Army had put her now in her right place, somewhere well below the W.A.A.F.S. and the A.T.S. and the pretty Italian girls with whom he had fallen in love since, he could still imagine himself meeting her again and discovering that nothing had changed between them.

'I could give you news of them if you were interested.'

'Oh? Yes, I should like to hear.' He tried to sound indifferent, but already his heart was beating out an absurd message that she was here in Cairo—now! Was that the news?

Wells puffed at his pipe for a little, as if wondering where to begin.

'I could have told you this five years ago or more. In fact, I went round to see you, but you'd already joined up. Funny our meeting like this. I often wondered—when I asked you all those questions, did you know what I was after?'

'Not at first. I hardly ever bothered with the papers in those days. Afterwards, when I heard about the jewel robbery at Glendower House, I wondered if it was that.'

'It was.'

'And you thought Platt might have done it? I shouldn't have put it past him.'

'Well, yes and no. It wanted somebody quicker and neater and more active to do the actual robbery, but there was evidence to show that he had been interesting himself in the lay-out of the house—hanging around, taking her ladyship's maid to the pictures, that sort of thing. My idea was that he prepared the ground, and somebody else nipped in and did it. Possibly there was a third person in the background who organised it all.'

'But you never got them?'

'Oh yes, we did. Not then, but later on when they worked it

again in another part of the country, and we found some of the Glendower stuff on them. And then we got the whole story out of them, from Platt chiefly. A nasty bit of work, Platt.'

'Platt?' said Arthur, astonished. 'You mean he *was* in the Glendower show?'

'Oh, yes. The girl actually did it, of course, and it was Clyde who had worked it all out. A great organiser that man, and a great artist. Pity he had to go to prison, he'd have done well in the Army.'

'The girl?' cried Arthur. 'What are you talking about, Wells? What girl?'

'Lydia.'

Arthur gave a loud mocking laugh. Wells raised his eyebrows, shrugged, and said nothing. A little disconcerted, Arthur said, 'Perhaps I'm getting it all wrong. When did the robbery take place?'

'Everybody was at dinner, all the bedrooms empty. It was the night of the Hunt Ball, but the women didn't really plaster themselves with the stuff until they were ready to start. So she made a pretty good haul. Accidentally, as we thought at first, she knocked over the ladder as she came down. It crashed on to the terrace, and brought everybody out. The moon had just risen, and they saw a figure running, sex unknown. Time, definite and fixed, 9.15.'

'And twenty minutes later she was thirty-five miles away! Ha-ha!'

Wells didn't say anything, and Arthur asked a little anxiously, 'Glendower *is* thirty-five miles from Norton St. Giles, isn't it?'

'Ten miles due south of Kingsfield, and another twenty-five north. That's right.'

'Well, then!'

'This is the ingenious part.' He put a hand for a moment on Arthur's knee, and said, 'Don't think that you have anything to reproach yourself with. I was taken in just as badly, and I was a policeman.'

'What on earth do you mean?'

'Well, you see, Carstairs, you never were at Norton St. Giles.

You were never more than a mile from Kingsfield—and ten miles from Glendower House.'

'But—but, my good man, I went there with *you*!'

'Oh, next morning, yes.'

'To the same house.'

'No.'

'But I could swear——'

'You couldn't swear it was the same house, because you never saw the house that night. You saw one room.'

'All right, then, the same room.'

'No.'

'Really, Wells, I know I was an innocent young fool in those days, but I wasn't blind.'

'Everyone is blind to the things at which he isn't looking. What did you see in that room? That picture. What else? Go on, describe the room to me.'

'The other picture, the Corot. The chessmen on the table by the window. The big table with a check table-cloth—er—dammit, it was six years ago—oh yes, there were some patchwork cushions, and—er——' He tried to think, but all he could see was Lydia.

'You see? Everything you remember was movable. It could all have been put in a car, and taken from one house to another; from Clyde's house in Norton St. Giles to Platt's house outside Kingsfield. Oh, he knew his stuff, that man Clyde. He knew that a young bachelor living in lodgings doesn't take in a room as a woman does, or even as a married man might. Give him something to fix his eyes on, and the rest goes by. So he gave you the portrait of Lydia and the chessmen—your two loves, so to speak— and they furnished the room for you.'

'But she drove me there——'

'In the dark, to Barton Langley and back, same as when Platt drove you home. When Lydia left you and Clyde playing chess, she drove straight to Glendower House, ten miles, did the job, and drove back to Platt's house where you were just finishing your game. Platt, who was in the pub until nine, walked over and met her outside. Then they burst in together, straight from their supposed twenty-five mile drive, and full of it. Easy.'

Arthur sat there, trying to take it in, trying in the light of this revelation to remember all that she had said to him, all the lies which she had told him.

'Was he really her father?' he asked.

'Oh, yes, undoubtedly.'

Well, at least she had told the truth about that.

'Oh, sorry,' said Wells, 'I see what you mean. No, no, Clyde was her husband.'

'Her *husband*?'

'Yes, he's quite a young man. It was Platt who was her father.'

Lies, lies, nothing but lies! All lies!

'I daresay it didn't give the girl much chance, having a father like that. Just a common crook. Clyde was the genius, an artist in every sense of the word. He painted that picture, you know.'

'Oh?' He didn't want to think of the picture now.

'Typical of him.' Wells laughed gently. 'It wasn't the girl at all. Just a professional model for Dawn or Summer, or whatever he called it. He painted in his wife's face specially for the occasion. Thought that it would occupy your attention more. He thought of everything.'

All of it lies, and this the crowning lie of all! He could forgive her everything but this, this outrage on his modesty. Damn her! And who the hell cared? Edna was having dinner with him to-night. A really good sort. And quite pretty.

'Oh well,' he said indifferently, 'that was a long time ago. I was a bit younger then. What about another drink? It's my turn this time.'

The Wibberley Touch

It may be within the memory of my friends that recently I recorded the facts which led to my expulsion from The Towers (whither I had gone in all good faith on a Christmas visit) by the direction of the third Mrs Aldwinckle (Bella). It was a melancholy business, which reflected, as I showed, the greatest discredit, both on that lady herself and her step-daughter (Gabrielle). My indecision as to which of them I should marry being thus set at rest (as it would have been in one sense anyhow by the discovery at The Towers that Mr Aldwinckle, though senile, was still officially alive), I was now maturing my matrimonial plans in another direction; as it happened, the second and divorced Mrs Aldwinckle, Claudine. My feelings, therefore, can be imagined when I received a letter from her solicitor a few days ago, threatening me, on her behalf, with a writ for malicious slander! The idea of marrying a woman who goes about pursuing innocent and spotless men with writs for slander is so repugnant to me that I decided at once that I should have to look elsewhere for a mate; but further reflection showed me that first and foremost I owed my friends a plain statement of the facts. For once again I have been abominably treated by one of Mr Aldwinckle's many wives; once again I have been the victim of cruel circumstance. In an unfortunate situation in which anybody might have found himself I acted throughout, not only with discretion, but with a high degree of ingenuity— and this is my reward! Let my friends judge. Let the facts speak for themselves.

2

The second Mrs Aldwinckle, Claudine, had married again, and was the widow of a rich manufacturer called Pagham. It is an unlovely name, and the opportunity, which I proposed to give her, of changing it to Wibberley would no doubt have been welcome to her. At the time of which I write I was already calling her by her Christian name, and making a few careless enquiries as to how the late Mr Pagham had left his money. These were most satisfactory; indeed, by a flight of fancy one might say that the air was already charged with the distant music of wedding-bells.

On this fatal Wednesday evening (as it proved to be) I was taking her out to dinner. This was the first time that I had had this pleasure, so naturally it was to be something of an occasion. We were dining at a newly-opened restaurant unknown to either of us, of which I had heard a good account: the Hirondelle. I had already decided on champagne.

In good heart, then, I drove up to her house in Green Street, telling the cabman to wait. This meant a little extra on the clock, but at the time I did not grudge it; now, of course, I know that it was wasted money. We were both of us in evening dress, and made, if I may say so, a handsome and well-matched couple. Claudine, being what I may call the *ex*-mother of Gabrielle, was naturally some years older than myself, but remarkably well preserved; I, for my part, had been from childhood intellectually ahead of my contemporaries, and have continued to give an impression of maturity somewhat beyond my years.

I think it was Shakespeare who observed that the course of true love never did run smooth, and almost immediately I had an example of this. I had been hoping that after dinner I should not only see Claudine home, and thus have an opportunity of indicating the warmth of my feelings in the taxicab, but that I might even be invited upstairs for a moment, when I could make a more pronounced revelation of my passion. Indeed, I saw myself coming away from Green Street an accepted suitor and the happiest of men. How different the dream from the reality!

'Is that you, Cecil?' she called out from her bedroom. 'Where are you taking me?'

'The Hirondelle,' I replied. And I added, 'If that is all right with you?'

'Nice. Do you know the telephone number?'

'Yes. Why? Anything particular you want ordered?' I admit that I felt a little hurt at the suggestion that I could not be trusted in the matter.

'Heavens, no. I leave that to you. With confidence, my dear man. But Paul will probably be ringing up, and I said I'd leave the number. Give it to Annette, will you? And mix us both a drink.'

Her maid came in. I make a habit of jotting down the details of engagements in my book, and was thus able to give Annette the number she required. I may say that I objected strongly to the intrusion of this Paul, whoever he might be, and felt that some explanation was necessary.

Claudine joined me just as I had got the drinks ready, and I am bound to say, in the teeth, so to speak, of what has since transpired, that she looked extremely well. A propensity for issuing writs cannot disguise the fact that she had a good figure, a flair for dress, and a very clever maid.

'Here's to everybody,' she said as she drank.

'And to you above all,' I replied, my eyes meaningly on hers. 'Cigarette?'

I put down my glass and whipped out my cigarette-case; with a flick of the finger my lighter was ready for her. Women appreciate this sort of well-bred dexterity in their men.

'Thank you.' She blew out a cloud of smoke. 'About Paul. I was hoping we might have danced somewhere afterwards, or something, but I suddenly remembered this party I'd promised to go to, and Paul said he might be able to call for me. He's going to ring up and let me know.'

'My dear Claudine,' I said, 'I should have driven you home in any case, and I could have driven you equally easily to your party.'

'Not quite as easily, darling, it's right in the wilds of the country. Richmond or somewhere.'

'Would that be Richmond in Yorkshire?' I asked, not without irony.

'I shouldn't be surprised. It's an anniversary of something, and I'm hoping Paul will tell me before we get there whether it's a birth, a marriage or a death.'

I must confess that the 'darling' mollified me, though I still felt that Paul was not essential to the success of the evening.

We drove off. I took her hand in mine, but some sudden need to touch up her hair arose, and I was unable to retain it. In any case we had a very short way to go. As soon as we arrived, I mentioned that there would be a telephone call later for Mrs Pagham. A careless motion of the hand indicated the lady of whom I was speaking; and if I a little over-emphasized the ugly 'Pagham', there was an underlying suggestion both in my voice and in the glance which I gave her that the name was not irremediable.

I had ordered a table up against the wall, so that we should sit together. I was glad to find that ours was the last on that side of the restaurant, and that for the moment the table on Claudine's right was vacant. Though the place was otherwise crowded, and there was a pleasant hum of conversation, we were, so to put it, in a little island of our own. I think I may say that I am a good host; the food was excellent, and the wine, a vintage Lanson, above reproach. We talked gaily. I had been keeping a witty anecdote from *The Reader s Digest* for this very occasion, and it went well. We also had some amusing passages again about the Aldwinckle family. Once more she confirmed the severe judgment I had been compelled to pass upon the present Mrs Aldwinckle (Bella), and we laughed together over it. It was a merry evening.

However, all good things must come to an end. As we sipped our coffee the waiter arrived with the bill. Although it was discreetly folded, I caught sight of the final figure. It was, as I had feared, in the neighbourhood of £4 10s. 0d. I continued, however, to talk gaily, and she was smiling at my whispered comment on the hat of the woman now sitting next to her—(for I should explain that the Hirondelle does not insist on evening dress, and the two women who had taken the empty table were both in hats)—she was smiling, I say, at some pleasantry of mine on this rather ridiculous red hat, when the telephone summons came.

'That's Paul at last,' said Claudine, getting up—rather too eagerly, I thought. 'Forgive me, Cecil.'

I rose and bowed as she moved away. It seemed to be the tactful moment for paying the bill. Women must always feel slightly embarrassed when their menfolk fumble in their note-cases, and a man of the world seeks to spare them this embarrassment. I put my hand in my pocket for my note-case. —

My note-case was not there!

3

My cousin Bernard, the naturalist and big-game hunter, tells of an occasion when, faced by a charging rhinoceros, he whipped his trusty rifle to his shoulder, and then realized that he was armed with nothing more lethal than a butterfly net. I suppose that his feelings on that occasion were much as mine were now. Instinct told him what to do. He sprang behind a tree and climbed rapidly up it, remaining there until the rhinoceros wearied of looking for him, and returned to its former avocations. Instinct alas! was of no help to his cousin Cecil. To dive under the table and remain there until the restaurant closed would be of little ultimate value. To borrow the money from Claudine was equally impossible. One does not take a lady out to dinner and cut short her prettily expressed thanks at the close of the meal by saying 'I wonder if you could lend me five pounds.' I might have asked the *maître d'hôtel* to take a cheque, but we were both strangers to him, and I should have become involved in a considerable argument ending in the return of Claudine and an offer from her to lend me the money. This, and I am sure every man of spirit will agree with me, was not to be endured.

So, what? (as I believe the Americans say).

The Wibberleys observe quickly and think quickly. They are rarely at a loss. A little to my right, by Claudine's vacant place, was her bag, which she had left behind when called to the telephone. She had told me once that she always carried 'Five or ten pounds' with her, 'in case', to which I had retorted quickly, 'Where else would you carry it?' This *jeu d'esprit* came into my mind now. Here was a heaven-sent opportunity to borrow the money without embarrassment to her. For the moment I did not quite see how to return it with an equal regard to her feelings, but doubtless I should think of something. The immediate need was to pay the bill. I sidled cautiously towards the bag, therefore, while maintaining an airy nonchalance towards my surroundings; pulled the bag behind my back with the right hand, felt for it with my left, and sidled carelessly back to my original place. I now had the bag out of sight between myself and the wall. This manoeuvre was necessary; for the idea of prying into a lady's bag in her absence, and in the full sight of others, is abhorrent to a man of any feeling.

I opened the bag. In an inside flap there was an embroidered silk note-case. In the case (and you can imagine the sigh of relief which escaped me) were five £1 notes. I tucked them into the bill, and was about to return the empty case to the bag, when, as if from Heaven itself, inspiration descended upon me.

The late Duke of Wellington—or, more accurately, the early Duke of Wellington—said that it was necessary to know what was happening on the other side of the hill; by which he meant that we must deduce what goes on in the other person's mind. So it was now. My whole plan was visible to me in a flash. I foresaw exactly each move which would follow, and had my answer to it. Let me make it clear to less agile minds.

It is quite impossible to lose five separate pound-notes out of a note-case. It is not wholly impossible to lose a note-case out of a bag. I slipped the empty case into my pocket. At some time or other Claudine would discover her loss. When? Not to-night, for she was going on to a party. Presumably Paul (preoccupied as I was, I recognised gladly that such men may have their uses) presumably this interloper would drive her home. She would sleep until a late hour in the morning, thus making it unlikely that she would have need of the note-case until the afternoon. So far, I trust, my friends have followed me. So far, indeed, they might have reasoned for themselves. But now comes what I might call the Wibberley Touch.

Immediately on my return I should take five pounds from the note-case which I had left behind, and transfer them to hers. At 12.30 next morning I should ring her up from my flat. I should speak as from the Hirondelle, saying that I had dropped in there in order to engage a table for lunch in the following week. I had been told that a note-case had been found under our table last night, and I had been asked if it belonged to the lady who was with me. Would Claudine see if hers was missing, and, if so, describe it to me so that I could satisfy the management?

I could foresee what would happen. She would give a scream of dismay, rush for her bag, confirm the loss, give me a confused description of the note-case, and beg me to get it back for her. I would calm her down, and promise to call with it that afternoon. So active is my mind that even now I was shaping a few phrases appropriate to the restoration of her property, such as would lead gracefully to an expression of the hope that in future we should hold all our possessions in common.

The waiter came back. I pushed the plate towards him, magnanimously telling him to keep the change. I restored the bag to its original place. I lit another cigarette and puffed it luxuriously. No one, I think, will deny that I was extricating myself from an extremely unpleasant position with consummate address. It is true, of course, that my story to Claudine would deviate (or seem to the self-righteous so to do) from the strictest accuracy. Doubtless the Duke of Wellington was condemned by such people for misleading the enemy by a feint on this or that wing. I venture to think that our reputations will not suffer. Indeed, I do not mind confessing that for my part I experienced no twinges of conscience. I was, on the contrary, extremely pleased with myself.

It was at this moment that I saw Claudine weaving her way

through the tables towards me. *She was carrying her bag in her hand!* . . . .

I cannot pretend that I was immediately master of myself. Momentarily my appearance was such that Claudine associated it with an entirely irrelevant crab salad with which I had begun the dinner. I corrected her, pulled myself together, and lit a cigarette for her.

'Well,' I said gaily, 'what news from the Rialto?'

'Paul is coming round now. We'll give him five minutes.'

'Don't you want——' I began, and left it there tactfully.

'I tidied up when I went to the telephone. That's why I was so long.'

Of course! And that is why she took her bag with her. I should have realised this.

She thanked me for a delightful dinner. Little did she know how nearly she had paid for it! (Little did the red-hatted woman next to her know that she *had* paid for it.) For the few minutes remaining to us I tried to be my usual light-hearted self; I think I may say not unsuccessfully.

I accompanied her to the door, not stopping on the way for my hat and coat. There was a Rolls Royce waiting for her. I am not a Socialist, but I dislike ostentation. I said nothing on this subject, however, and Paul (as I suppose it was) got out. I bowed and left them. I returned to the lounge, lit a cigarette, and gave myself up to thought.

4

There was an unpleasant character on the air during the war who used to pose some trifling problem to his listeners, and then ask them 'What would *you* do, chum?' In less revolting language I will now ask my friends what they would have done in my place. I think they will agree that so far my conduct has been irreproachable, and it was an ill reward for my ingenuity that the lack of restraint with which this red-hatted woman scattered her belongings about

162

the restaurant should have brought me to such an *impasse*. Some of my friends may think that she would have been rightly punished if I had gone home and said no more of the matter. But I felt otherwise. It was my duty, I conceived, to return the note-case and the money to her, and to do this in the way which would cause us both the least embarrassment.

But how?

It was clear to me that I could not approach her with the case until I had replaced the money in it. This entailed either a visit to my Club or a return to my flat; and by the time I was back in the restaurant, the two women might have left. I was assuming of course that the other woman would have enough to pay for both of them. Charitably I hoped that she would; for the plan which I was now maturing would postpone the restoration of the note-case until the morrow. My friends will wonder how this could be accomplished without the ignominious confession that I, Cecil Wibberley, was to all appearances a penitent 'thief'. Well, they will see.

I took one of my cards from my pocket-book, and wrote on the back:

'*It is of urgent importance that you should get in touch with me. This will be explained if you will ring up between 11 and 12 to-night, or 9 and 10 in the morning.*'

I added my telephone number, and gave the card, together with a shilling from the loose change in my pocket, to a page-boy.

'Take this to the lady in the red hat,' I said, pointing her out to him through the glass doors. 'You need not wait for an answer.'

He seemed an intelligent lad, but I watched him until he had handed over the card. Then I collected my hat and coat and left the restaurant.

I had no doubt that she would accept the challenge. What woman could have resisted it? Probably she would have discovered by then that she had mislaid her note-case; for I have observed that, when two women eat together, the discussion as to which of them has been entertaining the other usually ends in each paying her own share. Even so, she would be unlikely to connect my message with her loss, but assume it to be an affair of gallantry. Was it likely that she would hesitate? Let us admit that there *are* unpleasant men about who pursue and prey upon women, and that, for all she knew at this point, I might be one of them. But what had she to fear? There was no need even to give me her name until she had heard what I had to say.

It was as I had foreseen. At 11.45 that night she rang up. I took off the receiver and said 'Cecil Wibberley speaking.'

'Mr Wibberley? I got your card,' a voice said, and gave a slightly self-conscious laugh. 'I'm wondering what it is all about.'

To put her at her ease I said: 'It is rather a long story, but no doubt you would prefer that I should give it to you over the telephone. I am entirely in your hands in the matter.'

With the same little laugh she said: 'Well, I think perhaps you had better begin on the telephone, and we'll see how we get on.'

'Then I will come to the point at once. Did you miss your note-case at the Hirondelle this evening?'

I am extremely responsive to impressions. I could sense the disappointment which underlay her surprise at this unromantic opening.

'Good gracious!' she said.

'Well?'

'I certainly did, and I've been looking for it ever since I got home. Why?' and her voice became a little sharper. 'What do *you* know about it?'

'A good deal,' I said calmly. 'In fact, I have it here by my side at this moment.'

'It had a lot of money in it,' she said quickly, for all the world as if I could be suspected of stealing it!

'It still has,' I said; and if there was a note of reproof in my voice, who shall blame me?

'Well, I'm glad of that, but I should very much like to know how you come to have it. You aren't a pickpocket?' she added with a forced laugh.

I laughed too, and said lightly, 'A pickpocket, dear lady, might return an embroidered silk note-case to its fair owner for sentimental reasons, but he would hardly return five unsentimental £1 notes.'

'Oh, I *am* getting them back, am I?'

'But of course.'

'That's good. And when may I expect it?'

'Whenever you say.'

'Well, there's nothing to prevent you posting it to-night, is there?'

'Addressed to The Charming Lady in the Red Hat, London?' I said. 'Certainly. I'll put it in an envelope and slip down to the pillar-box. Good-bye.'

'Mr Wibberley!' she called quickly.

'Yes?'

'Good Heavens, I thought you'd gone.'

'You could have rung me up again.'

'So I could. Listen, let's go back to where we started, shall we? You said you had rather a long story to tell me. How long?'

'Ten minutes.'

'Yes, well, it looks as though you'll have to have my name and address anyhow, doesn't it?'

'Not at all,' I said coolly. 'You invent a name for yourself like Florence Nightingale, you give me the address of your old nurse in Yorkshire, you write to her to-night asking her to send on all letters addressed to Florence Nightingale, and I delay posting your property until tomorrow night. It will be quite easy.'

'You seem to be a very ingenious person,' she said, with a laugh in which a faint note of resentment was to be discerned.

'I have to be in my profession,' I replied.

'Oh, what's that?'

'That is part of the long story, Miss Nightingale.'

She laughed in appreciation of my sally, and said, 'Then I think you had better bring the note-case and the story round to-morrow at, say, 12.30. I'm going out to lunch, but we could have a quick one first.' And she gave me her name, and the address of her flat in Chelsea.

'That's charming of you,' I said. 'We shall all be there at 12.30. Good-night.'

I will confess that I was not displeased with my share of the conversation, nor with the subtle way in which I had forced an invitation from her. For I felt that my story would need all the personal charm which I could exert, if I were to get, as they say, away with it.

I presented myself punctually at 12.30 next morning, and she opened the door to me. She was a Mrs Trant, living, I gathered, apart from her husband; much the same age as Claudine, but plumper and more provocative. She gave me a glass of indifferent sherry, and said, 'Well, now for the story.' She was evidently determined to be business-like. So was I.

'First let me give you this,' I began, and I handed over the note-case. 'I ventured to look inside,' I added, 'hoping to find some means of identification, and in this way ascertained that there were five £1 notes within. Is that as it should be?'

'Five, that's right. The story, please, I can't wait.'

'It is quite simple. Did you happen to notice the woman at the table on your left?'

'Naturally I saw what she was wearing and what she looked like. I didn't notice her particularly.'

'I did. I was sitting some way away from you, but looking in your direction. You had put your bag down by your side; and while you were talking to your companion, I saw her surreptitiously extract the note-case from it. Almost immediately afterwards she left the room and went to the telephone-box, presumably to contact a confederate outside. The man at her table, I don't know if you remember him'—to my relief she shook her head— 'I should say that he was innocent of his companion's character. I was not. So I followed her. We had a little talk together, and I persuaded her to give up the note-case.'

That was all. A perfectly simple, straightforward story. But obviously she would not allow me to leave it there.

'Persuaded her!' she said indignantly. 'Why didn't you have her arrested?'

'There are official reasons,' I said with a note of authority in my voice, 'why it is not considered advisable to arrest her just yet.'

166

'Oh!' Mrs Trant thought this over, and then said, 'Does that mean you're a policeman?'

'Temporarily,' I smiled. 'I am in M.I.5, but lent to Scotland Yard for special duties.'

'M.I.5—that's the Secret Service, isn't it?'

'That is so,' I bowed.

'Well, fancy! All the same,' she went on, 'it was very inconvenient being without the money last night. What I'm wondering is why you didn't give it back to me at once.'

I was wondering, too, but I couldn't very well say so.

'Isn't it perfectly obvious, dear lady?' I said, playing for time.

'Not exactly.'

Luckily it became so to me almost as I said it. The Wibberleys, as may have been remarked, are very quick thinkers.

'She returned to her seat by your side,' I explained patiently. 'If I had given it to you then, you would have demanded her instant arrest. As I have said, this was contrary to public policy. We are hoping that, if we leave her at liberty, she will lead us eventually to—well, to a certain organisation. She left altogether a little later, giving me just time to write you a note and follow her. Which, you understand,' and I finished my glass of sherry with an air, 'was why I had come to the restaurant in the first place.'

This last statement, of course, was strictly true. The fact that I was so ingeniously weaving truth and what in a sense might be called untruth into the fabric of my story may have gone to my head. For, without really thinking, I found myself adding:

'She is known to us at Scotland Yard as Flash Annie.'

5

If there were any justice in the world: if true character were rewarded according to its worth: if man's honourable love met with an equally honourable response: indeed, if any of Mr Aldwinckle's multitudinous wives had had a sense of humour, this story would either not have been begun or would have ended differently.

Last week I received the following letter:

'Mrs Arthur Pagham begs to inform Mr Wibberley that she met your friend Mrs Trant at a dinner party last night. She behaved in such a peculiar way to Mrs Pagham that I had to ask our host for an explanation. He took her on one side, and came back to Mrs Pagham later to say that the woman had had the impertinence to mistake me for a notorious crook called Flash Annie. Naturally she insisted on a full explanation from her.

Mrs Pagham has only two things to say to you. One— that she has instructed her solicitor to issue a writ for slander; and the other, that for the first time in my life I have come to recognise the sound judgment and good sense of the present Mrs Aldwinckle.'

Illiterate, too, you see. I am well rid of her.

Before the Flood

We are told that Lamech was 182 years old when he begat Noah, and that he lived 595 years afterwards. So we are not surprised when we read that 'all the days of Lamech were seven hundred, seventy and seven years: and he died.' It is just what we should have expected. But the next verse gives us material for more sustained thought. It says 'And Noah was 500 years old: and Noah begat Shem, Ham and Japheth.' Now it is improbable that this verse is meant to convey two independent items of news, for then the chronicler is merely telling us in the first one that at some time in his career Noah was 500; which we could have worked out for ourselves, remembering that he was 595 when his father died. But if, as therefore seems likely, the two statements are related, then he is giving us the really interesting information that at the age of 500 Noah begat triplets. As he says a few verses later, 'There were giants in those days.'

The present chronicler, however, finding it difficult to distinguish in his mind between a hearty, middle-aged man of 500 and an elderly gentleman of 840, and suspecting that it is arithmetic rather than nature which has changed so remarkably since those days, has thought it better to divide patriarchal ages by ten, in the hope of so arriving at some picture of the truth. He proposes, therefore, to regard Noah as a man of sixty when he entered the Ark, and the ages of his sons as 28, 24, and 20. And since the old chronicler has said little of the women, the present one, wishing to say more of them, would remind his readers that the name of Noah's wife was Hannah, of Shem's Kerin, of Ham's Ayesha, and of Japheth's Meribal. Now we can begin.

Noah was accustomed to dream at night, and to recount his dreams to the family over the breakfast table. These dreams were either straightforward prophecies of ill-fortune, or were so oblique that they would only be interpreted accurately after the event. For example, if a plague of locusts destroyed his crops, he would remind the family complacently of his dream a month earlier that he was emptying a bottomless well with a sieve; acknowledging that he had misinterpreted this at the time as meaning that his second son would come to no good. Noah never did like Ham much. Ham would argue.

One night Noah had a peculiarly vivid dream. He dreamed that the Tigris and the Euphrates had joined together and rushed at him, and that he and Ham were sitting on a log in the middle of the waters, and Ham was saying 'Why didn't you dream about this, and then we could have built a boat and saved my mother and my brothers, and my brothers' wives?' And, as an afterthought, he had added 'And Ayesha.' And then Ham had turned into a crocodile, and the crocodile said 'What about *my* wife?' And suddenly all the animals were saying 'And what about *our* wives?' But he wasn't sitting on a log, he was sitting on the top branch of a cypress tree, sawing it off so as to build a boat, and suddenly he found to his horror that he was sitting on the wrong side of the branch. And he gave a great cry as he fell, and his wife awoke and said 'Who is it?' and lo! it was a dream. So he said 'Just a dream, dear. I'll tell you in the morning.' And he lay awake for three hours pondering it, at the end of which time he had forgotten that it was a dream. He fell asleep again as the day was breaking, and this time Yahweh Himself spoke to him; and now all was clear in his mind.

'Shem, my boy,' he said at breakfast, 'what did you think of doing this morning?'

Shem was his favourite son. He was strong and willing; he could do anything with his hands, and had very little brains to do anything else with; so he could be trusted to do what he was told without arguing. Ham was cynical and unsatisfactory. He didn't seem to

170

believe any of the things which were commonly believed: among them that a father was the embodiment of wisdom, and should be honoured even when he differed from you. Japheth had just got married to Meribal, and Meribal had just got married to Japheth. They sat together and thought together and walked together; and neither of them had said 'I' for six months, but always 'we'. They were regarded as a temporary but total loss to the establishment.

Before Shem could collect in his mind the facts with which to answer his father, Noah went on: 'Well, I want you to put all that on one side and help me to build a boat. Ham, no doubt, will now wish to ask me why a boat, seeing that the only water we have here is a well. Ham, my boy?'

'My dear father,' said Ham, raising his eyebrows in that way he had, 'it never occurred to me to ask you why a boat. On the contrary, I have always thought that the one thing this farm lacked was a boat. Really we ought to have one boat each. Seven boats,' he explained, looking at Japheth-and-Meribal. 'You never know when a nice boat mightn't be useful.'

'You have spoken a true word there, Ham. You never know when a boat mightn't be useful.'

Hannah, scenting trouble between them again, said:

'Oh, you were going to tell us about your dream, dear. Was it about boats this time? I don't think you have ever dreamed about boats before.'

'I have had no occasion to, Hannah. But on the eve of the most terrible catastrophe in History, when a Great Flood is about to cover the face of the Earth and destroy all the people thereon, I have been mercifully forewarned, and instructed what to do.'

The family took it calmly, as if all that was to be expected from this dream was that a sheep would fall into the well. As a matter of academic interest Ham wanted to know where the water was coming from.

'Where everything comes from, my son,' said Noah sternly. 'From Heaven.'

'Amen,' said Hannah, feeling vaguely that it was called for.

'Oh, you mean it's going to rain?'

'For forty days and forty nights, until the waters cover even the crest of Ararat.'

'And we shall all be in our boat?'

'Not only we, but representatives of all the animals in the world, two of each, male and female.'

Japheth-and-Meribal had a secret smile for this.

'What's the idea?' asked Ham.

'As I understand it, Yahweh is weary of the wickedness of the world, and intends to destroy every living creature in it, with the exception of this household, and these—er— specimen animals I was telling you about. We, or perhaps I should say, I, have been fortunate enough to find favour in His sight.'

'And what happens afterwards, or do we live in our boat for ever?'

'When the waters subside, we shall all start again, and found a new generation.'

'Us eight and all the animals?'

'Yes.'

Ham looked at Ayesha and said 'Fancy that!' Ayesha looked away from him and said nothing.

'It seems rather a roundabout way of doing things,' said Hannah. 'You don't mean that I've got to start again, too?'

Noah ignored the question, and said sternly:

'Woman, do you dare to tell the Lord Yahweh how to do things?'

'Mercy, no, I just said it seemed rather a roundabout way of doing them.'

Japheth and Meribal had been whispering and laughing together, and now Meribal said: 'Daddy Noah, we want to ask you, are you going to save two scorpions?'

'Certainly, my child. Yahweh makes no exceptions.'

'We think,' said Japheth, 'that you ought to give scorpions a miss. We think that if Meribal's father and mother are going to be drowned, it is rather unflattering to save the lives of two scorpions. Couldn't you leave them out? Say you couldn't catch them, or got two males by mistake, or something?'

'What's the difference between a male scorpion and a female scorpion?' asked Ham. 'Does anybody know?'

'I thought,' said Noah coldly, 'that I had explained the facts of life to you on the night before your marriage.'

'Oh, was *that* what you were doing?' said Ham, a little surprised. 'I thought—well, anyhow, we never touched on scorpions.' He glanced at his wife, and added, 'It didn't seem necessary then.' Ayesha flashed hate at him, and dropped her eyes.

'Isn't one bigger than the other?' asked Hannah. 'Or is it smaller?'

'It might be younger, mother,' Shem pointed out.

'Well,' said Hannah, 'I can't see that Yahweh would mind very much if we all started again without scorpions.'

'He *would* mind. Very much,' said Noah.

'So would the scorpions,' said Ham. 'Don't forget that.'

'So will Father and Mother,' said Meribal brightly, making, she felt, a good point.

'Aren't you glad you married into our family?' Japheth asked her, kissing her nose. Meribal took a quick look round the room and bit his ear.

'All these matters,' said the Patriarch importantly, 'sink into insignificance beside the problem of building the boat. Obviously it will have to be a big one to contain all these animals. My instructions are that it shall be 450 feet long, 75 feet broad, and 45 feet high.'

Shem gasped. Hannah said 'Gracious!' Japheth whistled.

Ham said negligently: 'Oh, would you call that a big boat, Father?'

Though the patriarchs had seen to it that the lowly position of Woman in the Home was established by Divine Law, it is doubtful if her authority differed very much from that which her glorious emancipation has since given her. Hannah, it may be said, frequently confused Noah with Yahweh, and, regarding them both as children, felt it her duty to do what she could for them.

'Just a moment, dear, before you go off to your tree-cutting,' she said after breakfast.

'What is it, Hannah? All right, Shem, meet me at the Well Gate.'

'Yes, Father.' Shem shouldered his axe and strode off.

'Now, dear.'

'All this about the boat——'

'I think we'll call it the Ark. Yes, I remember now that that is what Yahweh called it. The Ark.'

'You really do believe it? You know, dear, sometimes your dreams—there was that prophecy of yours that Ham was going to be struck by lightning——'

'If you remember, my love,' said Noah patiently, 'Ayesha had a miscarriage shortly afterwards, which is exactly what the grief and shock would have caused, if Ham *had* been struck by lightning. There was nothing wrong with the prophecy, I just didn't follow the implications far enough.' Even now Noah could surprise his wife. She looked at him pityingly. How anybody over the age of five could suppose that Ayesha—couldn't he see how it was between them?

'You do believe in this Flood, then?'

'I was never more certain.'

'Naturally there will be preparations to make if we are all to live in this Ark for—how many days did you say?'

'The actual rains will last for forty days. But then, of course, the water has to go down again. I don't know how long that will take. It might well be a year before normal conditions were restored.'

'A year's provisioning for eight people and all those animals. Have you any idea of how many sorts of animals there are, and what they all eat?'

'N-no,' said Noah cautiously. 'I shall—er——' he brightened up and ended, 'I shall leave that to Ham. We must all do our share.'

'They won't bring their own food with them?'

'I—er—no. Don't think, my dear,' he added hastily, 'that I don't appreciate the enormous responsibility which this command of Yahweh's has placed upon you.'

'As long as you appreciate it, that's all I ask of you. It's just that, if some of the rarer animals, of whose habits we know so little, do happen to find themselves running short at the end of the tenth month, I don't want you to say "How like Hannah".'

'My dear, I shouldn't dream of saying it.'

'You dream of so many strange things, Noah, that that might well be one of them. Very well, dear, now run along and get your axe. Shem will be waiting for you.'

When he had gone, she went in to Kerin and said, 'It's serious this time.'

And now even the neighbours were beginning to take it seriously.

'You seem to be building something,' said Nathaneel one day. He was an observant man.

'Yes,' said Noah, wiping away the sweat which was running into his eyes.

'You won't have much wood left if you go on like this.'

'No.'

'What's the idea?'

Nathaneel was the thirty-second person who had said 'What's the idea?' and Noah was now a little tired of it. He said 'Oh, just an idea,' and went on sawing.

'If I blink my eyes rapidly, and then look away, I get a curious sensation of a house of some sort. Would that be right?'

'Yes.'

'Bit big for a house, isn't it? But perhaps you are expecting an addition to the family?'

'Yes.'

'Ah, that's good. I like to see young people——' he was about to say 'enjoying themselves,' but substituted 'realising their civic responsibilities.'

'Yes,' said Noah.

Nathaneel felt that he was doing most of the work. However, he had now arrived at the point for which he had been making.

'As I was saying, you will be running out of wood at this rate. I could let you have a couple of acres of cypress, if it interested you.'

'The North wood?' asked Noah, straightening up and showing interest.

'Yes. Matter of fact it's a little over the two acres.'

'What do you want for it?'

'You've got some good-looking sheep,' said Nathaneel cautiously.

'I dare say we could do something on those lines,' said Noah. The fact that all his sheep but two were doomed anyway offered, he thought, a good basis for bargaining. The fact that Nathaneel was equally doomed might also be worked in somehow: post-dating delivery or something.

'Come along to my place to-night,' said Nathaneel, 'and we'll talk it over.'

Noah nodded a little condescendingly. It was hard not to be condescending when the Lord has told you that you are the only man in the world worth saving. The only man, that is, with a beard.

'How are you getting on?' Ham asked his brother at dinner some weeks later.

'Oh, all right,' said Shem.

'If you worked as diligently as your brother,' said Noah —'your elder brother,' he explained, glancing at Japheth- and-Meribal who were still one, 'then you would be getting on all right too. You are responsible for the animals, and so far you seem to have done nothing.'

'On the contrary,' said Ham, scratching his elbow, 'I have collected a flea. Whether male or female, and with or without companion, I cannot say. But it's a start.'

'Tchah!' said Noah through his beard.

'Well, there's one thing,' said Hannah. 'With all these animals I needn't provide food for the fleas.'

'That's just what I wanted to ask you, Father. Don't imagine that I have been idle. I have been thinking. And, believe me, this needs a great deal more thought than anybody had yet given it.'

It was so obvious that 'anybody' included Yahweh that Hannah was a little frightened. You never knew with Yahweh. He was so

176

easily offended, and *so* impulsive. She hastened to substitute herself, saying that she had had to think about it a great deal, with all that food to provide.

'Exactly the point, Mother. Father insists that there must be two of everything. One male, one female. No more, no less.'

'Yahweh insists,' corrected Noah.

'Quite so. But some of these animals eat each other. If we are to satisfy a couple of lions for a year, we want more than two gazelles. Otherwise you will end up with no gazelles and no lions. Lions, I have estimated, want about a gazelle a day each. So, merely looking at it from the lion's point of view, we shall have to start with 730 gazelles.'

'Yahweh distinctly said two only,' repeated Noah obstinately.

'Take it or leave it,' shrugged Ham. 'Why should I mind either way?'

Noah scratched at his beard. ('This is the other one,' Japheth whispered to Meribal, and they both giggled.) 'The solution is obvious,' he said, as soon as he had thought of it. 'There is always a way if you look for it. Dead meat. Yahweh said nothing against dead meat.' He looked round at them triumphantly. There was a heavy silence.

'I am only a woman,' said Hannah very clearly, 'and my one desire is to obey the Lord's and my husband's commands. But if I *should* be offered the choice of drowning comfortably with my friends, or living for a year in a box with 730 dead gazelles——'

'Oh, why don't we *all* drown, and have done with it!' cried Ayesha passionately. Amazingly she burst into tears and rushed from the room. Ayesha! Ham felt a sudden lightening at the heart. If she were unhappy too——! He started up to follow her. But what was the good? She would only say, 'Oh, leave me *alone!*' He sat down again, but still with that strange excited feeling. Ayesha!

Noah said bitterly: 'I have walked with the Lord all the days of my life. I have obeyed His testimonies. If the commands of the Lord are now to be as naught with my own people, then it were indeed better that we should all drown/

'Yes, dear,' said his wife soothingly, patting his head, 'but we shan't. Not when you've built that nice boat.'

'Ark.'

'Yes, dear, ark. That boat you're building so cleverly.'

Ham said, choosing his words carefully, 'Nobody would be so foolish as to set up his wisdom against that of the Creator of All Things. But if He seems to have given us an order which no man can possibly carry out, do we not follow the path of wisdom by telling ourselves that the order cannot have been fully heard, fully understood, fully interpreted?'

Noah combed his beard with his fingers, saying nothing.

'May we speak, Father?' asked Japheth, holding up his hand.

'Yes, my son, let us all speak.'

'Well, we've been talking it over, and what we think is this. Fleas. You can't have an ark full of all sorts of furry animals, and only have two fleas. Then think of flies. *Flies!* Can you see Ham examining all the million flies in the ark until he's got one boy-fly and one girl-fly—' (Meribal giggled)—'and then trying to catch and kill all the others? Think of birds. You can let two of each in by the front door, but what of the hundreds which settle on the roof? Cats! How many kittens are you letting yourself in for? And how can Ham be sure of finding all the animals anyway? There may be a particular sort of rare beetle, which lives in a hole at the top of a mountain a hundred miles from here—what does he do about that one?'

'I shall be up there anyway,' said Ham, 'getting that second eagle.'

Noah was silent. There was nothing to say. He looked up and saw that Shem seemed to be in trouble with an idea.

'Well, my boy?'

'I was just thinking—if we didn't have to have all those animals it would mean a much smaller ark, and we could do with the wood we've got.'

Noah nodded.

'Kerin? Have you any contribution to make?'

'May we just say one more thing, Father?' Japheth interrupted.

'Well?'

'We just want to know. When the flood is at its height, and Meribal's father and mother drift past us on a barrel, what do we do? Wave?'

'Kerin? You were going to say——?'

Japheth, realising that he had been snubbed, restored confidence in himself by pointing out to Meribal what an unanswerable point he had made. She agreed, and kissed his nose.

Kerin was fair, and her hair came down in two plaits over her shoulders. She was very beautiful. Not dangerously, frighteningly beautiful, like the dark and passionate Ayesha, but tranquilly beautiful, as if she knew what she was and where she wanted to go.

'In the end,' she said slowly, 'we have to trust to our own minds and hearts and consciences. If it be Yahweh's will to destroy the whole world, then we can neither help Him nor hinder Him. But if He gives us, and us alone, the opportunity of saving ourselves, then we must use all our efforts to save ourselves, efforts not only of body, but of mind and judgment. Our judgment may be wrong, but we shall have done our best, and nothing which we do or leave undone can alter His plans for the world.'

They were all against him. All!

T think, dear, if I may speak again——'

'Yes, Hannah?'

'Wouldn't it be better to wait until you have had *another* dream, one in which things are made *much* clearer?'

Even Hannah!

'I cannot have dreams to order, Hannah! I cannot summon Yahweh to speak to me!'

'No, dear, but I have noticed that that sort of thing so often happens after you have been eating Lebanon honey. Kerin, dear, you will find the jar on the top shelf of the larder. Would you mind? Just put a little out on a plate.'

In the end Noah did what mankind always ends by doing. He compromised. He had Divine Authority for this; that is to say, he

179

put the difficulty before Yahweh when he went to bed, talked it over with Hannah until they both went to sleep, and in the morning came to a decision. No man could have done more.

'About the animals,' he said at breakfast.

'And Meribal's father and mother,' murmured Japheth.

'I have now received clearer guidance.' (Hannah looked across at Kerin and nodded.) 'The wisdom of the Lord is too deep for the mortal mind to comprehend it at the first instruction, and in substituting his own imperfect wisdom for so much of the Divine wisdom as he does not understand, Man may fall into grievous error.'

He paused a moment, as if for comment, but since it was not quite clear whether reverent assent or polite dissent was called for, nobody said anything.

'As should have been plain to you all from the first, my reference to animals was to domestic animals only. If it be Yahweh's will to destroy all evil men, must it not be equally His will to destroy all evil beasts and creeping things? Ham, you should have seen this. Is it not also manifest that among beneficent cattle and sheep no distinction of goodness can be made, and that the numerological reference, the mention of "two", applied therefore to the sex, not to the individual? Japheth, my boy, I am surprised that this did not strike you. Moreover Hannah, my dear, it was always obvious, or so I should have supposed, that we could not sustain ourselves unless we had a surplus of living animals from which to replenish our stocks of fresh meat. This of itself would have made the idea of two sheep only—' he waited to get it under full control, and then gave an amused chuckle—'quite ridiculous!'

'Of course now that you put it so logically, dear, I do see,' said Hannah. 'Men,' she went on to Kerin, 'are so much more logical than women. Such a help. Meribal, darling, when I see you eating Japheth's ear, I always feel that it is a reflection on my housekeeping. You should keep that in reserve, in case the Flood lasts longer than we expect.'

'I have the Divine Authority,' announced Noah a little pompously, 'for saying that, after all, we may be back on dry land in as little as eight weeks from the beginning of the rains. Eight weeks, Hannah. Nevertheless,' he added, 'you should cater for the whole year, so as to be on the safe side.'

'Of course, dear,' said Hannah. 'As you will find later on, Kerin, when you set up house for yourself, it is these little authoritative hints which make housekeeping so much easier.'

'Now as to the human element,' Noah went on, 'and this of course includes Meribal's father and mother. Whether owing to my intercession or of His own bounteous mercy (and it is not for me to say), Yahweh has relented towards them. Our friends and neighbours are to be warned of the Flood, and so to be given a chance of saving themselves.'

'Very handsome of Him,' said Ham.

'Oh, thank-you, Daddy Noah,' said Meribal, after being nudged by Japheth, 'that *is* kind of you both.'

'Do you mean, dear, that they are to be given a chance of saving themselves in *our* boat——'

'Ark.'

'—ark, or a chance of building and stocking one for themselves?'

'Well——' said Noah, and left it at that, not being quite sure.

'You do see the difference, dear?' Hannah asked anxiously.

'I think, Hannah, that we might leave that point for the moment. The immediate duty is to warn them.'

'Surely by this time,' said Ham, 'everybody knows why we are building an ark. Don't they, Shem?'

'They come and ask me, and I tell them, and then they scoff.'

'Isn't that good enough, Father?'

'In a general way, yes, my boy, but I feel that in certain cases the situation should be explained in a little more detail.'

'To Nathaneel, for instance.'

'I wasn't thinking so much of Nathaneel, as of Meribal's father and mother.'

'I agree,' said Hannah firmly. 'I shall call upon your mother this afternoon, Meribal, and make it all *quite* clear to her.'

So Hannah called on Meribal's mother, and no two people (you would have said) could have been more delighted to see each other. When they had got over their delight, Hannah began:

'What lovely weather we are having, but of course we could do with a little rain.'

'I understood,' said Meribal's mother archly, 'that we were going to have some.'

'Oh, you've heard our news?' Hannah laughed. 'Forty days and forty nights? Fancy!'

'Is it—official?' asked Meribal's mother, glancing up at the ceiling.

'I'm afraid so. But then everything is which Noah thinks of. It makes things *so* difficult.'

'Shobal used to be like that, but I got him out of it.'

'You're so clever, Tirzah,' sighed Hannah. 'If only I had taken it earlier! But it's too late now, I'm afraid. I shall have to go on saying "Yes, dear", for the rest of my life.'

'You don't believe it, of course,' asked Tirzah, with the uneasy laugh of one who didn't want to.

'About the Flood?' Hannah's laugh sounded much more genuine. 'Darling, how can you ask? Raining all that time!'

'I said to Shobal, "Whoever's heard of rain for forty days?"'

'Who indeed? Oh, but you haven't heard the best of it. With all this rain, there's going to be a flood which will cover the top of Mount Ararat, and everybody in the whole world is going to be drowned! Isn't it amusing? The things Noah thinks of!'

'Oh, is *that* why you're building this extraordinary box? What did Shobal call it? It made me laugh so. "Noah's Ark", that was it.' She tittered, and said again, 'Noah's Ark! I think that's a wonderful name for it. "Have you heard about Noah's Ark?" he asked me. I didn't know what he meant.'

'My dear,' said Hannah grimly, 'it may be a joke to you and Shobal, but it's no joke to me. I've got to provision that box for a whole year!'

'I thought you said forty days——'

'Yes, but the water has to subside—I think that's the word —and apparently that takes another year.'

'Hannah! It's crazy!'

'Of course it is, but what can I do?'

'I said to Shobal when I first heard of it, "Well, our daughter has married into a crazy family".'

'I'm afraid she has, poor girl. And such a sweet nature. But, Tirzah, can you imagine us all shut up in that box for a year or more, with as many animals as we can squeeze in, shut up in a box for a whole year?'

'Horrible,' said Tirzah with a shudder. 'But, of course, if it *doesn't* rain——'

'Oh, but we shall have to go into our box just the same. Noah is determined on that. Just sit there boxed up, and wait for the rain to begin. And then wait for it to stop. And then wait for another year. And then—Oh, Tirzah, how I envy you and Shobal, such a nice sensible man, Shobal, with none of these strange ideas.'

'I'm thinking of Meribal. It's very hard on her.'

'It is. Luckily she can't see an inch beyond Japheth's nose at the moment, so she's quite happy. But as for the rest of us—*and* all those smelly animals—oh well, dear, I mustn't bother you with our little troubles. It has been lovely to see you.'

She got up, laid her cheek against Tirzah's, and moved towards the door. But suddenly she remembered.

'How silly of me, darling!' she laughed. 'I had a special message for you from my husband, and I had forgotten all about it. Well, the fact is, I'm ashamed to give it. You'll think I'm making fun of you.'

'Oh, go on, Hannah, you know I'm not one to mind.'

'Well, do forgive me, dear.' She paused, and then went on quickly, 'Tirzah, it's really too absurd, but Noah says that if you and Shobal like to join us all in our box—for the whole year, of course, and I'm *afraid* you'd have to bring your own provisions, men never think of that, but *you* understand, darling—well, you know how delighted we should all be to have you.' She took a deep breath and ended, 'There! I've done it!'

'Oh, dear!' said Tirzah. 'Of course, it's sweet of you, Hannah, but—well, I know Shobal is rather busy this next week or two—and, as a matter of fact, I'm supposed to be out in the open air

183

as much as possible just now, no, nothing serious, but you do see, dear——'

'Of *course*, darling! Don't think any more of it. But my husband insisted that I should ask you, so naturally I had to do it. Good-bye, darling. My love to Shobal, please. Good-bye!'

So at dinner that night Hannah said:

'I'm afraid it's no good, Meribal darling. Your father and mother just *won't* believe about the Flood. So foolish of them.' She caught Kerin's eye, and added, 'I did my best.'

'I'm sure you did,' smiled Kerin.

The words 'father' and 'mother' came to Meribal from a long way off. She was smoothing out Japheth's eyebrows for him.

The Ark was nearly finished. The neighbours had stared, and made their jokes, and lost interest. Shem was resting for a moment when Kerin came down from the house with a jug of milk in her hands.

'You will be thirsty,' she said, 'and tired. Sit for a little and talk to me.'

'I'm all right,' he said. He took the jug from her and they sat down together.

'How much longer will it be?'

'Just the roof to finish off,' said Shem. He drank and said, 'That was good. Well, say three more days.'

'And then——?'

'How do you mean?'

'Then we all go into the Ark together, and there we all are. Together.'

He nodded and said, 'The same as we have always been.'

'Don't I know? But even so, you and I have managed to be away by ourselves sometimes. Now, for a whole year——'

'Oh, I expect we shall be all right. Bit crowded at first perhaps.'

'If it is to be for a whole year,' began Kerin, 'I don't think I——' and then suddenly, 'Shem!'

'Yes?'

'Will you promise me something?'

'Anything I can. Of course.'

'When it is all over, will you come away with me?'

'Where?'

'Anywhere, so long as it is a long way, and we are alone.'

He looked at her in astonishment.

'Why, what's the matter, Kerin? Aren't you happy with us?'

'I think that Husband and Wife should be alone together.'

'Yes, dear, but with their children. Like Father and Mother.'

'No, no,' she said urgently, 'not with their children, not when the children are grown up.'

'It is the custom,' said Shem, a little bewildered.

'Is it? Then why isn't Meribal with her father and mother? Would you like me to be with mine, if they were alive?'

'Oh, daughters, no.'

'Oh, daughters, no,' repeated Kerin. 'So you see, children don't have to be with their parents for ever. There is no Divine Law about it.'

Shem scratched his head, took another draught of milk, and tried again.

'What's wrong with being all together? I don't understand. Everybody loves you. Who is it who makes you unhappy? I know Mother loves you.'

'I like your mother very much. I admire her, and she amuses me a great deal.'

'Amuses?' said Shem, shocked by the word. One oughtn't to think of Mothers as amusing.

'And of course everybody respects your father. He's a dear old man. Sometimes he amuses me too,' she added, with a reminiscent smile.

That word again! 'Kerin!' he cried. 'I don't know what you're saying!'

'Yes, I like them both very much; I have been very lucky. But you see, dear, I don't *love* anybody but you.'

Shem groped his way after her as well as he might, but he was still in the darkness. All he found to say was, 'I thought we were all so happy together'; but he didn't sound happy as he said it.

'All!' she said scornfully. 'Ham and Ayesha never speak to each other! Japheth and Meribal are only happy because they can still behave as if the rest of us weren't there. For all they mean to anybody else they might be gone already.'

'You don't want us to behave like Japheth and Meribal?'

'Do you ever wish that I did?' she said softly.

Shem turned to her in surprise. He found himself looking into the depths of her deep blue eyes, and was lost. Suddenly he took her in his arms, crushed her until she could scarcely breathe, and kissed her. . . .

'All right, I promise,' he said. 'Now I must get on with the roof.'

Kerin went singing back to the house, swinging the empty jug.

'I have it on High Authority,' said Noah that evening, 'that the Ark will come to rest on the summit of Mount Ararat. This may not be until the seventeenth day of the seventh month. From that moment the waters will gradually subside.'

'And what do *we* do?' asked Japheth.

'We gradually get out, darling,' giggled Meribal.

'And there we all are on the top of Ararat,' said Ham. 'Mother, how good are you at climbing down a 17,000-foot mountain?'

'Not very good, dear. I haven't been practising lately. But I expect to be a little better than some of the cows.'

Noah pulled at his beard.

'I may have got that bit about Ararat wrong,' he said reluctantly.

'I hope so, dear,' said Hannah.

Ham came into his wife's room. She looked round and said coldly: 'What do you want?'

'Not to disturb you,' he said. 'And not to annoy you; at least, not before I have begun.'

'Begun what?'

'Saying what I want to say.'

'Oh, are we talking again?' said Ayesha. 'How nice! It will be the first time for months.'

'And it may be the last time for ever. But perhaps it was a bad moment to choose. You're packing.' He had come to rest at her

186

dressing-table, and now, sitting down in front of it, he picked up a carved wooden hair-brush. 'I made this for you. Do you remember? It's rather good.' He looked at it appreciatively.

She took it away from him, saying, 'Don't muddle things up, please. And wouldn't it be better if you got on with your own packing? We move in to-night.'

'You do, perhaps. I don't.'

She was startled. She said, 'What do you mean?' putting the brush down, and backing away from him. He got up from his seat and said, 'Sit down here and brush your hair. It will give you something to do, if you don't want to listen to me. Here!' He gave her the brush again, and she sat down. 'I used to like watching you brush your hair —your serious, so remote, face, and the ripple of your arms. But I won't watch you now. You're alone, and I'm alone, and——What were you asking me? Oh, about the packing. Well, I shall have very little to pack. You see, I'm not going into the Ark.'

'You mean you don't believe there's going to be a Flood? You wouldn't, of course.'

'Sometimes I do and sometimes I don't. What I don't believe is that I'm a particularly good person to save. I can't help thinking "Why Ham?" I can see why Father and Mother, and why Shem and Kerin; they're good. I am not so sure about Japheth and Meribal, because, when you are as happy as that, it seems to me rather a good time to die; but they are nice children and have never done anybody any harm. And I can see why Ayesha, because beauty, sheer beauty, is the one thing which mustn't be destroyed. But when I think of Ham, then I begin to doubt. Then I begin to feel that it's absurd and wrong to choose a little group of eight people out of the whole world, and to set them above all the rest. There are wicked men on the earth, and I daresay I'm one of them, but not children, not babies. I can't quite believe in a God like that.'

'So you're taking a chance?'

'Yes. . . Ayesha, I want you to take it with me.'

'Now?'

187

'Yes.'

'Why?'

He said, as if to himself, 'I should never have dared to ask you. But when you cried, "Oh, why don't we all drown, and have done with it?" then I knew that you were no happier than I, and that there was still a chance for us. I want you to come with me and take it. To put it in another way,' he went on more firmly, 'I'm damned if I'm going to live with you in that damned Ark for a whole damned year, watching Japheth and Meribal, and knowing that I love you a hundred times more than he will ever love her, and that without some help from you I shall never have the courage to do anything about it.'

The brush had ceased its regular motion. There was silence. Then slowly her hand moved again, and, still looking in her mirror, she said, 'Stand where I can see you.'

He came and stood behind her, a little to one side. They looked at each other in the mirror.

'Is that where you used to stand when you liked watching me brush my hair?'

'Yes.'

'I don't think you ever told me.'

'I thought you knew.'

'Never think that of me. Never think that I know.'

'You know now.'

'Yes. All the same, I think that we will go into the Ark together. Just to be safe. Will you mind?'

'Not now.'

'Perhaps,' she smiled, 'Japheth and Meribal will be able to give us a few hints on how to be happy.'

'I don't think so. I have a very good memory.'

'So have I. Oh, so have I!'

'Ayesha!'

'When it is all over, then I promise that we will go off by ourselves—oh, a long, long way—and start that family.'

'Thank you, my very lovely one.'

'Is your courage coming slowly back?'

'Slowly,' he nodded.

She turned round to him and said:

'Show me.'

Under a cloudless sky that evening, they all went into the Ark. After they had seen to the animals, they assembled in their own living-room; and when they were together, Noah said:

'Let us now call on the Lord God to bless our enterprise. Let us pray that the light of His countenance may be a shining beacon, our faith in Him a sure shield, through all the perils which confront us.'

Young or old, thoughtful or frivolous, believing or unbelieving, they fell upon their knees, each of them in his separate way moved by a sense of his own littleness, the knowledge of his own ignorance. And, as Noah prayed, it seemed to them that the beating of their hearts kept time to his words, at first gently, then more loudly, until the words were lost in the monotony of its rhythm . . . and they knew that what they heard was just the beating of the rain upon the roof.

The Balcony

Albert Edward Wilberforce Pyrke C.B.E. (Albert Edward after the Prince of Wales, and Wilberforce after the Bishop, both parents having taken a hand) was 62 when he fell out of a balcony on the eighth floor of Cavendish Mansions. Although his death was accidental, this did not immediately explain to his widow why he arrived on the pavement without coat, waistcoat and shoes, nor relieve the shareholders of Pyrkes Ltd., of the fear that their Chairman was thus avoiding prosecution. In fact, he had often told Sheila that her little balcony was dangerous, but she had only laughed at him. Now he had proved it. The shares went down and up again, nothing was wrong there; and Mrs Pyrke, assured by Sheila that the shoes had been hurting him, and that it was a particularly hot afternoon, soon forgot the unpleasantness of those first few days. So relieved, indeed, were the shareholders, and so pleasantly surprised the widow when the will was proved, that Justice demanded a revised verdict upon him; in whose white light the text on his tombstone began to seem not so ironical as was at first feared. Meanwhile Albert Edward Wilberforce Pyrke was awaiting a more impartial judgment in another place.

This was, or seemed to be, a large, empty reception room on an upper floor. He remembered dying, all but that last, awful moment, but he was not sure whether he had immediately woken up to find himself here, or whether centuries of oblivion had passed while he waited with all the others for Judgment Day. Seeing himself, as he had seen himself through life, as a special case, he doubted if he were the sort of person one would keep waiting so long; nor could

190

he believe that his memory of that last hour with Sheila would be so clear if it had happened so long ago. In a moment, then, the door would open, and a voice would say 'Mr Wilberforce Pyrke, please', and he would be passed along to St. Peter; alone, not with a million jostling dead. It was St. Peter, wasn't it, who received you, asked you a few polite questions, and gave you the freedom of the place? One ought to know for certain; nobody liked being called by the wrong name. He could ask the attendant casually, emphasising at the same time that he had dropped the Albert Edward in his own name years ago. He didn't want that dragged up against him.

He was not frightened. He had made his fortune as honestly as anybody in the City; no shareholder had lost money in his companies save by his own stupidity; he had given a helping hand to most of his poor relations. Not to all of them, of course, not Muriel the suffragette, nor Howard who hadn't joined up in 1914, nor that damned parson cousin who preached at him; but all the deserving ones. Yes, and helped them again, if they had shown their gratitude properly. He had subscribed to charities regularly; and though he did not go to church himself (because he played golf, and you can't do both), he had given the Vicar £100 a year for the good of the parish, and an extra £100 for repairing the tower. Presumably St. Peter had all that down. The only serious fault which might be found with him was in the matter of Sheila, and her two—two, that was all—her two predecessors. Well, one couldn't help one's nature; and if Agnes ceased of her own wish to be a wife (though a dear, good woman, all the same), what was one to do? St. Peter was a man of the world, he would make allowances. Of course, if they passed you on afterwards to St. Ursula or St. Teresa or one of those, he would have to look out. They just wouldn't understand.

So he waited; not frightened, yet not complacent; just pleasantly assured, pleasantly interested. At any moment now his name would be called, 'Mr Wilberforce Pyrke, please' . . . .

He was standing, and had now been standing for some little time, in the middle of a room which seemed to be about 60 feet long and 30 feet wide. Behind him was the door from which presently he would be summoned. In front of him were long windows opening on to a balcony, whose parapet hid from him all but a violet-blue sky: the sort of sky which he had noticed sometimes abroad (when he had leisure to look at the sky), but which was rarely to be seen in England. Evidently the weather here was good. He thought of walking to the balcony and seeing what the country was like, but feared that this might take him out of hearing when his name was called. 'Plenty of time for looking about later,' he told himself. All the same, he had been here now for—how long was it? Automatically his hand went to his watch; automatically the thought flashed through his mind that he had left his watch on Sheila's dressing-table, silly of him; and, with the thought, he looked down, and found, to his shocked surprise, that he was naked.

For the first time a trickle of fear crept round his heart. Until now he had had as support the assurance of a hundred contacts with other men, teaching him that he could hold his own with any. He had discussed production with Cabinet Ministers, he had talked without embarrassment to the King when receiving his decoration, had made speeches, opened bazaars, given away prizes. An interview with St. Peter was just another occasion. But now— naked! It was damnably unfair. There was St. Peter covered from neck to ankle in the sort of bath-towelling which Saints seemed to go in for, and there was he, Wilberforce Pyrke, feeling a perfect fool, catching the devil of a cold, and not even a handkerchief to blow his nose on. How could he stand up for himself under cross-examination, however mild, knowing all the time that at 62 one's figure didn't look at its best? Better than most men's of his age, he thought, looking down at himself with a slight renewal of complacency, but not what it was once. Now if he had died at 30, he could have shown St. Peter something.

Yes, it was unfair. Not cricket. Leaving behind a nasty feeling that they were going to take every advantage which they could. Tricky, that's what they were. And then to keep him hanging about for all this time—bad staff work? Or trickiness again? Trying to work on his nerves. All right then, if that's how they treated you up here, they couldn't expect courtesy in return. He would sit out on the balcony and enjoy the view, and they could damned well come and fetch him when they wanted him.

He walked to the window, looking about him as he went. The walls of the room were queerly opalescent, seeming to have no positive substance, no final resting place for the eye. All the colours of the spectrum were there, until one tried to give one's impression of any particular colour an abiding form; then it was there no longer. A phrase which he remembered from some book came into his mind: 'Its walls were of jasper'. Was this jasper? He went closer, in order to feel it; half a dozen strides, and . . . and he was still in the middle of the room. He laughed uneasily, hoping to reassure himself, and went quickly on, as had been his first purpose, towards the balcony . . . But he was still in the middle of the room.

Then he was really frightened. He called out, 'St. Peter! St. Peter!' and then, 'Here, for God's sake, somebody!' He bent down to touch the floor, wondering if it was so slippery that he could not walk, or if it was just that the room moved as he moved. He touched nothing. He realised suddenly, surprised that he had not noticed it before, that his feet felt nothing, neither heat nor cold. Very cautiously he tried to sit down, and found that though he still felt nothing, he was in a sitting position, and somehow sustained. It was the same when he lay down, and when he stood up again. He put a hand on his leg and up his side, and felt nothing. Yet he could see himself as clearly as he had seen himself in Sheila's room—was it a few hours ago? But now he was a ghost, a disembodied spirit. It came home to him then, as it had not yet come, that death made a difference; that all the pleasures of the flesh had been put away for ever. Well, he must get used to the idea, difficult as it might be at first. After all, ghosts had their advantages. They could not be imprisoned. They were free to walk through walls, so he had always understood. Yes, but if the walls were ghosts too? If all were unreal, but the invisible self within himself? What then?

Suddenly he began to cry in a weak, helpless sort of way . . . and put the back of his hand to his eyes, but could not wipe away the tears which he knew were there.

Days, or weeks, or years passed—how could he tell when there was neither day nor night, sunrise nor sunset, to mark the passing of time? He was still there in the middle of the room. It was clear to him now that Judgment Day and St. Peter and all that was just a tale for children. Nobody was coming for him. Nobody would ever say 'Mr Wilberforce Pyrke, please'. Nobody bothered about you when you were dead. When you were dead, they took everybody and everything away from you, and left you alone in empty, infinite space. Yes, but you weren't dead; that was the horror of it.

He remembered a text from one of the many funerals and memorial services which he had attended (not that he liked them, but it was bad form not to show up): 'We brought nothing into the world, and it is certain that we can carry nothing out.' St. Paul, wasn't it? In one of those letters he was always writing. But he was alive when he wrote it, he didn't really know. Of course one left one's property behind, one's friends, one's credit, in a way one's name. One would expect that. But this absolute nothingness was different. If they had let him keep a pencil, a pack of cards, a dictionary: dammit, even a piece of string to tie and untie, a wall to touch, to examine, to make marks on with a finger-nail—if they had left him anything! What Heaven, it seemed to him now, prison would have been: surrounded by solid walls; in front of work, however lowly, waiting to be done; spoken to however roughly by real people, however much unloved. But nothing was left to him— *nothing*! An eternity of doing nothing, and nothing to do it with.

But wait! Something *was* left to him. His mind. They had had to leave him that.

His mind. Well, they could have that too, if they liked. If he went out of his mind—and it wouldn't take much more of this to make him—then he would be all right. He would be imagining himself Julius Caesar or a poached egg or something, and be perfectly happy. But even as the idea came into his mind, he resisted it. They had left him this one thing, and now let them take it away

194

from him if they could. He would fight for it; he had always been a fighter; my God, how I shall fight for it!

If only he had been a poet, a novelist, a musician, he could have sat here happily, writing, composing, as happily alone with himself as he would have been in the real world. If only he had read as he should have done, he could have comforted himself now with poetry—*Paradise Lost,* Shakespeare and *The Lays of Ancient Rome*—for hours at a time. Of course, some of those poets would look pretty silly now, lacking his expert knowledge; he would be able to criticise them, and tell them where their imagination had failed them. Paradise! He knew a bit more about Paradise than Milton did.

Yes, but what else did he know? How else employ his mind? The arts, all the worlds of the imagination, were closed to him; a pity, he saw now, that he had neglected them; but what about the world of affairs? What about —figures?

He laughed aloud (or so it seemed to him) as he thought of figures. He put his tongue out, and made a face at St. Peter. (For some reason, St. Peter was to be regarded as his chief enemy.) He almost said 'Sucks to you, old man.' For here was occupation for the mind, occupation without end. He would begin in a small way, multiplying 123456789 by itself. Keeping all the figures in his head. Remembering nine lines of figures, keeping them all in their proper places, and then adding them up. Talk about Mental Arithmetic; there was an example for you! It would take him—how long? Hours, of course; perhaps days. And so he could go on, making up other problems for himself, for as long as he liked. Sucks to St. Peter.

He multiplied by 9, and found to his bewilderment that the answer was 1111111101. Extraordinary! He multiplied again to make sure, and it still was. Apparently it always had been, and always would be. And he had never known! 'Well, well,' he thought, 'we live and learn,' and then laughed at himself, and said ruefully, 'We die and learn.' Eight ones, a nought and a one, easy to remember. He started on the next line, wondering if something equally remarkable was coming out. It began promisingly 21345 —could it possibly be 6? It was. And 7?——7. Well well, well! To think of it! 987654312! Another easy one to remember. It simply couldn't go on like this. Absurdly excited, he began to multiply by 7. His excitement died; the great thrill was over. It took him several attempts, and a good deal of mental crossing out, before he had committed the answer to memory—864197523. Nothing there . . . Except that every figure came once and once only. That was odd. Would it always be like that? And why? He had never thought of figures in this way before, and now it was all becoming rather interesting. In a sudden burst of enthusiasm he cried, 'Damn it all, I'll *cube* it!'

Days passed, weeks passed, years passed—who could tell when there was neither dawn nor dusk, sleeping nor waking, when the deep violet-blue of the sky beyond the balcony never wavered, never changed its intensity. He had done the task which he had set himself; something which nobody had ever done before. All of it meaningless, he saw now. It told you nothing, it led you nowhere. Surely there was something better to do with his time than this?

Something he had heard somebody say once: 'Every man has at least one book inside him.' Something like that. What did it mean? That every man could write a book? No, that was nonsense. He certainly couldn't, for one. Or did it mean—yes, surely that was it—that every man's life was material for a book? Well, it was the one thing which a man would know, his own life. No need to invent anything, no need to wonder what happened next. One just put down all that one remembered. Exactly as it happened. . . .

Why not? . . .

Why ever not?. . . .

Of course, it wouldn't do just to go on thinking aimlessly, picking out a scene from this or that year: nursery, school, office, army: as it happened to come into his head. It must be consecutive; it must be 'written'; it must be committed to memory, so that at the end he had the whole book complete in his mind. Could that be done? If it were written in short paragraphs, each paragraph learnt by heart as it was finished, and then repeated to himself, and then repeated with all the preceding paragraphs: one; two, one-two; three, one-two-three; four, one-two-three-four; yes, it could be done like that. It would mean that he would be saying the first paragraph over to himself thousands and thousands of times. Well, he had eternity in front of him. But it would be something to do, something tremendous to do, something (he felt with complete conviction) good to do.

It would be a book whose like had never been seen. Every autobiography ever written was less than the truth. The author was making himself out greater or smaller than he really was. He was boastful or deprecating. However he had lived, there were things in his life, if only thoughts, which he dared not reveal to others. But this time there were no others. There was not even a posterity to discover and decipher the manuscript after he was dead. He was dead now, and there would be no manuscript. He could 'write' uninhibited, perhaps the first man who ever did. He would have nothing to hide, because there was nobody from whom to hide it.

How long would it take him? Ten years, fifty years, a hundred years, what did it matter? What were years to him? A phrase came into his head, which he had used himself when addressing shareholders: "The immediate future is amply provided for." Immediate—ten years! He laughed happily. He felt very happy suddenly.

Now then, to begin. He would begin with a short paragraph, because of saying it so many times.

'I was born on May 15th, 1886. My father was Joseph Preston Pyrke, M.A., the Vicar of Withamsted in Somerset. My mother was Grace Brackenbury before she married my father. I was their only child.'

He said it over and over again until it was part of himself. Then he went on to the second paragraph.

'Withamsted is a small village in the north-east corner of Somerset. We lived in the Vicarage. I was christened Albert Edward Wilberforce. . . .'

*

How many years? But he was nearly at the end.

'. . . I told her that it was the last time. I was paying her well, and I don't think she minded, because of course I was getting a bit old. I told her that that was why. The real reason was that I had just heard that I was in the running for a knighthood, and of course I shouldn't get it if Agnes divorced me. So I was taking no more risks.

'It made me feel very noble that I was going to be faithful to Agnes again. I wandered to the window and stood for a moment on the little balcony. You could look right over London. It was the last time, so that was why I was looking. I didn't throw myself down—at least, not meaning to— but something made me fall. I am not very clear about this. I don't mean Sheila, of course; I mean giddiness, or perhaps some sort of devilish compulsion. But the balcony was dangerous. I had told Sheila so.

'Well, that was my life. At least, all that I can remember of it.'

It was finished. How many years? Well, it wasn't quite finished yet. Now he had to go right through it from the beginning:

'I was born on May 15th, 1886. . . .'

And as he reached the last words, the summons came. Not from the door, as he had once expected, but from the blue immensity outside.

Albert Edward Wilberforce Pyrke!

Eagerly he jumped up, and walked with firm, quick steps to the balcony.

Printed in Great Britain
by Amazon

63753252R00125